THE RUSSIAN CRUCIFIX

Richard Freeborn
THE RUSSIAN CRUCIFIX

A Victorian Mystery

A · THOMAS · DUNNE · BOOK

ST. MARTIN'S PRESS
NEW YORK

Library of Congress Cataloging-in-Publication Data

Freeborn, Richard.
        The Russian crucifix.

        "A Thomas Dunne book"—
        I. Title.
PS3556.R3829R8   1987   813'.54   87-16266
ISBN 0-312-01156-3

First published in Great Britain by Macmillan London Limited.

First U.S. Edition

10 9 8 7 6 5 4 3 2 1

Part I

1

Dr Hodgson was ambitious, though he did not like to admit it. As soon as he heard the coach coming down the Belgrave Road he slipped out of his house to take a look at the new arrivals. It was Sunday 12 August, 1860, a pleasantly warm day, and Sunday arrivals were usually foreign and wealthy.

'This is Ventnor, sir,' the coachman announced. He addressed a tall, broad-shouldered man with a fine head of nearly white hair who was stepping down from the carriage. 'There's the Marine 'Otel, sir, just up the road, and down there, sir, is the Esplanade.' He pointed towards a steep, narrow lane which went down to the sea past some cottages. Fronting the sea itself, and seeming almost directly beneath where they were standing, a line of sunlit rooftops indicated the buildings along the esplanade. 'The Esplanade 'Otel, sir, is the very best 'otel in the 'ole of Ventnor. But of course you might care just to take rooms, sir.'

The tall man nodded at this advice. He was clearly not English. His large stature and his general air of innocent bewilderment, not to mention his fashionable French topcoat, large sunhat and silver-knobbed stick, were foreign, that was clear, but he was not French, the doctor thought. The one piece of separate luggage being unloaded from the back of the coach confirmed the doctor's suspicions: he was Russian, like so many others in Ventnor this summer. The name on his luggage was clearly visible: 'I. S. Tourgueneff.'

'I will take rooms.'

'Well, sir, there's Rock Cottage just up the road. Look, it's got a sign out.'

Rock Cottage was advertising through a modest painted sign hung on the gate that 'Rooms are rented to the Gentry'. This seemed to satisfy the new arrival. He thanked the coachman. The latter offered then and there to help and sprang down from the coach-box in expectation of a good tip. He knew one when he saw one.

Dr Hodgson simultaneously saw that the Russian gentleman did not look ill and since he chose to stay at Rock Cottage would probably be very unlikely to afford expensive treatment. So the doctor slipped back into Alto House, stopping for a moment to glance at the new brass plate fixed next to the bell-pull, *Dr J. S. Hodgson, Medical Practitioner*, before striding through the cool tiled hallway and into the drawing room at the back. The french windows were open on to the garden. His wife and daughter were sitting there in the sun.

He had been a doctor in Ventnor for a number of years, but it was only this year that he had acquired a practice for himself. His reputation for the treatment of tubercular conditions was beginning to be acknowledged. As he usually did at weekends in the summer months, he picked up his telescope and surveyed the Ventnor sands. It was a powerful telescope and he could easily make out features, even the colour of eyes. He had no difficulty also in seeing the colour of complexions. By this means he could identify not only those visitors who were already patients of his but those likely to qualify as such in the near future.

On the rock-studded shore, with its line of huts and bathing machines and beached boats just below the esplanade, parasols mushroomed above the bell-like shapes of women strolling in their silks and crinolines and men raising their stovepipe hats with the formality of plumed horses. Family groups sat decorously in deck chairs, the women minding the children, the men with raised chins surveying the sea. A Sunday scene of holidaying English gentry. The only unusual movement was supplied by four donkeys. Riding on the leading donkey in side-saddle fashion was a tall, bonneted lady wearing black boots. Each of the remaining donkeys carried a child perched on it. In their childish solemnity they acted out the roles of miniature Queen Victorias and Prince Alberts for admiring onlookers.

'I see Molly Ford's out with the donkeys again,' said the doctor.

His wife, Mrs Rose Hodgson, seated on a bench just behind him, gave a very slight sniff and gently touched a handkerchief to the tip of her nose. 'She is *such* a kind dear thing. I am so pleased for her. Whatever you may think about relationships of that sort, it is always pleasant to see two people who are happy together. Of course, she still suffers from sore feet, poor thing. After what she must've gone through last year! They say she came all the way on foot from Southampton and in such rags and tatters! But she's *such* a kind dear thing! So good with the donkeys!'

Neither the doctor nor their daughter Susan showed any sign of having heard. It was as if the remarks had not been made. One or two gulls cried noisily and the sound of waves rose softly through the afternoon heat.

'Good heavens!'

'What is it, James dear?'

'Do you remember that boy ... what was his name? He was friendly with Miles from next door.'

'I believe his name was ... was ... Susan dear, do you remember?'

'Guy,' said Susan sharply. She was using scissors equally sharply in preparing roses for display in a large glass vase.

'Of course – Guy Seddenham. And I see those two girls, the twins, are both riding the donkeys.'

'Jane and Edwina,' said Susan, again sharply. 'Their mother died last year.'

'Oh dear, I'd quite forgotten about that!' exclaimed her mother. 'What a tragedy! So like the Fentons.'

The doctor moved his telescope slowly and was drawn, as if he were the eye of God peering as much into their souls as into their faces, to look directly at two figures, seeming flat and depthless, like silhouettes against the whitely flashing waves.

'I can see the Misses Bosanquet. They're here again this year.'

'I can't say I'm very fond of them,' his wife said.

'Ah, that's most interesting!'

'*What* is most interesting?'

'Very, very interesting.'

'Oh, you can be such a pest when you're using that thing!'

'It's that young lady who stayed with the Fentons last year. The French governess.'

'Oh, you mean Marie,' said his wife.

'Marie Valence,' added Susan, demonstrating her French accent.

'She's with ... let me see ... ah, yes, von Fricken, who's just along the road at Wellington House, then there's Prince Bariatinsky from the Esplanade Hotel, and the Princess, of course, and then there's Colonel and Madame Rostovtzoff from Somerset Cottage, and then there's Mr and Mrs Kruze and their children ...'

'You mean the ones from Grove Road?' asked his wife.

'Exactly.'

'I think he has fine eyes.'

'I don't know about his eyes, my dear, but medically speaking it's his chest that worries me. Ah, there's Count Rostopchine! Oh, and I see our next-door neighbour's down there. I'm glad he's better.'

'It is,' said his wife, sighing as she dabbed her handkerchief at her cheeks and temples, 'quite a catch for little Ventnor – having Russian counts and princes here, I mean.'

Her husband snapped shut his· telescope and also wiped his face. 'All we need is to have the railway brought through. Then we'd be able to offer treatment all the year round. That's the way to make money.'

'Father, you shouldn't!'

His daughter looked severely at him, snipping a rose stem as she did so. Dr Hodgson laughed.

'It *is* business, no matter what you say.'

'Other people's misfortunes can never truly be a source of profit.'

This kind of remark from his daughter might have sounded prim, but she made it sound as if it had all the innocent charm of a motto in an embroidered frame. He gazed down at the amphitheatre of steeply layered houses and streets which comprised the town of Ventnor as it opened itself towards the sparkling sea.

'I do try to help,' he said.

'Susan dear, you're being unfair to your father in saying that,' her mother remarked. She slowly waved her handkerchief in a fanning motion before her face. 'If we are to have foreigners here in Ventnor, we should at least be nice to them. That's why your father invited that young Russian doctor as a locum.'

Dr Hodgson swayed on the balls of his feet and leaned forward to peer over the garden wall.

11

'Good afternoon, Mrs Flint, Mr Flint. A beautiful day, yes.'

He waved to those below in Belgrave Road. The horses for the return journey to Ryde were being led out of a small field adjoining the graveyard of St Catherine's church and were just about to be harnessed to the coach. There was a certain amount of shouting, stamping of hooves and neighing. The doctor opened his telescope again and directed it towards the west, to the limit of its magnification.

What he saw was a layered series of cutouts, grey upon grey, and here and there intervening splashes of white where the sea kicked up a jet of spray among the rocks. He looked in that direction, the area to the west of Ventnor sands known as West Hill and the Undercliff, because he had been told his new Russian locum made a habit of swimming there. It was dangerous, as everyone knew, but the man seemed to enjoy such danger. He had been here just over a week and yet he had already acquired a reputation for strange behaviour and an intimidating manner. Rome, Heidelberg, Dr Hodgson thought, in addition to his Russian qualification. An expert on pulmonary diseases and brilliant with a scalpel, that's what his letter of reference had claimed. But it hadn't said he was mad!

'I think he's a nice young man,' Mrs Rose Hodgson added after a pause. She sounded doubtful. 'It is true he speaks very little, but whenever he's spoken to me I've always found his English quite correct. Oh, how tiresome the flies are today!' She made shooing movements. 'And I can never pronounce it properly – his name, I mean.'

'Eugene, Mother. We talked about it at dinner-time.'

'No, no, I don't mean his Christian name. Bazaar something.' She spoke her doubts to the garden at large.

'It is strange to think of someone called Bazaar.'

'Bazaar-off,' said her husband. 'Bazaar with an "off" at the end of it.'

'Bazarov,' said Susan, 'that's how he likes his name to be pronounced.' She had by now completed her arrangement of the roses and was studying them.

'Bazarov,' her mother murmured to herself as if it were something she'd just tasted.

Dr Hodgson continued his scrutiny of the rocks beyond West Hill, attracted by glimpses of some pale indistinct figure apparently diving from a rock.

'Don't they smell lovely!' cried Mrs Rose Hodgson.

'I wish,' said her daughter, touching the roses slightly with the tips of her fingers much as she might primp and tidy children's clothes before a party, 'his room had a lovely smell.'

'What do you mean?'

'He smokes those dreadful cigars there, Mother. And he's collecting something in bowls.'

'I haven't noticed any bad smell.'

'He won't let anyone into his room, that's why. He has a microscope and he talks about dissecting things. Sea anemones.'

'He's a very gifted fellow, I'm sure of that,' said her father, snapping shut his telescope once again. 'But I'm not sure he's exactly the sort of fellow I'd wanted.'

What he meant was that he had decided to employ a Russian locum because he wanted to attract some of the wealthy Russian visitors to Ventnor, but Eugene Bazarov had had exactly the opposite effect. He had offended all the Russians staying at the Esplanade Hotel by refusing to attend them in their rooms and he had even befriended some of their servants and hangers-on. In short, he wasn't the sort of fellow Dr Hodgson needed as an assistant.

He gazed up at a dozen or so gulls crying as they circled in rising air currents above them. Every year, like Russian visitors, the gulls had increased. They scavenged along the shore, in the town itself, among the back gardens and refuse tips. But now, as they swung in the rising air, they appeared to look down on the Sunday activities of the town like tiny recording angels, watching and noting. They noted, for instance, the people out strolling along the sandy strand, the parallel lines made by fishermen's sledges and wheels of bathing machines and the few people brave enough to enter the frothing waves. Captain Stringer Fenton and his daughter Elizabeth noted the same thing.

'It is good to see how our little town flourishes,' he said. 'Have you seen yesterday's *Ventnor Times*, my dear?'

'I saw it this morning.'

'The list of visitors grows apace.' He laughed at two young men splashing water at each other. 'That's the spirit! Let him have it! Oh, what it is to be young!'

'You are young, Father,' she said, her arm through his, and when he turned to acknowledge her compliment he saw her earnest pretty sixteen-year-old face look round at him absolutely calmly, with all her mother's gentle sensibility of feature and expression, and for a moment he was made to wonder whether she had any of his own hot temper and masterfulness in her.

'Forty-one is not young. A man can pretend to be young at that age, but he can't have the vigour of these young fellows,' and he pointed to a couple of young men thrusting their heads and shoulders above the waves at each breaststroke. 'All I hope is that I can do something for this little town of ours. Shall we go back now?'

'Are you feeling tired?'

14

'Just a little. The lingering effects of that cold, you know.'

'Then we'd better go back.'

At that moment they were met by Mr Ellis, smart as ever in his tight, well-fitting uniform with its polished silver buttons. He saluted the Captain, raising one hand to his peaked cap and leaning his red, bearded face slightly forward.

'Good afternoon, Constable. Nothing to report, I hope.'

Captain Fenton was chairman of the Ventnor Watch Committee. He liked to receive personal reports on the criminal happenings in Ventnor and, in the temporary absence of the sergeant, it fell to the constable to make such reports. One was due in the coming week.

'Nothing very serious, Captain,' said Mr Ellis without complacency, but with a responsible constabulary air. He had a somewhat military bearing. 'Just one small matter, sir.'

'Can it wait till next Thursday?'

'Oh, yes, sir.'

'Thank you, Constable.'

Mr Ellis saluted again and the Captain raised his stick. They treated each other politely, but the constable's deference was ever so slightly obsequious. He continued his stroll along the sand, nodding towards people he recognised and surveying visitors with a mildly awesome backward tilt of the head, due to the fact that the steep angle of the peak of his cap obliged him to peer down the length of his nose if he wished to see them clearly.

'Unimaginative, but conscientious,' the Captain whispered to his daughter. 'It was a stroke of luck we found him last year. Well, well, do you know who I think I can see?'

'Who?'

Elizabeth followed the direction of his gaze and saw Marie Valence further up the sand. She was in the company of several smartly dressed Russians. One of them, an elderly man supported as he walked by a much younger man, seemed to be her companion, but as soon as she caught sight of Captain Fenton and his daughter she immediately waved and left her Russian group behind her. Dressed in a voluminous checked skirt and holding aloft a frilly parasol, she danced lightly down the sand towards them, her dark eyes and long shapely mouth breaking into a smile.

''Ow are you, Captain Fenton?' she gushed. 'And you too, Miss 'Lizabeth?' Her accented English had a music-hall French ring to it.

'I'm very well, Marie, but my father's just recovering from a cold.'

'*Mais vous ne parlez pas.* . . . Ah, well, you forget your French, yes?' She turned with a showy, concerned smile to the Captain, her chin lifted a little to look straight into his face. 'I am so sorry, Captain Fenton, to 'ear of your illness. Are you better?'

'Oh, much better. It is a pleasure to see you again, my dear Marie. Are you on holiday?'

'I am with Count Rostopchine. I came two weeks ago. I 'ave been 'ere and in Shanklin. Now I am 'ere. I am staying at St Martin's Villa.' She waved loftily towards one of the three-storey houses along the esplanade. ''Ow is Miles?'

There was a momentary silence. It was perhaps due not so much to embarrassment as to a lack of preparedness for the question.

'Miles,' answered Elizabeth, 'is becoming an officer in the navy. He is not at home now.'

There was some sharpness in her tone, except that her attractively musical voice dispelled any harshness. If her

16

voice did not convey her exact meaning, her eyes showed her annoyance.

'Miles always wanted to be an officer,' Captain Fenton said. 'He entered the navy in April. But Elizabeth has decided she does not wish to have any French lessons this year.'

' 'Ow sorry I am! But I understand. So I will 'ave the opportunity to see you, will I?'

Marie's dark eyes, though surrounded by lines crinkling into a warm smile, had the pure bland clarity and sparkle of glass. Elizabeth had never been able to fathom them. She'd never been able to escape the feeling that Marie's behaviour was artificial. She imagined that men might be fooled by her, as her brother Miles had been, but she simply couldn't put up with all the dazzling smiles and little ingratiating mannerisms.

'Do come and see us whenever you have the time,' said Captain Fenton, rising, so Elizabeth thought, to Marie's bait just as she'd hoped.

Marie danced away from them up the sand and rejoined the party of Russians. The elderly man, supported by the younger, had waited for her and yet obviously disapproved of her behaviour. He appeared to speak curtly to her while she, tossing her hair, walked on grandly beside him.

'How attractive and talented,' said Captain Fenton. 'She can speak English perfectly, if she wishes. And since she regards both Russian and French as her native tongues, what gifts for a woman to have!'

'I think you are exaggerating, Father.'

Elizabeth's remark closed the matter. Captain Fenton discerned from the look on her face that she was adamant and the two of them walked slowly up the sandy shore towards the esplanade. People were already beginning to return home. The sun was still bright and hot, despite a suddenly rising onshore breeze. The bottle-green waves developed slightly longer white crests and the circling gulls perhaps cried a trifle more stridently. The combination of sounds meant that neither Elizabeth nor her father heard a woman's voice just behind them until Elizabeth, recognising a renewed call, exclaimed:

'Oh, Father, it's Molly with the donkeys!'

'Thank you, Miss Elizabeth,' said the woman called Molly. She was no longer riding the leading donkey but walking along with it, a child having taken her place on the donkey's back.

'How are your feet?' Elizabeth asked.

'Oh, I'll be seeing the doctor tomorrow. Come on, Jonquil dear!'

And then Elizabeth recognised two of the little girls riding on the donkeys and vigorously waved, calling out:

'Jane! Edwina! How are you?'

'Very well, thank you,' the twins answered almost in unison.

'Father, it's Jane and Edwina, remember. They were here last summer. And where's Guy?' asked Elizabeth.

They pointed to their brother who was following in the wake of the donkeys. He was a tall boy dressed in a jacket and trousers that had obviously grown too small for him. At the sight of Elizabeth, whom he presumably had not expected to see, his handsome sunburned face seemed to darken and he grew noticeably tenser.

'How nice to see you again!' was Elizabeth's airy and rather hearty greeting, which appeared to embarrass the boy still more, but before he had time to reply Molly Ford was busily persuading them to make way for the donkeys, saying:

'If you'll please stand away from Jonquil, Miss Elizabeth, Dandy, Herbert and Pretty can come by.'

So she stood back from the leading donkey and all

four animals then carried the children, waving and smiling, away from them. Swaying in easy motion, the backs of the children astride the donkeys seemed so intently concentrated and dignified that Elizabeth was surprised when Jane suddenly twisted round, her bonnet blown back on her head, and waved at her, a single tiny hand-gesture highlighted against the dark background of the West Hill rocks. She waved back spontaneously.

'We didn't know you would be coming back again this year,' said Captain Fenton. 'Ventnor seems to be attracting more and more visitors every summer, I'm happy to say.'

'Well, sir . . .'

The possible embarrassment of such a formal exchange was curtailed by Elizabeth asking how long Guy Seddenham planned to stay. She held out her hand. He took it. Feeling her soft fingers in the grasp of his callused hand, he feared she would despise him for betraying such signs of his recent farm work, something which his sunburned complexion and the abundant growth of his chestnut, almost red, hair must also have proclaimed to the world. He held her hand awkwardly in his own for a moment, but her smile as he released it made his heart jump.

'Perhaps a week, perhaps two weeks,' he blurted out.

'You've grown, haven't you?' said the Captain.

'Almost five inches, sir.'

'Good heavens! You mustn't outgrow your strength, as they say. Last year I could just about look you in the eyes, now you're far above me! Where are you staying?'

Guy Seddenham said he couldn't say.

'Oh, dear, why is that?' asked Elizabeth.

'It seems there are a lot of foreign visitors this summer.'

'Oh, it's the Russians!' exclaimed the Captain.

19

'Yes, the Russians,' agreed Elizabeth. 'We've just seen Marie. Do you remember her? She was with us last year.'

'I do.' Guy's bright smile altered to one less straining for his lips. 'How is Miles?'

The Captain explained about his decision to go into the navy.

'I'd been hoping,' Guy said, 'we'd be able to . . .' He was going to mention how he had looked forward to going sailing with Miles, as they had done last year, but instead he found himself sounding serious. 'I have to look after the twins, you see. We have a maid, but very often she's having to attend to my aunt's needs.'

Such admissions were a sign of the change in their family fortunes since the previous summer. He glanced down at his worn boots and the ends of his tight trousers.

'We're poor, you see, that's to say . . .'

'I understand, I really do,' said Elizabeth, perceiving at once what he meant. 'I was so sorry to hear about your mother. It must've been such a shock.'

He nodded. To his surprise, her concern pleased rather than saddened him as such formal condolences usually did. He looked deeply for a moment into her clear blue eyes and recognised in them not only a genuine sympathy, but also an awareness of bereavement similar to his own.

'Yes,' said the Captain, 'we offer you our deepest . . . deepest . . .'

Before the commiserations were completed, Guy heard his name being called. Their maid Joan was standing on the esplanade calling out 'Master Guy! Master Guy!' like some screeching parrot. She looked frantic and Guy at once excused himself.

The Captain raised his hat and Elizabeth gave a little

bow. The two of them, almost the same height and with similar slender builds, walked off towards the steps leading up to the esplanade. Joan was meanwhile gesticulating. She was signalling that Guy should collect the twins. As a matter of fact, that particular ride had just finished and they had been lifted down. They ran towards him at once, their heels kicking up sand.

'Fun?'

'Oh, lovely fun! Marvellous fun!'

'Joan's waving, you can see,' he said.

It turned out that their aunt, Mrs Emily Whitehouse, had told Joan to fetch them immediately. There wasn't a single room to be had in the Esplanade Hotel and all they could find overlooking the sea were top rooms at Belinda House and a back room, and would Master Guy go at once to where the Mistress was, at the Esplanade Hotel, and see that all the cases were brought from there to Belinda House. Guy resented receiving such instructions from a maidservant, especially since they were given in a high-pitched, truculent manner, as if somehow he were personally responsible for their failure to find rooms. But he was glad somewhere had been found. Swallowing his resentment, he went off to the Esplanade Hotel where he discovered his aunt at the entrance surrounded by a trunk and three cases. She greeted him with some relief.

'We have to move to Belinda House, Guy, my dear.'

'Yes, I've heard.'

'The people here say they never received my letter, but I really can't believe them.' She was a portly woman with a large florid face who delivered herself of these remarks in a whisper loud enough for the manager and the porter to hear. 'They say the hotel is full to bursting. Well, I've never heard anything like it in all my life. They are most disagreeable here. So I've decided we'll

21

take rooms further along the esplanade. So, Guy dear, the cases are waiting.'

She said it as if the fact of waiting were an insult to the cases themselves. To Guy, though, the remark had a different meaning. It meant that his aunt was not prepared to spend any of her money on paying for a porter from the Esplanade Hotel to carry the cases along the esplanade. The fact that they were on holiday at all was a privilege wrested only at great cost from Uncle Charles Augustus and every penny had to be spent with the greatest care.

A very elegantly dressed woman with an aristocratic, sternly beautiful face watched Guy and began to smile slightly as he bent to pick up the cases. Another woman shook some sand from the hem of her skirt and a tall gentleman with sideburns tapped sand from the heel of his shoes with a thin walking stick.

'Russians,' breathed Aunt Emily. 'That's why there are no rooms.' More loudly she added: 'Leave the trunk, Guy dear. I'll send for that.'

Guy obediently lifted the cases, finding them less heavy than he'd expected, and walked slowly out into the heat of the esplanade. Meanwhile his aunt kept up a running commentary on the several ways in which Ventnor had caused her offence since their arrival.

'I know you were here last year, but it has become a lot more crowded since *I* was last here. And such a lot of foreigners! And that Esplanade Hotel, what pretensions it has! "We regret, madame, we have no accommodation available, none whatsoever." Such snobbish behaviour, Guy dear. They are quite above themselves.'

They walked past Pelham House, Alma Cottage, Medina Cottage. His aunt mimicked the manager's voice to perfection but Guy was too encumbered with luggage to laugh. She went on to comment unflatteringly about the noise of the gulls and the way the breeze was shaking her parasol.

'Oh, here we are, I think,' she said. 'It isn't anything like as far as I'd thought. Well, here we are. Yes, here's St Martin's Villa already. They said it would be a nicer place than Belinda House, but Belinda House is reputed to have good, simple food and the lady doesn't mind children. So I chose Belinda House. A pretty name. What did the twins do? Oh, rides on donkeys. Isn't that common, Guy dear? Only common children like rides on donkeys.'

Guy was relieved of the cases in the hallway of Belinda House where the proprietress, Mrs Rees, was waiting to greet them. The twins looked sullen and subdued, as they usually did when Joan had charge of them. Mrs Rees herself, recognising that Mrs Emily Whitehouse was a lady of quality, suppressed her reluctance at having to cater for children.

'Such good-mannered girls,' she remarked, 'I'm sure. And I do so like to cater for the better sorts of person, I'm sure you know what I mean, Mrs Whitehouse. Er, you will have the large front room, of course. I'm afraid there is nothing at present on the first floor. But it is very pleasant, with a good view of the sea.'

They were led up the stairs. Childish fingers were urged not to touch the brass ornaments set out on tables on the landings. Sand was not to be brought into the house on shoes, which should be wiped carefully on the mat provided by the front door. There was a bathroom and a water closet, but the usual amenities were provided for guests in each bedroom. Hot water would be available each morning and evening. And so on. Then Mrs Rees turned to Guy.

'I'm afraid there is only one room remaining. It is at the back on the top floor, very sunny in the morning. This way, please.'

Guy's room turned out to be small. It had one

23

window, which overlooked the side wall of the adjacent house, St Martin's Villa, and gave a view of the sea and the esplanade if one squinted sideways. It was clean. It had a flowered jug in a flowered washbowl standing on a marble-topped washstand. A small wooden bed had been crammed into one corner, largely in order to accommodate a bulky dark wardrobe with a full-length mirror. A bamboo chair and a towel rail completed the furnishings.

'Ah, there, aren't we nicely settled!' said Aunt Emily. 'How very kind of you, Mrs Rees.'

But Guy, when the door had been closed behind them, stood by the little window and stared at his reflection in the long mirror, feeling annoyed and apprehensive and ashamed. 'Guy sweet in feature, sweet in nature,' his mother had been used to saying. But his mother was dead and his father had gone to Australia. He was simply Guy Seddenham. He was nearly sixteen, tall, chestnut-haired, with dark brown eyes and a round face. Ordinary. His hands were big-fingered. He was strong. He had worked at haymaking and harvesting after his tutor, Mr Prendergast, had departed for the continent to 'broaden his horizons', though what that meant exactly Guy was not sure. He had liked Mr Prendergast as much as he had liked any teacher, but Mr Prendergast had been sacrificed to the demands of thrift just as Guy's schooling had. A year ago, before his mother died and his father's business had finally collapsed, he had dreamed of becoming a doctor. Now his horizons were reduced simply to this promised Ventnor holiday, when he had hoped to go sailing with Miles, and then his uncle's office in Lambeth where he would start work as a copying clerk. Until they heard more from his father, that was the sum total of his future. He and the twins had been brought on holiday as

24

a favour grudgingly allowed them by Aunt Emily (with the equally grudging permission of Uncle Charles Augustus) and they were expected to be grateful. Thousands of children never had such a chance. Guy acknowledged this, but why, why had this all happened to him, Guy Seddenham? Why had he been taken away from school? Why had he been put in this cramped back room? He stared at himself, filled his lungs with air and then expelled it in one short gasp. The world was like that, he supposed.

He stared dreamily out of the little window. There was the tall adjacent house and there was a glimpse of the sunny esplanade and the blue sea between the houses. By peering downwards he could see the only window in the side wall of the adjacent house. It was two floors below him. The sash was open. Standing in the window, holding aside the curtains, was a naked woman. She was looking directly across at Belinda House, showing herself, it seemed. Her body was slender, shapely, firm-breasted and gleaming white. All Guy could not see clearly was her face. His eyes consumed her. He had never before seen a naked woman or seen a woman preen herself in her nakedness, moving her hips seductively, lifting her shoulders so that her full breasts swayed and the little crucifix hanging between them shook. The sexual thrill of the blatant nakedness was like an electric shock. He felt a mixture of excitement and shame and disbelief. Then the curtains fell back into place and the woman vanished. He went crimson, thinking she might have seen him and imagining he knew who she was. But at that moment the gong suddenly sounded for tea.

2

By the end of tea, consisting of some fruit cake as well as cucumber sandwiches ('special for Sundays,' as Mrs Rees assured her new guests), Mrs Emily Whitehouse had succeeded in discovering practically everything she wanted to know. She learned from the Misses Bosanquet the names of the other guests and which rooms they occupied, what was happening in Ventnor, who went to which church or chapel and which doctor to consult for which ailment. They gave it as their opinion that Ventnor was going downhill. Apart from the weather, which had not been good and promised to be worse, there were the Russians. One Russian, Miss Adelaide and Miss Henrietta whispered simultaneously, both with handkerchiefs raised daintily to their mouths, was actually living in Belinda House. He was occupying the small room on the first-floor landing. Some kind of manservant, it seemed. 'A very common person,' said Henrietta Bosanquet. 'And such table manners!' added the other. They described in detail how he ate soup with his chin almost level with his bowl and spooned the liquid in noisy slurps into his mouth, accompanied by much munching of bread. 'But he is quite smartly dressed,' Henrietta explained. 'They say he is employed by a Russian Count who is staying at the Esplanade Hotel. It is hardly what one would expect of Ventnor, is it?' Adelaide added: 'To be asked to share the dining room with a manservant!' Lowering her voice, she went on: 'He had to be taught to use the water closet! Oh, it is too much, too much!'

The Misses Bosanquet's account ended with both of them succumbing to the racking coughs which were the reason for their visit to Ventnor this summer. Aunt Emily, always wary of illness, sat very upright with pursed lips. She gave Guy sitting beside her one quick severe glance. After a while the coughing subsided and the conversation turned to the question of doctors.

'There is even,' said Henrietta, appalled, 'a new *Russian* doctor here this summer. He is working for Dr Hodgson.'

'Can you understand what he says?'

'Oh, he speaks very good English and is most polite. But of course he is quite uncivilised.'

Aunt Emily expressed surprise.

'He is . . .' said Adelaide Bosanquet and searched for a word ' . . . unusual.'

'Uncivilised,' her sister insisted. 'This very morning, when we went for a stroll shortly before the early service, what did we see? We saw him . . .'

'Oh, but you know we couldn't be sure!' Adelaide protested.

'We saw him without a stitch on, as naked as the day and as bold as a Hottentot, standing there on the rocks below West Hill. It was absolutely shocking, Mrs Whitehouse.'

'But what on earth was he doing there?' exclaimed Aunt Emily, who was clearly showing more than usual interest in such a revelation.

'I suppose he was engaged in sea-bathing.'

Henrietta Bosanquet spoke briskly, as if she were making a swift purchase in a shop with a rather unpleasant smell. Almost immediately she succumbed to a further attack of coughing. In order to distract attention from her sister's illness, Adelaide asked how long Mrs Whitehouse intended to stay in Ventnor,

27

adding in a lowered voice, obviously for fear that Mrs Rees might overhear, that they themselves were probably not staying more than a few days. 'The weather is simply not conducive, you know.'

Sitting as they were in the small room behind the dining room, described by Mrs Rees as the parlour, they did not exactly look as if they were dressed for summer weather, although the window beside the fireplace was open and admitted almost as much heat at five o'clock on this Sunday afternoon as did the fire which burned somewhat dimly in the cast-iron grate. All the ladies used handkerchiefs to dab at their cheeks.

'We are here for two weeks,' said Aunt Emily. 'Did you say the man was not wearing any bathing garment?'

'None that we could see,' answered Henrietta, now recovered.

'Very remarkable.'

'He has a nasty habit of smoking cigars,' said Adelaide. 'I do hate men who smoke. Mrs Rees is not as particular as she should be about smoking. That Russian manservant smokes, you know.'

'I find it an offensive habit, I must say,' Aunt Emily agreed, again exchanging a glance with Guy as if intimating that she hoped *he* would never develop such a habit. Guy tried to give his face an expression of polite distaste while not appearing to make it seem too real. Throughout the conversation between the elderly women he had been conscious of the dusty old-maidish odours which exuded from the Misses Bosanquet. He did not like to diagnose their separate, olfactory constituents, being equally fascinated in an appalled way by a wart on Miss Adelaide's chin which sported a few dark hairs, and a livid uprising, like an unswallowed raisin, that appeared on Henrietta's lower lip as she spoke and seemed to obtrude slightly as if she were about to spit it out. Engrossed by these reflections, he suddenly found he had become the subject of their attention.

'Such a good-looking nephew you have,' remarked Henrietta, making Guy feel instantly ashamed of having been so distracted by her lower lip. 'I imagine he is still at school.'

Aunt Emily shook her head. Usually, whenever the subject was raised in his and the twins' presence, she would announce that she was *in loco parentis* so long as her brother, their father, was away in Australia endeavouring to recoup the fortune which an unscrupulous agent had stolen from him. She would explain, perhaps a little piously, that she had not been able to deny him the earnest wish that his poor orphaned children should be looked after as well as possible in his absence. Now, a little to Guy's surprise and relief, she simply said:

'No, Guy is not at school. His tutor has been dismissed and he will begin working in my husband's Chambers as soon as this holiday is over. I am afraid there is no other course. The twins will receive some kind of education, though it has not been decided what it may be. You see, their mother – the most devoted mother, you can imagine – caught a cold last autumn, neglected herself and was soon, all too soon...' She patted her temples with her handkerchief and touched it to the tip of her nose. 'I have tried to take her place, but it is not easy.'

'Oh, how very noble and charitable of you, Mrs Whitehouse!' exclaimed Henrietta.

'Thank you. It is not everyone who appreciates the sacrifice, you know.' Again Aunt Emily glanced at Guy. Blushing, he said a little too emphatically: 'We do appreciate it, Aunt Emily, you know we do.' She went

29

on: 'He has been working on a farm belonging to a relative. Haymaking.'

'You can tell he has been out in the sun,' remarked Henrietta. 'We so seldom see such healthy faces among the young people in our neighbourhood. We live in Holborn, you see.'

All of them now looked at Guy and he found himself embarrassed by their scrutiny, even though it was intended to be admiring. What embarrassed him was the fact that his blue velvet jacket which had been purchased last summer before his mother's death was now stretched as tightly over his back as a child's garment and the sleeves had grown so short that at least three inches of his forearms and wrists were left bare. Although he tried to pull the sleeves down, the effort was clearly useless. He tried folding his arms in a slightly defiant way, but a commotion of running feet and laughter on the stairs saved him further trouble.

'Oh,' cried Aunt Emily, her voice rising powerfully, 'that's those naughty twins! I do wish Joan would exercise more control! Guy, take them out, there's a good boy! But be sure to be back by six!'

'Yes, Aunt Emily,' Guy said and did as he was told. The twins had been racing down the stairs from the second floor in the hope of escaping from Joan. As soon as he entered the hall he took charge of them, told them to be quiet and led them out on to the esplanade.

It was such a relief to be outside after the stuffiness and embarrassments of the parlour that he felt like running at once right down to the sea. He was restrained by the sight of several groups of people dressed in formal Sunday clothes on the seaweed- and rock-strewn sand, but more restraining still was the need to set an example to the twins. He turned to them severely:

30

'You mustn't tease Joan so much.'

Joan was a standing joke to them no matter what he said. A large-thighed, heavy girl of eighteen, she was always complaining about the twins' liveliness. At that moment she had managed to get as far as the low esplanade wall before exclaiming in her usual way: 'I'd like a real sit-down, I would,' at which the twins both gave way to little salvoes of giggles.

'Do please behave yourselves,' he said. 'People will notice.'

That was a very severe stricture and the twins knew it. They might be poor and their clothes might be too small for them, but they owed it to their mother's memory to be as well-behaved as possible. She had always insisted on it. Since her death they had become united against the rest of the world in a kind of conspiracy designed to ensure that no one should separate them or belittle them or hold them up to ridicule, least of all Aunt Emily or Uncle Charles Augustus or even Joan.

'You're not on her side, are you?' whispered Edwina, looking up into Guy's face.

He squeezed her hand.

Jane said: 'Of course he's not.'

'Please say you're not,' Edwina insisted.

'I'm on your side,' he agreed, but it was grudgingly admitted, because he found the twins' attitude rather childish. He felt they did not have a proper idea of what this visit to Ventnor ought to mean. To him it meant recovering ever so little, tiny fragment by tiny fragment, the memory of their mother. In the stillness of the summer heat which filled the whole area of sand at that moment he felt her presence. The tall white thunderheads rising like Alps on the horizon reminded him in particular of one of her remarks last year, 'If it's not

31

wind in Ventnor, it's thunderstorms,' and at that moment he was sure he could hear distant thunder above the soft lapping of the waves.

'Oh, look, the donkeys've all gone!' said Edwina.

'So what'll we do?' begged Jane.

'Play with the seaweed,' he said rather curtly, and to his surprise they seized eagerly on this suggestion, beginning to trail long strands of seaweed behind them as they ran about among the small rocks. Then Edwina, always the more inventive of the two, suggested they start making their own names out of the seaweed. This activity soon absorbed them and Guy found himself on his own. Feeling hot and sticky in his tight jacket, and upset by the recollection of his mother, he wandered idly away along the shore in the direction of the rocks below West Hill.

The previous summer his mother and he had walked in precisely this part of the shore on three or four occasions. They had always gone as far as the rocks, never any further. She had expressed her fear of slipping on the seaweed and the tide had always been higher than it was this Sunday, so the wide area of rocks had been out of bounds to them. Instead, what he remembered about those walks was the pleasure of being able to talk freely about the private things of their lives. It was on one such walk that he confessed how much he wanted to be a doctor when he grew up. His mother had said they would do all they could to make it possible, and she had spoken of her worries about the wool-importing business and the dishonesty of the Australian agents. He had also noticed then how frail she was, though he knew she never wanted to discuss her health. They avoided the subject as they avoided the rocks. Once he had seen her face lifted to confront the wind and he had suddenly felt his heart ache for her and had said quite spontaneously, 'I love you, Mother. You're the best mother in the world,' and she had given an amazed trill of laughter like a girl and quickly pressed him to her side. 'You're a very sweet boy, Guy,' she had said quietly, almost to herself.

He turned and looked behind him, feeling slightly embarrassed by the recollection, and saw the twins were still playing with the seaweed although they seemed very far away, well out of earshot, while the sea, in the stillness, seemed very close and listening. The dazzlingly bright sun of the late afternoon caused a glitter and sparkle among the rock pools directly ahead of him. He was drawn towards them as much out of excitement at their brilliant silver surfaces as out of curiosity to see what they contained. Separate from the area of sand and only accessible through a wide stream flowing out of the cliffs of West Hill, they were like a different world. They were also taller than he remembered, or perhaps it was that the freshwater stream which flowed among shoals of sand and rocky outcrops had washed away sand from their base. He knew his only choice was to wade through the stream, so he removed his boots and stockings, pulled up his trouserlegs and danced his way from shoal to shoal across the wide water.

Clambering on to the lip of the first plateau of rocks, he found what seemed to be an empty area. Overhead a couple of gulls floated and towards the horizon were fishing boats with their dull white triangles of sails sharp as flints against the seascape. He felt himself completely alone and his imagination began to play tricks on him. He imagined he would find mermaids beside the glassy pools. Mr Prendergast had ridiculed the idea of mermaids, he remembered. Miles, though, had told him last year some story about fishermen finding one in their nets. What Mr Prendergast admired were the Greek gods. He would insist they had dwelling-places even in England. Could this silent area of rocks be a dwelling-place for the gods? Guy dismissed the idea for the quite obvious and strictly practical reason that no gods in their right minds would want to live in a place which the sea covered twice a day. His imagination ran on beyond Mr Prendergast's book full of plates of naked Greek statuary to the thought of the naked woman he had seen in the window of the house opposite. If he were to find anyone, he hoped he would find her stooping beside one of these pools, her lovely body arcing white over the water and her long hair trailing its dark tresses right to the water's surface. Enchanted, he would watch, trying not to be noticed, but he knew she would slowly raise her eyes and see him and her eyes would be as green as the eyes of Circe. If he were not transformed into an animal, like the sailors of Odysseus, he would still remain at the mercy of her enchantment. If she were to rise up and seize hold of him and carry him down into the depths of one of the pools and then through cavernous pathways beneath the sea, he knew he would be unable to stop her. If he were to become her prisoner in some coral palace, the only human companion for her nature that was half fish, half human, he would become what was called in books her 'lover' and be glad, he supposed, for her to lean over him and kiss him and press her sea-cold body to his body's warmth.

Jumping from rock to rock while immersed in this daydream, he failed to notice that the seaward promontories had risen slightly. At the same time he heard voices. The very idea that there *could* be mermaids – or mermen – with voices suddenly caused him to stop dead, frozen in shock. He was old enough, almost sixteen after all, and he was certain there could be no

scientific proof of the existence of mermaids or mermen. At that instant, piercing his sense of shock and
increasing it, a gull screamed loudly overhead. Other
cries followed like echoes from other gulls, as loud in
the stillness as gradually dying rolls of thunder, and he
saw how the sea itself, scarcely ten yards from him, rose
and fell indolently, like an animal basking, and touched
white fingers of wave lightly against the sides of the
rocks, splashed here and there into gullies with unexpected vigour and then beat again softly all along the
shoreline of sand towards the white house-fronts of
Ventnor. Glancing downwards from what he now
realised was a rock promontory approximately ten feet
above the sea, he recognised the source of the voices.
Two naked boys were standing on a spit of sand partly
submerged by incoming wavelets. They were eleven or
twelve and their heads were bent over something one of
them was holding. Guy stood absolutely still, knowing
the slightest move from him might attract their attention. Then the boy holding whatever it was they were
studying called out suddenly:
' 'S an arrer, sir! An arrer!'
He ran off with a loud splashing through the shallow
waves at the foot of the rocks, followed by the other
boy. They both disappeared beyond a further promontory of rock and Guy heard their shouts in an adjacent
inlet, answered by a man's voice, but neither what they
said nor what the man said made any sense to him. He
turned round immediately and retraced his steps across
the rocky plateau of seaweed and pools, knowing he had
intruded.

35

3

The next morning, after some thunder in the night, a fresh breeze from the sea swept along the sunlit Ventnor esplanade and rustled the curtains of Count Rostopchine's bedroom in the Esplanade Hotel. He stood on the small verandah for a moment, surveying the almost empty shore, the esplanade with its butcher's cart and one or two strolling people, the bland, shimmering sea, and wondered what on earth he was doing here in this insignificant English seaside resort on the southern coast of the Isle of Wight in this year of Our Lord, 1860. The foreign look of the sea and the houses reminded him that he was here to contemplate the liberation of the Russian people, the so-called emancipation of the serfs, which the Tsar was due to announce in the following year.

'My liberal conscience,' he said aloud, addressing an imaginary crowd of loyal peasants below the window, 'obliges me, my dear friends...' and then he turned back into his bedroom as he noticed one top-hatted English face glance up towards the sound of the unfamiliar Russian words. Fedya, his manservant, was standing waiting for him, a clothes-brush at the ready.

'A hair. On my sleeve.'

Fedya brushed obediently.

'Today you were late. Why?'

The fellow started mumbling. '... Russian doctor...'

'What was that?'

'The doctor, sir.'

'What about him? Are you ill?'

There was a mumbling which contained a denial and a mention of someone called Masha.

'Aha! No, no, no, and again no!' The Count wagged his finger at this manservant of his. Fedya represented to him both a living reproach for his past and a sense that, through the smartness of his suit, he signalled the liberal future for which the Count hoped. But before that could happen, he must be taught who was master. 'I'm not giving you a penny. The claret, if you please.'

He saw his own figure in the long oval mirror with the gilt frame. Remarkably young for forty-five, the prime of a man's life, you might say, and aristocratic of feature, the sparse, tinted, very straight hair macassared sleekly over the small skull, the trimmed moustache, the soft collar of the expensive silk shirt neatly setting off a loosely tied cravat, the navy-blue blazer with brass buttons and the smart white flannels. English, you might say, urbane, unpretentious, confident. A snap of the fingers and Fedya brought him a tray of cold meat and a glass of wine and then withdrew into an anxious stooped position just beside the door, his shoulders slightly hunched. The Count sat down, fixed his glittering eyes on his manservant and raised his glass.

'I will drink to your health, Fedya. Your master drinks to your health. The health of our liberated people.' He drank. Fedya blinked his eyes. 'Oh, I know about you and Masha.' Again the finger wagged. 'You have misbehaved. You have allowed her to seduce you, haven't you?'

Fedya turned away his eyes.

'Look at me! Tell me I'm wrong!'

Fedya mumbled something.

'You are twenty-two years old. I have been a father to you, haven't I?'

The mumbling sounded like 'You are my father,' but the Count waved his hand, a pink handkerchief fluffing

37

from his sleeve, sipped more wine and declared: 'It's neither here nor there. You will soon be free to ruin your life just as you wish. Discipline, that's what the Russian people need. I have provided, have I not? Your clothes, your room, your food, haven't I provided them? And haven't I provided Marie's as well? And how am I repaid?'

Fedya did not even offer a mumbled answer.

'By licentious behaviour,' said the Count. 'By demands for money.'

He gave a long sniff which was followed by a short bout of coughing. The pink handkerchief was raised to his lips, then tucked back again into the cuff with a few fidgety movements which suggested the Count did not like to be reminded of his illness. He raised his chin in defiance of Fedya's possibly reproachful, possibly callous look. But his manservant's expression betrayed only stoniness. The Count contemplated Fedya for about a minute. He speculated on exactly how much of this curly-haired, red-cheeked, strong young man in his tight English suiting was *his* progeny, how much the peasant girl's whom he'd seduced when he was approximately Fedya's age. Fedya seemed so little like him that he found it easy to disregard his supposed paternity. In any case, the girl hadn't been a virgin.

'I think perhaps I have allowed you too much freedom already,' the Count said quietly. 'If there'd been more room in this hotel, you'd have been found somewhere here. Not a room of your own as you have now. And I'd have made sure you weren't free to enjoy Marie's company. In view of which,' he sipped a little wine, savouring it with his lips, 'I think we ought to be leaving. The discussions, well ... Ah, see who it is, please!'

Fedya sprang towards the door and opened it as soon

as Russian voices were audible on the other side. Two men stood there, a little startled by the suddenness with which the door had been opened even before they had tapped, but the Count rose at once, extended his right hand in an English greeting and Colonel Rostovtzoff, the taller of the two, accepted the handshake with formal warmth, his eyes blinking hurriedly. The second man, smaller, more portly and older, introduced himself in a clipped, bureaucratic fashion with a slight bow:

'Kruze, Nikolay Fyodorovich.'

They exchanged the usual greetings and introductions. Colonel Rostovtzoff explained that he had taken the liberty of inviting Kruze to accompany him because they had felt it best to impart their news jointly. The Count invited them to be seated and offered refreshments, which they refused.

'News?' he asked, fingering his cravat and feeling the soft collar of his silk shirt.

'Unsatisfactory news,' Colonel Rostovtzoff announced in a cultivated, drawling voice. He played with the starched cuffs of his shirtsleeves, drawing them forward sharply under the cloth of his fawn topcoat. 'I assume we can talk freely?' He glanced towards Fedya.

The Count assured him that his manservant could be trusted, but for safety's sake he ordered him to leave the room until his visitors had left. The Colonel leaned forward, smoothing his moustaches:

'We cannot take unnecessary risks, Count Rostopchine. Especially since we understand' – at this point his voice was lowered – 'we understand Herzen will not be coming here this summer. He may have got wind of some special surveillance measures. The authorities are suspicious, you know.'

He eyed the Count from under his brows and drew

his lips tightly together. Then he exchanged a look with Kruze. The Count knew exactly what they were thinking. They were wondering whether he could be trusted. He was no friend of Alexander Herzen, the famous London exile and publisher of *The Bell*, unlike Kruze, or the famous writer Ivan Turgenev, so the news that Herzen would not be coming to Ventnor this summer mattered little to him. But the idea that their own presence in Ventnor was known to the Tsarist authorities and might have given rise to special surveillance measures was alarming. He tried to suppress all signs of such alarm as he said:

'Ah, that is a blow, isn't it? Without Herzen's support, if not his active encouragement, our discussions will lack ... er, will lack political weight, don't you think?'

'I understand,' said the colonel, 'he is opposed to our discussions here, more's the pity. He plans to take his holiday in a place called Bunmoss.'

'Bunmoss? Where's that?'

'On the mainland.' Colonel Rostovtzoff crossed his legs. 'He considers we're merely ·so many dilettantes and amateurs, so many liberal charlatans, you might say, who've come here to make plans for our country's future without any real understanding of the people's needs. So we have to ensure that our discussions are fruitful and that we are men who can be trusted. There must be no breath of scandal associated with our gathering here. Above all, we must ensure there are no spies in our midst. I don't think I need say any more, need I?'

'No, no, of course not.'

'Precisely,' said Kruze in a sharp, authoritarian, bureaucratic tone of voice, 'precisely my own sentiments. We have a duty to show we're statesmanlike.

40

But we must be on our guard.'

'I assume you are with us, Count,' said Colonel Rostovtzoff, 'even though we may have to forgo the pleasure of Herzen's company.' The mild, patrician sarcasm elicited a quick response.

'I have to confess I have often thought of him as a charlatan.' The Count realised that this might sound a trifle bald and added with a faint smile: 'A charlatan with convictions, of course.'

'Precisely, precisely,' Kruze agreed. 'But it is precisely through his fundamental belief in democracy and freedom that our country will be saved. He is a charlatan only in the sense that he is equally convinced of the peasantry as the true focus of revolution in our country and derides, not to say actively opposes, any attempt by other sections of society to assume a guiding role. He is opposed to our discussions for that reason. If we are to ascribe his reaction to jealousy, not to say sour grapes, then we may well regard him as betraying an unseemly degree of charlatanry at this crucial moment in our nation's history. It is easy to bandy about terms of that kind. As an impartial servant of government I always felt it my own personal duty to see both sides. On Herzen's behalf it must be said that he chose exile out of conviction. He has asked us to respect him as a free voice. *The Bell* is a tocsin summoning our great nation to a crusade for freedom at this momentous juncture in our destiny. He is our liberal conscience, gentlemen, and we forget that at our peril. But it is my own sincere conviction that Herzen has been outside Russia too long. He does not understand what is happening. He is deficient in practical political sense. There is also too much *amour propre*, a certain self-regarding preening, not to mention some failure of magnanimity, in my opinion.' Kruze took out a

41

handkerchief and blew his nose. 'As I once told His Imperial Majesty, what he should most fear is the peasant waving an axe, not the intellectual waving a bell.'

Colonel Rostovtzoff gave a polite laugh. But the reference by Kruze to his former role as a confidant of the Tsar had a subduing effect on the conversation. The Count looked down nervously at his fingernails and tried to think of something to say in the momentary silence. Before he had time to make a renewed offer of a glass of wine, the door was abruptly flung open and Marie Valence in a brilliant red dress flounced in, carrying a parasol. Her broad-mouthed smile, sparkling, actressy eyes and long black hair, which she now swept away elegantly from her face, brought her instant attention.

'I wish to speak to the Count!' she declared.

All three men rose, Kruze and Colonel Rostovtzoff with the dignity of polite but slightly offended gallantry, the Count with evident annoyance and a series of dismissive hand-movements.

'You can see I am busy. Fedya, be good enough ...'

'I must insist,' Marie said in a determined voice, giving a challenging shake of her dark hair. 'I have been kept waiting too long.'

'Ah, it is never wise,' said Kruze, bowing towards her, 'to keep a lady waiting.'

'Thank you, sir. You are wiser, in that case, than the Count.'

It was clear that Count Rostopchine showed no inclination to introduce Marie Valence to his guests, so the Colonel said diplomatically:

'We can leave our discussion for the time being. Perhaps till tomorrow? You will have to excuse me, by the way. The news that Turgenev has arrived ...'

'Turgenev has arrived!' echoed Marie, raising a hand to her mouth in astonishment. 'Do you mean the famous writer?'

'Yes, mademoiselle,' said Kruze. 'I heard it this morning. He arrived yesterday.'

'Where is he staying?'

'At Rock Cottage. In Belgrave Road.'

'What a strange place! I would've thought...'

'The town is very full, you know,' Kruze said softly, 'and you and I and our compatriots are to blame.'

Marie acknowledged the justice of this at once. 'Oh, but to have someone so famous staying here! It is so exciting!'

Her spontaneous elation at the news proved infectious. The Colonel smiled broadly.

'I'm sure our famous writer would be greatly flattered to know his presence here gives you such pleasure. But now please excuse us.'

The guests withdrew suavely despite the Count's attempts to detain them. As the door closed, the Count knew only too well that his trustworthiness as a participant in their private discussions must be in doubt. He glowered at Marie. Of course, she read his thoughts and had probably interrupted the discussions on purpose. With a brusque gesture he directed her to sit down.

'Why did Fedya let you in? Didn't he tell you I was busy?'

'I insisted.'

She challenged him to deny her the right to be treated as a lover, a mistress, even a wife, for all practical purposes. Part of her challenge of course involved his political ambitions, as he well knew and recognised, but more serious was the challenge to his social reputation. Her relations with Fedya were involved here. He knew they had had an affair, his mistress and his illegitimate son. It had been unwise of him to allow them so much freedom, he supposed, though he felt aggrieved at such sordid betrayal of his trust, tending to blame it all on the general liberal atmosphere of the time. He recognised clearly enough that his own liberalism was just an expediency and it would take little to make him wash his hands of it altogether.

'So?'

He took his seat again, offered her a glass of claret, which she refused, and then leaned across to the little table on which Fedya had earlier set the tray. He cut himself a small slice of cold meat. As he put down the silver knife, the chink of metal on china made a very faint bell-like sound.

'You know perfectly well why I wish to speak to you,' she said, sitting very upright and folding her hands primly in her lap. He knew all her mannerisms. Chiefly he knew how much of an actress she was. She had special gifts, there was no denying that, and among them was her gift for languages. She spoke better English than he did. He knew how she liked to pretend to be French in England and English in France. But she was as Russian as he was, no better than a peasant for all her Frenchified airs and graces, with her 'Marie' instead of Masha, her 'Valence' instead of Ivanovna.

'I am listening, my dear.'

He let himself smile momentarily, accompanying it with a bright fixed look of the eyes. It amused him to note her intent expression and the way her hands pressed against each other in her lap.

'I want money! Money for myself!' Her voice was much too loud. Her hands, raised suddenly from her lap in eloquent gestures, made it seem that she would tear her clothes and her trinkets and her perfume from her if she could and fling it all in his face. 'Look at me – *your* clothes, *your* jewels, *your* perfume! Everything is *yours*! I want money of my own! I want to be myself! I want to be free!'

'My dear, of course you'll be free! Aren't the Russian people being freed? Surely that's why we're here... to discuss the future of our country when it's free.'

She raised her eyebrows in scorn. 'You talk about it, but what do you *do* about it?'

He leaned forward, suddenly venomous. 'I do not give you money! I do not let you betray my trust!'

She looked startled. But the next moment she had recovered enough to raise her chin defiantly at him and say:

'You're jealous, that's all. I'm very fond of Fedya. Why shouldn't I be? If I have his child, won't it be a grandchild of yours? Won't you feel some responsibility? After all, you brought us together.'

She rose and walked with a swish of her long red pleated skirt over to the window. Watching her, he said, knowing it wasn't true:

'So you want me to support your bastard child? That's why you want money?'

'Haven't you already?' she said to the fluttering curtains.

He took another sip of wine and replaced the glass slowly. Then he wiped his lips with a napkin, controlling his rising annoyance.

'You may open old wounds if you wish.'

'No, that's not what I...'

A flag flapped in a brief gust of wind somewhere outside and there was a sound of waves and gulls. She sighed and stared vacantly out at the sea.

'I did once love you, you know.'

'There is no need for such intimacies now.'

'I did once love you. But all I have of you now is Fedya's love. Oh, he loves me, the poor idiot!'

'Do you love him?'

'Of course.'

'You pretend to love him, is what you really mean.'

'Your cynicism, your beastly cynicism, that's what did it! It killed our love.'

She made one of her actressy gestures, her back still turned to him, but the sincerity of her feeling was obvious. He felt stung by it. Determined to curb his feelings as much as possible, he licked his lips and composed his features into a replica of haughtiness. When he spoke, it was in a tone of voice which suggested that he took no pleasure in explaining the obvious.

'I brought you here, my dear, so that you might meet some of the leading political figures of our society. You like to be what is called an *emancipée*, I think, a liberated woman, as they say. We are gathered here, we Russian patriots of liberal persuasion, to consider the future of our country. As a liberated woman you have much to contribute. It is unseemly of you to talk of my cynicism or to distress me by talking about our love as if it ever really mattered to you whether we felt anything for each other or not.'

'You are heartless!' She swung round towards him in a fury. 'Do you think I wanted to come here to meet your political friends? You forget I was here last year, and last year I was independent, I earned my own money, I did not need to humiliate myself by begging for money from you!'

'I suggest in that case you find some means of supporting yourself. It should not be difficult.'

His facial muscles were quite taut as he spoke. His hatred for her literally made his heart beat faster, though

46

he still refused to allow any sign of petulance or ill-temper to show in his manner. With great self-control he raised his glass again and sipped the claret.

'And you imagine that I can simply, like that . . .' She snapped her fingers. 'You owe me, you know you do!'

So, he thought, studying her figure, this full pleated red dress of hers has a purpose! He recalled that two or three months ago, when they had been in Paris at the start of their European tour, she had been particularly ardent in her love-making. Perhaps at that time she had been betraying him by her affair with Fedya. The thought was black and sickening because it reminded him not so much of her fickleness as of his recent illness and impotence.

'I do not owe you anything,' he said softly and put his glass down on the tray. 'So you are free to go.'

'You owe me money,' she insisted, holding out her hand in a melodramatic show of threat. 'Otherwise I will tell the whole world. I will tell them about Fedya and how mean you are.'

A muscle just above his right eye began to quiver but otherwise he controlled himself. He managed to say in a low voice: 'In Russia I would have you flogged for that!'

She laughed right in his face, leaning down slightly towards him. 'This is England! England! People are not flogged in England!'

'Sit down!' he ordered.

This had exactly the opposite effect. She strode towards the door, flung it open to reveal a startled Fedya waiting on the landing and then, with one hand raised like a Joan of Arc, she shouted down the stairs:

'Let everyone hear! Count Rostopchine has ordered his mistress to be flogged!'

The Russian words did in fact echo down the stairs. Colonel Rostovtzoff and Prince and Princess Bariatinsky who were standing in the hallway heard them and exchanged troubled looks. The manager came out of his office and glanced up the stairwell.

'Nothing, nothing,' said the Colonel soothingly in his best English. 'It is nothing.'

The manager smiled, nodded his head and returned to what he had been doing. As he did so Marie appeared at the top of the stairs. She looked down with raised chin at the three aristocratic Russian faces upturned towards her. They seemed to her so characteristic of their type that she could just as well have laughed at them as she had done a moment before at the Count. Instead, she deliberately smiled and flashed her eyes with her customary dazzling sweetness as she came slowly down the stairs. They looked affronted and turned hastily away.

She stalked past them, holding her head high and twirling the knob of her parasol. It was easy enough for her to despise them, but she scarcely bothered to expend any energy on such a pointless emotion. All she had at this moment was the dignity of her demeanour and a few smart clothes to give it credibility. In all other respects her life was being utterly wasted, she thought. It should have been fulfilled through some consuming, deep emotion, through some great love, not wasted in trifling relationships. Save for Fedya's devotion to her, to which she knew she could never fully respond, what was there in her life? One perfect moment of true pleasure would redeem all the little squalid surrenders, she felt. If only, she thought, she were capable of surrendering herself like one of Turgenev's heroines!

But no, it wasn't to be like that. She had to concentrate on first things first, as the English were so fond of saying. The first of these things was money. When she took stock, she knew she had nothing – no money, no position, that is – but what she did have was a sense of freedom. In the fresh onshore breeze from the sparkling sea, she felt freed for the first time from the Count and ready to enjoy the simple beauties of this Monday morning. The tide was out and so she crossed the esplanade and stepped slowly down the wooden stairway leading to the sand.

Some of the bathing machines had been wheeled down into the waves and the horses temporarily unhitched, but the majority stood further up the beach. A family was bathing. A middle-aged woman was being carefully helped down the steps into the waves while a group of children splashed around her. It was a decorous scene of innocent seaside enjoyment. A few family groups strolled along the sand. The sun was warm and shone out of a lustrous china-blue sky, but the breeze took the edge off the warmth and gave the whole morning a fresh, exhilarating briskness. She realised it was hardly the sort of morning for a parasol. Still, she persisted in keeping it open as if it were part of her challenge to the stuffy little customs of this seaside town. At moments like this she resented the fact that she had been obliged to come back here to Ventnor for a second summer. Last summer she had at least been in employment. Now she was – or had been until this moment – provided for, but it was humiliating, hurtful, degrading, and in any case ... in any case, there had been one essential change. She felt the deep, urgent excitement of it and knew that was the real change between this year and last.

Then she saw the boy. He was sitting on one of the low rocks that dotted the beach, his knees drawn up to his chin.

'Do not I know you?' she asked, looking down at the chestnut hair and meeting the brightness of the raised eyes. 'It is Guy?' She gave the French pronunciation. 'You remember me?'

'Guy,' he said, standing up. 'Guy Seddenham. You're Marie.'

'You are having a holiday here?'

'Yes, with my aunt and twin sisters.'

He pointed to Jane and Edwina who were busy pulling long strands of seaweed around behind them.

'Oh, how big you are!'

'Big?' It embarrassed him to be reminded how fast he'd grown.

'You are a man, not a boy!'

She implied so much by the rising accent of her foreign voice that she realised she might be thought of as flirting. It was ridiculous, though, to flirt with this boy whom she'd met once or twice last year when she was engaged to teach the Fenton children. Yet there was a look of recognition suddenly in his fresh, direct gaze and she grew interested in him at once and began to smile, saying as she did so:

'Miles is not at home now, I think. You were his friend, weren't you?'

'Yes, he's gone into the navy.'

'Will you go into the navy too?'

He shook his head.

'Why not?'

'I think I will go into my uncle's business,' he said, looking away.

She recognised the note of bitterness in his voice. 'You do not want that?'

'No.'

'Perhaps it will be different. Or perhaps you will be rich.'

She had noticed the tightness of his jacket, but she

also recognised that her interest in him had aroused a matching undercurrent of feeling in Guy. The air between them, as they exchanged direct looks, grew full of little electric shocks.

'No, I don't think . . .'

'You are becoming very handsome, Guy, very beautiful . . .'

Although she was trying to provoke him into smiling at her, she realized she had used a word more appropriate to a girl. He blushed. At that moment she had an impulse to kiss him on his bright red lips, but instead twirled the parasol and watched the small windmilling shadows from its bamboo struts flicker across his features. Gazing straight at her, he said with appealing frankness:

'No, you're beautiful, Marie. You see, I saw you . . .'

Then he could not keep his eyes directed at her and looked away. The compliment so took her by surprise that she lifted one hand to her bosom, literally catching her breath.

'Oh, that is so nice, dear Guy! I feel . . .'

It was then that she saw Elizabeth Fenton approaching and realised why Guy had looked away. She knew she could easily have brazened out an encounter with the girl, but instead she held out her hand in a formal English way and said:

'I'm so glad we met.'

They shook hands in rather embarrassed haste. She turned immediately with a brief wave. Although Guy had seen Elizabeth, he supposed his compliment must have offended Marie and with a puzzled look his eyes followed the supple, elegant motion of her slim figure in the red dress as she climbed up the sand away from him, the parasol held in one hand and her other hand holding up her skirts. She *was* beautiful, he thought.

'Who was that lady, the red one?' piped Edwina's voice.

'Probably you don't remember. She was here last year.'

'She was here last year,' Edwina shouted to Jane.

'There's no need to shout,' he said.

'I wasn't shouting,' Edwina said primly. 'I was telling.'

'Then there's no need to tell so loudly.'

'I have to tell loudly, otherwise she won't hear. Oh, look . . .'

Guy was being directed to look at Elizabeth who was coming along the sand towards them. Now he did begin to feel self-conscious, especially as she came directly towards him. He was self-conscious about his clothes and about the recent encounter with Marie.

'Good morning,' he said, trying to smile.

'My father thought he might have lost a cufflink yesterday,' she said as she approached, 'but it's worse than looking for a needle in a haystack. How are you, Guy?'

'I'm afraid I haven't seen anything – I'll ask the twins . . .'

But the twins had already gone back to their game with the long strands of seaweed.

'No, don't trouble. It's quite impossible.' She gave him one glance with her deep-blue eyes and then looked away quickly, fingering her dark hair busily while the breeze played with the curls.

'Guy,' she said.

'Yes?'

'We *are* friends, aren't we?'

'Of course.'

'I mean, *we* are friends, aren't we? It's not just because

52

you were friends with Miles?'

'No.'

Elizabeth and he were friends, that he knew for sure, but apart from knowing her last year when he had spent so much of the summer holiday with her brother he had no other claims to friendship with her.

'Excuse me for asking such questions,' she said, still not looking directly at him. 'I'd hoped you'd be here on the beach. You see, I'd been wondering . . .'

He just stopped himself from speaking in the interval of silence.

'I'd been wondering how bad things are, you know . . .'

It was then that he knew exactly what she had been trying to say. They had not only felt a natural sympathy for each other last summer, they had been more aware than Miles of what they had in common.

'Since my mother died . . .'

'That's what I mean,' she said.

'And since my father went to Australia, we've become poor.'

She put out her hand and touched his arm. 'I'm sorry.'

It was hard for him to face her, though he knew she could see the look in his eyes. She withdrew her hand.

'I think I know how you feel.'

He could not say anything. Tears rose in his eyes.

'You will come and see me, won't you?' she said in a melodious, self-assured way.

He nodded. She walked off quickly along the sand, calling to the twins. They waved back at her. He suddenly began sneezing.

4

The following day, Tuesday, Marie Valence spent most of the morning making up her mind. About noon she walked up to Belgrave Road. She knocked on the front door of Rock Cottage and asked to speak to Monsieur Turgenev. He was at home, it seemed, but busy, and if she wouldn't mind waiting a couple of minutes he'd be able to see her (so the landlady informed her). In fact, he came out into the hallway immediately he heard her beginning to speak in Russian, as she did deliberately when informed of the delay.

'At your service, young lady. What is it I can do for you?'

'Marie Ivanovna Valents,' she said by way of introduction. 'An admirer.'

'Ah, yes, I think Rostovtzoff . . .'

He showed her into a spacious, airy front room where he had obviously just been writing. The window opened on to a verandah and gave a view of the entire Ventnor bay.

'I am here, you know, for a holiday,' he explained. Despite his tallness, the big head of greying hair and the imposing, rather majestic, features, he spoke in a disconcertingly high-pitched voice and accompanied his words with occasional inelegant finger movements which suggested that he was familiarising himself with some invisible stringed instrument. There was, though, a natural authority in his words which gave them a ringing sense of child-like, earnest gravity. 'I am hoping for the arrival of my friend Annenkov, who promises to come next week, and I have tried to persuade Marie Alexandrovna' – the name was mentioned a little shyly, as if it were assumed that his guest would be bound to know who she was, but Marie had no idea – 'I have tried to persuade her to join me here. Without her I fear that my holiday will prove dull and boring. I also fear that the English summer will give me a cold. I am always full of all manner of worries when I find myself in a strange place. My friends Rostovtzoff and Kruze are here, of course, and very anxious that we should discuss certain, er . . .' at which point he fixed his blue eyes on her as though he suspected for a moment that she might be there to spy on him, 'certain, er, questions, you understand. I have told them that I am here for a holiday. And I wish to do some sea-bathing if the weather permits. As for my being a writer' – he did not exactly dismiss the idea, no matter how busily his fingers worked, but he gave a sigh and slightly shook his head – 'I had to tell them that a writer who finds it painful so much as to pick up a pen is of no use to himself and worthless to others.'

Bright, animated, Marie Valence leaned forward, resting one elbow on an arm of her chair. She cupped the palm of her hand under her chin in an exaggerated display of intentness.

'But,' she protested, 'you write so beautifully. You are our greatest writer.'

'I have had the good fortune,' he admitted modestly, 'to have enjoyed some success recently.'

'We have all read your novel *On the Eve* – youth, love, sacrifice, so inspiring, so noble! I dream of being a heroine like Yelena! Oh, if only I could sacrifice myself as she did!' Though she knew she had struck a wrong note in her eloquence, the sincerity evidently appealed to Turgenev, for he smiled patiently and nodded while contriving to suggest through a faintly sardonic shaping of his lips that it was exactly what he expected and, perhaps, deserved. 'We are able to sacrifice ourselves, all Russian women can sacrifice themselves,' she continued, impelled by her enthusiasm. 'I have had to sacrifice myself to the base desires of men,' she added with pursed lips. 'Oh, I am not proud of my life! But Yelena – what strength, what devotion, what love she had! Once she found someone she could love with all her heart, she gave up everything for him! All women want to know that kind of love. And you are able to understand our poor female hearts so well, to look into their depths! That is why we all admire you so greatly!' She looked deeply into his eyes with genuine passion, shaking her head slightly in admiration. Then she looked down. 'It was only a pity, you know,' she sighed, 'that Yelena couldn't find a *Russian* man with the same qualities. She'd have been able then to dedicate herself, as so many Russian women wish to dedicate themselves, to the task of liberating our country from slavery and tyranny!'

The exultant moral tone obviously upset her listener. Turgenev responded with a brief, dismissive shake of the head.

'Our younger critics have not been slow in pointing out my inadequacies as a writer. As for a Russian man with the same qualities, do you think such a man exists in the present day?'

'Oh, yes!'

'You know such a man?'

She paused before replying. 'Yes, I think I do.'

'I should be most interested to meet him.'

'He is here.'

'Here?' Turgenev looked incredulous.

She nodded eagerly. With deliberate slow movements

she pulled off her red gloves and laid them carefully one upon the other in her lap.

'Yes, he is here.'

'Please tell me.'

She took her time before saying:

'There is a young doctor here. He was involved in secret political activities in St Petersburg. That is what I have been told.' She spoke softly, scarcely above a whisper, slowly smoothing her gloves with her fingers. '*He cannot go back.* I'm sure you know what I mean?'

Turgenev stroked his beard and indicated with a forward movement of his head that he understood.

'He went first to Heidelberg, but he could not find employment there, so he came to London. He is now working for the English doctor, Dr Hodgson. Just over there.' She pointed towards Alto House. At that very moment a maidservant in a black dress and white apron was busily rubbing the brass plate by the front door with a cloth. 'He is a very brilliant scientist, a medical doctor who is also interested in – what is the word? – *la biologie.* He is collecting specimens, you see. He tells me he is able to find them in the deep pools. Of course,' she gave a delicate wave of the hand, 'if he could return without fear of arrest, he'd have a great future in our country. He is not rich, you see, but I think he is one of the "new men", as they're called. If only Yelena had known him. . . .'

Turgenev raised his eyebrows.

'So he is a "new man"!' he exclaimed, giving a short, slightly embarrassed laugh. 'Yes, they're certainly making their presence felt among us! They believe only in scientific progress, it seems. Those of us who attribute importance to the search for beauty in this life are no doubt too old to appreciate all the advantages of scientific progress. I regret to say,' he sighed, 'that my

57

own generation has already made its exit. We have played our roles. Now it is for the younger generation, the "children", as I call them, to take the centre of the stage.'

'Oh, they will!' She knew her exclamation was too loud and she quickly rephrased it in a softer voice. 'Oh, we will, of course, but you must educate us, teach us, guide us, dear Ivan Sergeyevich.'

'I am flattered.'

'It is your role as a writer. Education is so essential at the present moment. . . .'

'Ah, yes.' He grew instantly thoughtful.

'And we,' she went on, 'will of course learn. It is our duty to learn from the older generation.'

She was on the point of explaining the real reason for her visit when he suddenly stood up and walked over to the table by the window. He used a quill pen to jot something down. The pen made a slightly squeaky sound as he wrote.

'I am very grateful,' he murmured after several seconds. 'You reminded me of . . . well, it doesn't matter. Forgive me for interrupting our talk.'

Marie decided that she had no other chance. She rose and stood before him.

'I have a request to make.'

'Yes?'

She gave an uncertain smile as he also stood up and came towards her. She looked down at her gloves, pulling on first one, then the other.

'I am in need of money, Ivan Sergeyevich. I have come to ask you for money.'

She knew it was wrong and she felt wretched. With an effort she raised her eyes and looked him directly in the face. He returned her bold look with a sad compression of the lips and averted his eyes towards the window and the grey sea.

'I know I have a reputation for meeting all requests for money . . .'

'I am sorry, very sorry. . . .'

'No, you mustn't apologise. I know how difficult it is to ask for money. It is equally difficult, you see, for me to say no.'

'But perhaps,' she said, biting her lip. She found herself beginning to blush. 'Perhaps . . . Oh, there he is!' She caught sight of the young man she had just mentioned and instantly forgot her embarrassment. She pointed through the window. 'There he is, the young doctor! Forgive me, I have to speak to him!'

'If you must. . . .'

'I am so grateful to you for receiving me, Ivan Sergeyevich. Please forgive me for making such a request. It was . . . so insensitive . . . so . . .'

'We will talk about it later perhaps,' he said quietly.

'Yes, yes . . . Now I really must speak to him.'

She swept quickly out of the room and out of Rock Cottage and ran across Belgrave Road, calling out the doctor's name. He turned and saw her just as he was about to ascend the steps to Alto House.

Turgenev watched her dashing figure with the long hair suddenly blown in all directions as she danced on quick feet across Belgrave Road. He would have described her as a Russian *emancipée*, a liberated woman, except that she seemed in her dress and her manner both more experienced and more brittle than the typical 'new woman' of his acquaintance. As for the 'new man', the young doctor whom she had been so anxious to see, he was indeed a remarkable sight. He was wearing a kind of loose cloak, of some coarse canvas material, and he was carrying two large glass containers yoked over his shoulders, looking for all the world like some quack purveyor of patent nostrums. She was imploring him to do something, it seemed, while he nodded, tried to placate her with the occasional remark and all the time shifted his weight from one foot to the other. Turgenev was struck by his face. He peered at the young man, noting his features carefully. Then he sat down again and began writing.

That evening, at Belinda House, the Russian doctor made his presence known in a different way. At dinner-time he joined the young curly-haired Russian at his table by the door. Their talk was lively and loud. The other occupants of the little dining room, including the Misses Bosanquet and Aunt Emily Whitehouse and the Seddenham children, were a largely silent audience. The Russian doctor, dressed now in a sober dark suit, with tie and tie-pin, was accompanying expansive gestures, supposedly of swimming and diving, with equally eloquent Russian explanations.

'I cannot stand their faces,' said Aunt Emily Whitehouse. She had been studying the red-cheeked Fedya and the long face of his talkative companion.

'He has a very nice face,' whispered Jane.

'It is very, very rude to stare,' said Aunt Emily. 'Nicely brought-up children do not stare. I will not have you staring, my dear Jane.' She wiped her mouth with the edge of her napkin. 'As for his face, you may think it nice, but I have much more experience in such matters and to me he has a labouring face, a common, labouring face. Now that will be enough, Edwina. Do please stop twisting in your chair.'

Edwina stopped trying to twist round to see the two Russians and deliberately held herself still, looking very prim, as if she were holding her breath. Jane tried not to giggle. The Russians both spoke loudly and then began laughing. The Misses Bosanquet at the next table exchanged distressed looks.

Aunt Emily adopted a pose of straight-backed indignation. 'Such deplorable manners! Really, they are the limit!' But she spoke almost to herself. Then she said loudly: 'Guy, I wish you would tell those two men to stop making such a noise!'

Guy tried to disregard this summons. He made an indeterminate movement that combined a shake of the head and shrug of the shoulders. Aunt Emily looked at him fiercely.

'Go on, boy!'

'I, er . . .'

She did not deign to repeat her command.

'Yes, Aunt,' he said, rose and walked over to the table by the door. The two Russians were talking so busily they did not notice him at first. He cleared his throat.

'My aunt would be grateful if you did not make so much noise.'

The man with the long face stopped what he was saying, having clearly understood these English words, and turned his greenish eyes towards Guy. The eyes were brilliant, like seawater, but they seemed also depthless and at first glance even sightless. Slowly, though, as the long face creased into a grin, the eyes seemed to be the points into which all the features concentrated their vitality.

'Your aunt? Who is your aunt?'

The voice was deep and accented but not hostile. Trying not to appear that he was making any movement at all, Guy indicated where his aunt was sitting. Aunt Emily was not herself watching, though the twins managed to keep their sparkling eyes on everything that was happening at the other table.

'So she is that lady?'

'Yes.'

'Be so good to tell her . . .' he rose as he spoke,

revealing himself as taller than Guy by as much as six inches, and pushed his chair back into place '. . . tell her, please, Dr Bazarov presents his compliments. He is sorry his voice is too loud. He is leaving.'

He bowed towards Aunt Emily who disregarded him completely. Smiling at the lack of reaction, he gave a keen, amused glance in Guy's direction and then strode out of the room.

Conversation resumed instantly. Everyone glanced at Fedya, but he unconcernedly continued with his meal. Guy's success in putting an end to the loud foreign talk had come as such a surprise that he received looks of awe and respect even from the Misses Bosanquet. Aunt Emily was very impressed.

'Very well done, Guy. Of course, it always takes a man to handle these matters.' She patted him on his frayed sleeve, which she carefully did not notice. 'Now Jane, Edwina, off to bed with you like good little girls!'

The twins were for once so respectful of Guy's grown-up behaviour that they made no attempt to beg for more time and left the table without any of their customary mumbled complaints.

'I suppose really I should not let them stay up beyond seven o'clock. But it is so convenient for us all to have dinner at the same time, isn't it?' Guy was finishing a pudding of stewed apples. 'You were like your father, my dear Guy, in the way you talked to those Russians.' A loud sigh. 'Russians! Who'd have thought it! Only five years ago I thought we had quite defeated them in the Crimea and now here they are all over little Ventnor! I have no idea what the world is coming to.'

Guy finished his stewed apples, which were rather sour, and wiped his mouth with his napkin. His aunt, who liked to confide in him, gazed into a space intermediate between Guy's head and the half-open sash window through which slanting, evening sunrays were pouring.

'We see such changes nowadays. I'd supposed Ventnor wouldn't be affected but I can see I was wrong. Why do you think there are so many Russians here this year?'

Guy could not say.

'I'm sure they must be hatching some kind of plot. They have inscrutable faces.'

As she spoke, conversation in the dining room was again interrupted, this time by the arrival of a startling figure in a red dress. Guy knew at once that it was Marie Valence. She swept into the dining room, to the consternation of the landlady who protested that her guests had not yet finished their dinner, went straight up to where the red-cheeked Fedya was sitting, said something to him in Russian and both of them went out into the hallway. Guy followed all this with his eyes.

'Who is that woman?' asked Aunt Emily. 'Do you know her, Guy?'

He nodded, trying not to blush.

'How do you know her?'

'She was here last year. She taught French to my friend Miles.'

'Miles – ah, of course!'

Marie and Fedya had now moved out on to the pavement just beyond the open sash window.

'How is Miles? Have you seen him this year?'

'He's gone into the navy.'

'He's gone into the navy! Well I never! I suppose his father can afford that kind of career. Didn't you say he was a retired sea-captain?'

'Yes.' Marie and Fedya were talking together very earnestly.

'I should like to meet him. What did you say his name was?'

'Fenton.'

'And didn't you say he was a widower?'

'Yes. He is chairman of the Ventnor Watch Committee.' Fedya appeared to be gesticulating and Marie seemed to be pleading with him.

'Really.' The information no doubt lifted the Fentons socially in Aunt Emily's eyes. 'I think you said he brought his wife here because she was unwell.'

'Yes, she had consumption.'

'Poor woman!' She added doubtfully: 'I suppose it *is* a healthy place, this. I wouldn't've chosen to come here myself, as you know. You and the twins, Guy, you were the ones who wanted to come to Ventnor, didn't you?'

It was true and Guy couldn't deny it. They had come to Ventnor because he'd mentioned his friendship with Miles and last year's holiday.

'I didn't know Miles wouldn't be here,' he said defensively.

'Well, now, what are they doing?' She was remarking on the behaviour of Marie and Fedya. They were openly arguing, even shouting at each other during some of their exchanges. Then Fedya broke away and strode off along the esplanade. 'Whenever I see those Russians, they're always arguing and shouting. Or perhaps it's their language, so full of hisses and gutturals. By the way ...' she turned back from her scrutiny of the window '... didn't you say the Captain had a daughter?'

Inquisitive questions of this kind were a stock feature of Aunt Emily's conversation and Guy was used to them. They usually popped out like little sniper shots at the end of longer fusillades.

'Yes. Elizabeth.'

'Have you seen her since being here?'

Guy lowered his eyes. 'Yes.'

'I see.'

His aunt was not subtle. She sniffed, folded up her napkin and inserted it neatly in the napkin ring. Then she lightly drummed her fingers on the tablecloth.

'I think we shan't be able to stay here longer than a week. I only promised a week, you know. It'll depend on your father, *if* we hear anything from him. As for this place, quite pleasant, but not really my style. Simple, plain food. We can't expect anything more for what we're paying, of course. Oh, I must write to Charles Augustus, so as to catch the early post tomorrow.'

She rose quickly from the table, saying she would be down in an hour to play cards with him. It was always her habit to play cards in the evening and it had become one of Guy's functions to join her in this habit. He knew she liked to have his company, provided he was polite and did not aggravate her by winning too often. She had her fits of temper and her bouts of complaining, but on the whole she made life agreeable for him and the twins. In Lambeth she was their only defence against the insinuations and complaints of Charles Augustus, for which, of course, Guy was grateful. But he knew that the only chance he and the twins had of becoming a family again, as they had been last summer, was if his father returned from Australia.

He walked out into the rays of the brilliant sunset and a fairly stiff onshore wind. It was colder outside than he had supposed and the sea was noisier. High waves were breaking frothily about halfway down the beach. The sea had a surging, menacing appearance, even though towards the horizon beyond West Hill its surface reflected the sharp-edged white circle of the setting sun. The suggestion of menace came not from the sea itself,

65

he realised, but from long black strips of cloud through which the sun's false brightness came as if through shutters.

The freshness of the air and the dying light suited his mood. He was reminded again of his mother. The air had her freshness when she had been healthy, the light possessed her eyes' shining quality. Her spirit was in the evening atmosphere – for one instant, at least, while he stood by himself facing the sea. It seemed to him that whenever he recalled her she came and stood close beside him and he could even hear her voice saying in her amused, lightly scolding way, 'Oh, Guy darling, you're such a sentimental old thing, you know,' and he would feel a vague sense of alarm that his love for her might be able to bring her back to life in some unreal spectral form.

'Guy?'

He looked round in momentary fright. There was no one else on the esplanade at that moment.

'Guy?'

The very sound made him jump. Could it be his mother actually calling him?

Then he realised the sound was coming from below him. He looked down and there was Marie Valence leaning back against the wheel of a bathing machine, waving to him. Relieved, he waved back, but she persisted.

'Guy,' her accented voice called.

He went down the wooden steps to the sand and into the long, bulky shadows cast by the bathing machines. Her long hair was blowing right across her face in a gentle flailing motion. She made no effort to hold it back but stood there looking at him as if she were on the prow of a ship, her figure in the red dress boldly profiled by the wind. He went up to her. The waves pounded and frothed only a few yards away though they sounded loud enough to be right under their feet. It was then he saw that her eyes glistened with tears.

'Marie, what's wrong?'

She shook her head and gave a pretend smile. 'I'm going away, Guy. I wanted to say goodbye.'

'Goodbye?'

'I was rude yesterday morning, Guy. Are you angry with me?'

'Rude?' He had no idea what she meant.

'Say you're not angry.'

'I'm not angry, honestly.'

'Everyone seems to be angry with me. So I think it's better I go.'

'Where?'

'Oh, to London, to Paris, it doesn't matter!'

She looked so directly at him with her glittering eyes that he felt challenged by them not to look away but to meet their sadness with a similar strength and directness.

'Why must you go?'

She shook some of the strands of hair away from her face, stretching her neck back as she did so. He had the impression she was giving a silent laugh.

'Money, dear Guy. I need money. I will sell a dress, some jewels. And then ... then ... how is it you say? ... then I will live happily ever after!'

She gave a short laugh when she said this and there was a gentle, rather fond smile on her face as she turned her eyes back to him again. He suddenly felt overwhelmed by a desire to comfort her in some way.

'Marie, of course you will! You're bound to be happy!'

'Ah, Guy, the things you say!' she said, as if to herself. She let her features relax into an expression of dreamy absorption. 'Tomorrow perhaps I'll go to Ryde. I'll sell my jewels. Perhaps it'd be better in

67

London. . . .' She looked again at him, realising she should not be talking to herself. 'So, Guy, you see, I'm going. Will you be sad?'

'Yes.'

It was spontaneous. He remembered her standing in the window and the vision of her nakedness merged with the present look on her face to make her seem suddenly so personally and intimately real to him that her absence would be almost the same as her death.

'Ah, but I can't stay,' she said, holding out her arms to him. She put them round him and hugged him to her. Even in the wind, with the smell of the sea so close, he could smell her perfume. Her blown hair flicked tickly ends against his face. 'I have no employment here, you see. And I can't stay here just because of you, can I, Guy?'

He wanted to say yes again but he knew she was right.

'I want to be free, you see. I want to be truly an *emancipée*. Then I will feel independent. I will live my own life.'

She pressed him still more tightly and it surprised him how passionate the embrace was.

'Will you remember me, dear Guy?'

'Yes, of course I will.'

'You won't forget?'

'No.'

'My friend is staying.'

'Who?'

'The Russian doctor. Zhenia. He will stay here. He can be your friend.'

How could she possibly know of his loneliness? Guy wondered. How could she know that he needed friends?

'And one day perhaps I'll come back,' she said. 'But

you must promise to remember me. Always. Promise me.'

'Yes.'

He agreed in alarm at the ferocity of her hugging and the strange way she insisted on his making such a promise. Suddenly she released him and with brisk finger-movements started unbuttoning the front of her dress. He felt chilled by the wind, sneezed, apologised and stood quite still in amazement in front of her. From round her neck and from the parting in the front of her dress, so that he saw the whiteness of her breasts and the subtle cleavage between them, she drew the small crucifix with the slanting crosspiece which he had seen her wearing at the window. She held it out to him.

'Kiss it,' she said quietly. 'If you kiss it, we will be friends for ever.'

He leaned forward and kissed it. It was wooden and warm to his lips. Then she quickly tucked it away and seized his face in her hands and kissed him strongly on the lips. The sensation was one of sudden, deeply stirred excitement running through him as fast as light.

'Never forget,' she murmured.

'I won't, Marie, I really won't. . . .'

She laughed. For a couple of seconds she seemed to hesitate, as if she were debating with herself whether or not to tear herself away, and in the same few instants he understood for the first time in his life what it could really mean to love her, to be her lover, to know love, to hold her and keep her for ever, and then she turned from him, her fingers busily rebuttoning the front of her dress, and with quick, compulsive strides walked away into the now deep shadow and ran back up the steps to the esplanade.

5

Mr Ellis, the town constable, went to Connaught House as usual on Thursday morning to make his weekly report to Captain Stringer Fenton. The wind was brisk and as he glanced down from Belgrave Road at the sea beyond the tall new houses on the esplanade he saw the white crests of waves, a few fishing boats bobbing, threads of smoke blown from chimneys and the steel-grey blue of the sea itself little different in tone from the blue of the slate roofs. As he approached the steps leading up to Connaught House, Mr Ellis could not fail to notice Dr Hodgson's new brass plate beside the front door of the adjacent house. He surveyed for a moment the entire façade of Alto House, wondering if he might discover any clue from the appearance of the windows, but he saw nothing unusual. So he rang the bell of Connaught House and the door was opened very quickly by Dora the maid. She told him that Molly was downstairs in the kitchen.

'Thank you, my dear.'

He went slowly down the stone stairs into the warm kitchen. The noise of the wind and the sea was shut out now and all he heard was the soft hissing of a kettle on the hob. The cosiness and sweet comfortable smells of the kitchen were as warming to his heart as the sight of the woman seated at the table peeling potatoes. Though his metal-heeled boots made a noise like horseshoes on the stone stairs she did not turn her head and was obviously startled as he leaned over her and kissed her on the cheek from behind.

'So you've come to see the Captain! You're early,

Bill, aren't you?'

'No, it's you I've come to see.'

He sat himself down opposite her, his back to the stove. The wind, suddenly gusting, made something tap against the outside of the window. He looked round just to be sure it was only a branch. Seizing her right hand, he drew it up to his lips, kissed it and then let her withdraw it.

'You shouldn't, Bill,' she whispered. 'That girl'll see. What if the Captain . . .'

He shook his head. 'He won't, Molly, he won't. So . . .' He gave her a serious, caring look. 'Are you happy?'

She watched his lips and then smiled again and nodded.

'Good,' he said softly. 'He's right enough, of course, except for . . .' Lifting an invisible glass, he drank its invisible contents at a gulp. 'But if you're happy . . .'

'The Captain is a good man,' she whispered. The flushed appearance of her thin cheeks, the little tasting motion of her fine lips and her eyes, now shining with a confidence he had not seen in them for months, told him a great deal.

'Don't ever expect too much from these kinds of person,' he said in his firm constabulary way and loud enough for her to hear clearly. 'I've been here only a year and there's one lesson I've learned: they're very respectable here in Ventnor.'

'This is a respectable house,' she murmured. 'I don't like what you're hinting.'

'So long as you're happy, my dear. I see you're using the field next the church, the one just opposite. They're all right there, are they?'

'It's nice for them to have shelter. In the heat and in the cold.'

'Did you get much for the rides?'

'Four shillings Saturday, five shillings Sunday,' she said with a proud smile. 'Weekdays is different. And when it's blowing like this, there's no call for donkey rides, is there?'

'Ah.' He smiled back at her. 'I'm glad to see you so happy now, my dear. When I think what you were like last year, remember?'

She lifted her head, doused a potato in some water and began peeling it quickly. 'I remember. And I'm grateful.'

'Oh, grateful, Molly, my dear, no, there's no need to thank me. Just you think, though, what if they'd come after you?'

He watched her as she lowered her head and concentrated on the peeling. If he had not seen her as she had been a year ago, this Molly Ford, who had come to him with her story of having killed her husband, looking so gaunt and ragged and footsore as she was then, he could not have believed it was the same strong-looking woman he saw in front of him now. After agreeing to protect her, he had made certain discreet enquiries which confirmed that, though she had stabbed him with a butcher's knife, she had not in fact killed her husband and there were grounds enough in all conscience for her to have done so after the way he had maltreated and abused her. She had come to Ventnor from Southampton the previous autumn and when Captain Fenton needed a housekeeper she had come to Connaught House on Mr Ellis's recommendation.

'No one's come after me,' she said quietly as she slipped the white peeled potato into the saucepan, 'and no one will.'

'You're sure?'

'Yes.'

'I've made enquiries.'

'So?'

'They said they thought you'd drowned.'

She looked straight at him, blinking her eyes. 'How is he?'

'You're not still interested in him, are you?'

'I did love him once.' She spoke of her former husband in a calm, steady voice, as if she were talking about yesterday's weather. 'Now I love the Captain.' This was said just as calmly.

'Oh, my dear, do be careful,' he warned.

At that moment one of the bells rang above the door. He stood up. She seemed not to have heard anything and it was only when she saw where he was looking that she stood up as well. 'It's the Captain's,' she said.

'I know it is. You've not told him about us, have you?'

She had to watch his lips carefully. 'No, Bill, I haven't.'

'I thought perhaps we ought to.'

'You must decide that.'

He gave her a kiss, did up the button of his tunic at the neck and began to ascend the stairs. Dora the maid was dusting in the hall. She jumped to her feet from a kneeling position beside the hall table not so much at the sight of the constable emerging from the kitchen stairs, as at the sudden appearance of the black-suited Mr Hetherington coming from the Captain's study, or 'cabin' as he called it. She held out the shiny top hat, topcoat and stick which he had left with her on arrival. Mr Hetherington and Mr Ellis came face to face.

'A good morning to you, Constable. Brisk, isn't it?'

Mr Ellis agreed, straightening his tight jacket.

'Nothing to report, I hope?'

'Nothing, sir. No, sir.'

The Captain's voice came from the study doorway.

'You won't forget the contracts, will you? We mustn't delay.'

'No, no,' said Hetherington, both arms already partway through the sleeves of the topcoat held by Dora. 'I'll not forget about them, you may be sure. Good day, Stringer. Good day, Constable.'

Mr Hetherington sloped his tall way out through the front door to the top of the steps where theatrically, in silhouette, he raised his top hat, tipped it, swung his stick up in an arc and went off into the windy street.

The relationship between Mr Ellis and his superior was governed by stiff but friendly rules of etiquette. On the constable's side, gratitude and respect were dominant. On the Captain's, respect for the constable's conscientiousness and practical good sense was balanced by a suspicion that those very virtues might prompt him to look too deeply into the reputations and rumour which circulated as ubiquitously as gulls through the air of Ventnor. His own place in Ventnor society depended as much on his good name as on his money. A trim, youthful man in his early forties, the Captain seemed groomed for eminence in local affairs and was generally tipped to become chairman of the Council as a result of his successful chairmanship of the Watch Committee. But there were things in his former seafaring life which he preferred to keep private, among them the source of his wealth (derived mostly from quite legitimate trading but supplemented by some gun-running, narcotics and lucrative cargoes of precious metals). Since his arrival in Ventnor three years before he had increased his wealth through several successful property deals, and wealth can pay for secrecy, as everyone knows. It could not compensate him, though, for the one sadness that dominated his life. As he called for the constable to come into his study, he caught sight of the oil painting

of his wife above the fireplace and was again reminded of her death almost two years ago. The shape of
her face, the line of her eyebrows and the deep, wistful
blueness of the eyes (more like a china doll's, true, than
they had been in her living face) suggested a resemblance to his daughter Elizabeth. The placid warmth of
her presence emanating from the portrait was not
Elizabeth's and that very knowledge forced upon him
an old familiar ache at her loss. This he shut out from
himself by pouring a glass of port.

'For you, Constable?'

Mr Ellis declined.

'Then sit down, please, and tell me what you have to
report.'

Mr Ellis took his usual place in an upright armchair
facing the Captain who sat on the other side of the desk.
Holding a rather worn black notebook between the
forefinger and thumb of his left hand, which had been
injured by a Russian bullet on the Alma, he delivered a
gruff recital of petty thefts, childish misconduct and
other small demeanours.

'Not much to report,' observed the Captain when the
recital was over.

'No, sir, a quiet week,' said the constable. 'Except for
the Russians.'

'Yes, there are more here this year than last. No
trouble, I hope?'

'Well, sir.' The constable cleared his throat. It was
hard for him to broach a matter of some delicacy,
especially as it affected the Captain's immediate neighbour, Dr Hodgson of Alto House. He closed the
notebook. 'I have been informed by two elderly ladies
staying at Belinda House on the esplanade, the Misses
Bosanquet, Adelaide and Henrietta, that a week ago,
when out for an early morning walk, they observed a

75

man, er, an unclothed man, among the rocks below West Hill. They believe it to be the young Russian doctor who resides next door at Alto House.'

He watched the Captain closely. The Captain drank. A strong wind beat against Connaught House and made the study windows rattle. The view through them showed the whole of Ventnor bay and the grey-blue sea flecked with wave-crests.

'Unclothed. So?'

'The ladies were offended, sir.'

'Not a pretty sight, I imagine, no. But the town boys swim there, don't they, just as God made 'em? I've seen 'em myself.'

Mr Ellis was bound to agree. 'But an unclothed gentleman, sir, that's another matter. The town can lose its reputation as a respectable family resort.'

The Captain was impressed by this, nodded and for a moment or so looked preoccupied. 'What's he do there?'

'Swims underwater, sir. Collects, er, things. Scientific things.'

The Captain raised his eyes and looked straight at Mr Ellis with obvious amazement. He had not expected the constable to know the meaning of such a term, let alone use it. 'Scientific?'

'The Russian doctor, sir, it's what he said.'

'What sort of things?'

'Anemones, sir. He has two large medicine bottles. Yokes them over his shoulders. He puts the anemones in them and carries them up to Alto House.'

Evidently the constable knew all about it and had the doctor's activities under surveillance, but if there were any suggestions of indelicacy in what he was doing, let alone anything that might affect the reputation of Ventnor as a respectable resort, then it would have to be stopped at once.

'I'll speak to Dr Hodgson,' said the Captain. 'We can't have any indelicacy, nothing improper. Particularly with the meeting of the Watch Committee due next week. Thank you for telling me, Constable.'

'Thank you, sir.'

The constable was shown out of the Captain's 'cabin' and then let himself out of Connaught House. The tall, austere front of Alto House next door gave no sign of its occupation by such an eccentric fellow as the young Russian doctor, so the constable was glad to see, but the fact remained that he had been seen naked by two respectable elderly spinster ladies – gossips, naturally, the constable thought – and the thought rankled and alarmed him slightly as he strode out into the fierce wind blowing along Belgrave Road. He looked towards the shore. Very few people were about. A couple of fishing boats could be seen bobbing on the white crests of waves. Mild though it was, more stormy weather appeared to be in the offing. On the shore itself, strolling along the white strip of sand left clear by the outgoing tide, were two small figures, one of whom the constable instantly recognised as Elizabeth Fenton, the Captain's attractive daughter. The other was a boy.

As for Captain Stringer Fenton, he sat behind his desk, the empty port glass in front of him. Should he summon Molly Ford from the kitchen and confront her with what he suspected? He had looked very carefully at Mr Ellis's features during their recent interview and he was sure Hetherington (damn him!) was right. He had insinuated clearly enough that Molly Ford had a past and certain associations and had not become the Captain's housekeeper by chance. 'Damn him!' was the Captain's insistent thought. Yet he could not do a thing without Hetherington. Hetherington was the legal brains behind all the building contracts. Hetherington was a coroner. Hetherington owned several parcels of land where more building could be done. And now Hetherington was warning him that if he wanted to be received in the best local society he would have to find himself a wife from a good local family. Oh, the Captain knew what it all meant. There was gossip about, that's what it meant!

The Captain was a passionate man, passionate in his affections and his anger. But he was also a stricken man, stricken by the death of his wife and by his drinking. He knew he could not trust himself when he was drunk. Still, there were compensations. . . . His work on the Council, the possibility of social advancement, the love of women – he did not categorise such items or give priority to one or the other, save that when he looked at the portrait of his wife he recognised in her something deeper, more noble, more honest about himself, and in doing so he realised it was always to his daughter Elizabeth that his thoughts turned.

She looked so like her dead mother, true, but she had something of his own spirit and waywardness and he knew that not far below the pretty surface of the girl's innocence there was a passionate and wilful woman waiting to emerge. In a curious way, the only person in his life who seemed to menace his present domestic happiness was the daughter upon whom he doted. At that instant he heard the front door open, to be followed an instant later by a small brass travelling clock on the mantelpiece striking twelve tinkling chimes. Elizabeth's quick footsteps sounded on the tilework of the hall and she walked into the room to the accompaniment of a loud rattling of sash windows and a sharp hissing of logs in the fireplace.

'Oh, it's so windy, Father!'

She came across to him looking fresh and wind-blown and exhilarated and kissed him softly on the cheek.

'Where've you been, my dear?'

'Down on the shore. I knew it was your morning to see Mr Ellis so I thought I'd go for a walk. There was hardly anyone about.' She took off her bonnet, carefully withdrawing a large pin and letting the pink chin ribbons hang down. Then she shook back her hair. 'Father, do you think Miles will need his old jacket any more?'

The question reminded him how keen she was to assume all the duties of lady of the house since Miles had left. She spoke in the way her mother had spoken, a little loftily and airily, but always in a musical voice.

'You must write to him and ask him. I simply can't . . .' He stretched across his desk, opened the humidor and began to fill his pipe bowl with tobacco. 'I can't answer that, you know.'

'He's not likely to want to wear that old jacket now he's got such a handsome uniform, I'm sure.' She stood for a moment by the window, looking out. 'How was Mr Ellis?'

Again, it could have been his wife speaking. 'Well,' he said, striking a match.

'Didn't he have anything to tell you?'

'He told me . . .' beginning to puff, letting the tobacco smoke rise, '. . . he told me,' said the Captain, wiping out the match flame in the air, 'that the young Russian doctor collects anemones. Do you know anything about that?'

She laughed. 'Anemones! So that's what he carries in those bottles!'

'You've seen him, have you?'

'Yes, I've seen him twice. He wears a sort of canvas cloak.'

'Well, apparently he's . . .' But the Captain decided not to mention any further details. 'Strange behaviour by any standards, don't you think?'

79

'I think he's quite nice really.'

'It's a bad sign when someone's only been here two weeks and there's talk about his strange behaviour.'

'He's Russian.' It was said as if that settled it. 'It makes a change, though.'

He was puzzled by this. 'What exactly makes a change, my dear?'

'Ventnor seems to me to be so quiet,' she said, 'it's news if somebody sneezes.'

'Yes, that sort of thing's catching,' he agreed, quite pleased by his spontaneous joke even though she seemed to disregard it. She had in any case heard footsteps on the hall tiles. Molly appeared in the doorway and announced in a low voice that there was a young lady to see the Captain.

'A young lady?' asked Elizabeth. 'Who can that possibly be?'

Molly's expression gave no clue. It was like a mask. 'She says she's Miss Valence.'

No one in the room needed reminding. The name, though pronounced by Molly to sound like Vaylence, had the power to embarrass and antagonise each of them.

'Tell her we're not at home,' Elizabeth ordered with a spurt of temper which the Captain well knew she inherited from him. 'She is not someone I want to see.'

The Captain knew Molly had to be spoken to loudly due to her deafness but his daughter's commanding manner gave him deep offence.

'Please, please,' he insisted, 'that is not good manners, my dear. What,' he asked, turning to Molly, 'did she say she wanted to see me about?'

'In confidence, is what she said.'

'Father,' said Elizabeth, displaying some petulance, 'you really must not see her.'

80

'If she is good enough to come and see me on this windy morning, surely I ought to be courteous enough to receive her? I was her employer last year, you know.'

'That, Father, is why you shouldn't see her.'

He knew better than his daughter how right she was in saying that. Yet he was annoyed by her attitude and quite prepared to assert his authority for its own sake.

'I will see her, Molly. Please show her in.'

'In that case, I will stay,' Elizabeth insisted.

This annoyed him further. Molly, meanwhile, had done what she had been instructed to do. In an awkward silence between father and daughter, filled with more window rattlings and hissings from the fire, Marie Valence suddenly entered the room. She wore an incongruous, slightly faded, mustard-coloured coat with a grey fur lining at the collar. It was open and revealed a full flounced pink skirt and an attractive velvet jacket of the same shade. She was drawing off a yellow silk scarf which she had worn to protect her hair as she came in, but her entrance was crowned by that special dazzle of brightness which she was able to give to her eyes when she wanted to impress.

'Captain Fenton,' she announced in her Frenchified, actressy way, as if the words were a fountain she could barely hold in check, 'I am so very grateful that you have consented to see me. On such an unpleasant morning.' She walked across the room towards him, holding out her pink-gloved hand. It was then she noticed Elizabeth standing by the fire and paused. 'Oh, I am sorry.'

'There is no need to be sorry,' said Elizabeth, nodding curtly towards her and then turning back to contemplation of the fire. The Captain meanwhile welcomed her. He took her hand and kissed it, leaning on a stick with his left arm as he did so, and motioned her to a chair.

81

'I am very pleased,' he remarked, 'but also a little surprised.'

'Oh, it is surprising, yes,' gushed Marie, 'but I am needing your help, Captain Fenton.'

She sat down in one of several large armchairs, almost deliberately avoiding the upright chair in which Mr Ellis had sat, and carefully and very femininely arranged her skirt over her knees. As she was about to continue speaking, she looked up and obviously checked herself at the sight of Elizabeth in front of the fire. There was a momentary silence.

'I do not really have to stay,' said Elizabeth, slowly turning round. 'But if you have no objection I will.'

She looked down at Marie with her direct, intense blue eyes, as though artfully suggesting that no one could really take exception to such an innocent gaze. Marie simply had to acquiesce.

'No, no, I have no objection. I have come here to renew an old ... an old friendship. And for the sake of friendship I have to ask one little favour.'

Marie dazzled them both with her shining eyes and her smile, but her audience knew as well as she did that it was all an act. Elizabeth's formidably innocent gaze undermined her composure and the Captain's puzzled look, accompanied by a stroking of the chin, made her feel that she had perhaps been guilty of a misjudgement.

'What sort of little favour?' he asked.

'I need money, Captain.' Though the Captain raised an eyebrow and looked apprehensive, she added in explanation, 'A loan of some money, you understand. I will pay it all back and with interest, if you wish.'

She smiled at the Captain in a way which suggested she could exert some power over him, yet her manner also seemed quite ingenuous, as if all she were asking for was the loan of a book or an umbrella. The Captain puffed quickly at his pipe.

'I think this is really not the right time or place.' He glanced towards his daughter. 'Perhaps later . . .'

'Father,' interrupted Elizabeth, 'you must not give her any money. I insist that she has no right to any of your money.'

Both of them looked at Elizabeth, who wrung her hands together rather dramatically and returned their looks with an assurance and firmness that defied any attempt to contradict her. Then, apparently unwilling to say anything more, she stared hard at the fire. As a result she did not notice the effect that her words had on them. Both the Captain and Marie held very still, as if anticipating the disclosure of some extremely embarrassing information. Their eyes met, Marie's smiling a little insolently and his also bright, but with a light in them suggesting anger as well as passion. They were sharing a moment of covert intimacy which could easily have proved ruinous, had Elizabeth guessed anything about it.

'Father,' said Elizabeth, not even looking round, 'I think you should remember how Marie influenced Miles.'

'My dear, I don't see . . .'

'In what way?' asked an astonished Marie. 'In what way do I influence your brother?'

'You know perfectly well.'

'I do not know this!' Marie spoke with a defiance that was quite unfeigned in its sincerity. 'Captain, what is this influence?'

'I am not sure. Please, my dear, tell us what you mean.'

'I am talking about how you tried to . . . to influence my brother,' said Elizabeth, now looking directly at Marie once again. 'And you know perfectly well what I mean.'

Marie played with the yellow scarf, pulling it gently

through her fingers. It was clear she knew what Elizabeth meant, but she also sensed that the girl did not have sufficient confidence to make a direct accusation and wanted to avoid appearing foolish.

'I was most fond of your brother Miles,' Marie confessed calmly. 'He was a fine handsome boy. And he learned to speak French very well. I am sure he will be a very gallant sailor, a credit to his father and sister, *n'est-ce pas*? So if I influence ... well!' She gave herself a gay little hand-wave in commendation.

Elizabeth was straight-backed with disdain. 'I do not mean that and you know I don't mean that. You seduced my brother, that is what I mean.'

Marie's mouth dropped open. Perhaps she had misjudged the girl, or perhaps Elizabeth knew more than she had supposed. Whatever the truth, Marie recognised she had made a mistake in speaking so blithely about Miles. The Captain chose that moment to intervene, saying severely:

'Please, my dear, that's enough! You must not make such accusations!'

For once father and daughter displayed similar flashes of ill temper. That her father should reprove her in front of someone else, let alone in front of someone like Marie Valence, was almost inconceivable to Elizabeth. All the haughtiness of her nature took offence at her father's attitude.

'Father, how can you let this ... this ...' She could not think of a word beastly enough to describe the shocked and indignant-looking Marie.

'My dear, you will kindly leave!' her father commanded.

'No, no,' said Marie, rising, 'I can see that I'm the one who must leave. I do not wish to cause bad feelings of any kind. Perhaps later I will ...'

She had stood up into a suddenly tense atmosphere. The inreined violence of the father's and the daughter's emotions embarrassed each of them and made them speechless for a moment or so.

'At a more convenient time, per'aps,' Marie went on, giving the Captain a polite smile. 'But now I can see it is not the right time.'

She gave a little nod towards the Captain, who responded with a bow. He was on the point of turning to the bell-pull to summon Molly or Dora when Marie, pulling the silk scarf over her hair, strode as smartly from the room as she had entered it. Elizabeth ran after her, and the Captain heard Marie say 'There is no need, Miss Elizabeth, I know where the front door is,' as their two pairs of footsteps resounded sharply on the tilework of the hall. Then the front door slammed shut.

The Captain raised his pipe. As he did so he noticed how badly his hand was shaking. The visit had suddenly brought into focus so many of the fears about his reputation which had been little more than annoying blurs in his mind before. He poured out another glass of port.

'What,' he asked of Elizabeth, who had come back into the room and was closing the door, 'what d'you mean by using a word like that? Seduced? Do you have the faintest idea what it means, my dear?'

The gout in his knee attacked him agonisingly again and he sat down slowly. All manner of rebukes and admonitions occurred to him as he looked at his daughter, but she was such a picture of innocence – he simply could not bring himself to imagine she knew what the word meant.

'She knew what I meant,' she said haughtily. 'That is what matters.' Evidently she took some pride in having despatched Marie. 'Now I think I'll go to my room.'

'You shouldn't have said such a thing, my dear. I know you feel Miss Valence misbehaved, but you really mustn't spread such gossip about her relations with Miles. It reflects upon us all. It is bad for us.'

'I do not gossip, Father,' was Elizabeth's stern reply.

At that moment Molly appeared behind her in the doorway, excusing herself for having intruded, but Elizabeth quickly stood aside. Any further discussion seemed pointless. Elizabeth was not prepared to be lectured on the subject of Marie Valence, or on any matter of behaviour regarding servants and employees. Her father's behaviour had always been a source of puzzlement to her, especially when it involved his relationship with Molly, or his fondness for Marie. She simply could not understand how he could stoop so low. To Elizabeth it was as clear as daylight that a proper distance had to be kept between her father and herself and the below-stairs world for which she was now largely responsible as the mistress of the house.

'The mistress of the house' – she liked the expression. Her mother had told her that she would be 'the mistress of the house' one day and now that was exactly what she was, no matter what Molly Ford might think or do. She reflected on this as she slowly climbed the stairs to her room. Through the landing window she saw the strip of back garden with its one old apple tree and then, seeming almost directly below the end wall of the garden, the houses of the esplanade and the steel-coloured sea stippled with the crests of waves. It was cloudy and a strong onshore wind rattled the windows.

She went to her room, which faced the street. Marie was standing by the iron wicket-gate in front of Alto House. She was talking to the young Russian doctor who now wore an ordinary dark topcoat, the front lapels of which he was holding up to his neck against the wind. Talking Russian, Elizabeth supposed. For a moment she envied Marie the fur lining of her coat, however shabby it might be, as its nap was brushed from light to dark and dark to light by the playfulness of the wind. Even though the whole ensemble of mustard-coloured coat and yellow scarf and pink skirt seemed tasteless and foreign to Elizabeth, it reminded her how ordinary and dull her own clothes were. She felt tempted, as she had been often recently, and particularly since meeting Guy Seddenham again, by a desire to assert her femininity, to be the woman, the mistress, 'The Temptress of Men' as a picture in one of Miles's books was entitled. The woman in question bore a striking resemblance to Marie Valence.

She clasped her hands together again and felt perhaps she ought to pray. Her room had a crucifix, which had belonged to her mother, hanging above the fireplace. It was practically the only adornment in a room full of simple and rather old-fashioned things, such as the blue coverlet on the bed, the oak bedstead, the plain farmhouse chest-of-drawers and the severe dressing-table with its solitary mirror set on four little arched feet that made it look as if it were about to spring up in the air. Placed against this mirror was an ancient doll with a porcelain face, the only memento of her childhood Elizabeth allowed herself. All the rest of the room mutely announced her insistence on being a woman and in charge of her affairs.

As she drew back from the window her face appeared in the up-tilted mirror, the blue eyes seeming so brightly innocent, the dark eyebrows and the clear pale complexion seeming so impossibly youthful. I can't be like that! she thought. I can't possibly be such a little girl!

Meanwhile, downstairs in the study, the Captain sat

at his desk holding Molly's hand. The two of them did not speak. It was quite unnecessary for him to explain to Molly how anxious he had grown over Marie Valence's visit. Both feared that Elizabeth would discover the secret that united them. But Molly herself, after what Bill had told her, could not put out of her mind that hot August day a year ago, when the flies had been about in the still air of the evening and she had seen him driving the cattle into the pen for slaughter and her own ragged filthy clothes had had the smell of the carcasses on them, which she had humped daily for the butchery business, and he had come up to her in the slaughter-house among the flies and told her she shouldn't smell like a midden, that no wife of his should smell like a midden, and then he had hit her again over the ears and flung her down and she had seized one of the long butcher's knives from the wall and thrust it and thrust it and he had stumbled forward clutching his jerkin and she had thrown down the knife and run out into the long shadows and the red sunset and heard in her dull buzzing deaf ears the voices hissing: 'Murderess! Murderess!'

Part II

6

On the Thursday afternoon, at the insistence of Aunt Emily, Guy had been confined to bed. She was fearful of colds. There was no greater danger to health, in her opinion, than to neglect a cold. So Guy was sent to bed and he remained there throughout Friday and Saturday.

From his bed he heard the growing noise of the storm as if it were part of his own illness. The winds rose strongly on Thursday night and blew fiercely throughout the following two days, accompanied by torrential rain and high seas. The waves thundered up the sands and broke in such force against the low wall of the esplanade that Belinda House seemed to shake from the impact. Daylight appeared greenish, while the howling of the wind at night was an unending melancholy lament interspersed with cries and whimperings. The noise came out of blackness. It had a cavernous resonance that multiplied his fears and invaded his dreams with a feverish, tumultuous echoing. He feared the noise as if it were the sound of death. He dreamt of it as a force of nature that would shatter all man's futile attempts to discover its secrets. Mr Prendergast had insisted that all life began in the sea. It seemed to Guy that this noise was the sea's attempt to rise back over the land and enter once again into its rightful heritage.

Aunt Emily visited him twice each day. She showed a real concern for his health which surprised and pleased him. She also wanted to share her worries with him. The evening card games had to be abandoned, since she felt Guy was not up to them and in any case needed as

91

much rest as possible, but when it came to her money cares and the problem of Guy's father she was ready to share these with him. Charles Augustus Whitehouse had not been generous with the holiday money, which meant that they might have to leave Ventnor at short notice, and as for Guy's father, he had promised he would be returning to England in August. Would not it be better if they gave up their Ventnor holiday and returned to Lambeth?

So long as Guy was ill they did not have to decide. He was permitted no visitors, not even the twins or Elizabeth Fenton, who had called at Belinda House to deliver her brother's jacket. Aunt Emily described her as 'that hoity-toity young lady'. 'I sent her away,' she said with a sniff. 'Such impertinence! Leaving her brother's old jacket for you, as if we were paupers!' But the jacket was brought up to Guy's room as well as a mixture prescribed by Dr Hodgson. Guy had some of the mixture on the Saturday evening and by the next morning was feeling so much better that he realised he would not be able to sham illness any longer just to postpone the decision about their holiday. He had to be on his feet and outside as soon as possible. The early Sunday morning was, moreover, quiet and sunlit. The sea seemed inaudible. Peering down at the window in the side wall of the next house, where he had seen Marie standing naked on the Sunday afternoon of their arrival, he saw only drawn curtains. He supposed she had gone as she said she would, so that the strange excitement of her presence no longer worked to prolong their Ventnor holiday.

Pulling on his clothes, including Miles's old jacket which turned out to fit him remarkably well, he crept down the stairs of Belinda House. Though they creaked a little under his weight, it seemed that no one heard him and he felt so light-hearted and light-headed that all he could think of was the outdoors and the fresh morning air. It was half-past six. Not even early tradesmen were about. All the houses along the esplanade seemed to be asleep with their closed, curtained windows and their white-painted fronts looking so starched and still in the sunlight. The tide was out, perhaps at its furthest ebb, having left behind signs of the recent storm in the shape of piled shingle and seaweed just below the esplanade and several of the bathing machines overturned, with one of them smashed into what looked like so much driftwood just where the wooden steps had been. As he quickly discovered, the pile of wood served as a makeshift bridge giving unsteady but real access to the sand. The sight of the empty shore enticed him. He ran down the steep beach right to the water's edge.

The sea was almost as still as a lake. Instead of waves it sent long thin patternings of water up the slope of the sand and made its way into little indentations and gullies as if feeling them smoothly with its fingers. No sails were visible on its smooth surface and scarcely a white crest of breaking wave could be seen right to the horizon, which shone pale and blue against a featureless wall of white sky. He knew the cold had left him with a sense of being cocooned from the outside world and he supposed this might account for the unreal impression of quietness and confinement that sea and sky and sand now offered him, as if he were standing in nothing larger than a spacious, high-ceilinged room. To his ears every movement of his feet in the sand sounded clearly and his own breathing seemed to make almost as much noise as the slightly percussive cries of gulls over the rocky area below West Hill. The sense of space and emptiness, as well as the contradictory feeling that he was unobserved and therefore private, gave him a sudden, invigorating conviction that he was free. He was free now to go exactly where he wished. The whole world was his. He could do what he liked with it. Looking around, aware of the persistent noise of the gulls, he decided he would once again explore the area of rocks which had always been beyond the limits of last summer's walks with his mother.

The freshwater stream dividing the beach from the rocks was now snaking in racing, glittering lines across the sloping sand. It made no more than a soft trickling noise despite the fact that in places it seemed to run to a depth of a couple of feet or more. He untied his shoes, hung them round his neck and rolled up his trousers to above his knees. This did not prove high enough, for the streamwater at one point rose halfway up his thighs before he reached the rocks and clambered up them. Gasping from the effort and feeling his heart beating abnormally strongly, he sat down abruptly and stared at the brilliant sight which met his eyes.

The pools among the rocks were filled to the brim; they were motionless, not just mirrors but windows of clear glass, and they stretched one after another across the whole rocky landscape towards the whiteness of the sky. It took him a while to get his breath back. As he drew the fresh, harsh air into his lungs in short bursts, realising how weak the recent cold had made him, he felt that the fitful glitter of the pools was like so many star-shaped candles on a cake. At first their placid, glass-like brilliance, of small flames burning in a sanctuary, seemed awesome, but when he stood up and took several careful steps among the seaweed and shingle which littered the rocky surfaces he saw that the pools were as mysterious and exciting as the windows of shops full of Christmas decorations. For inside the first one he came to, as he leaned down and peered into its depths, he saw the apparently upward-hanging blossoms of the flora, creamy ivory, orange-flecked, amethyst and emerald, all caught in a glacial stillness that stretched right down to the faintly gleaming bottom of the pool. A perceptible, rhythmic motion stirred all the growths, yet seemed to emphasise the stillness as well. He clambered to his feet and approached a bigger pool. The surface brightness of the water dazzled him until, lowering his face almost into it, he peered again and saw sea anemones, shells, crabs, seaweed, especially the weed-curtains lining the perimeter, all stirring very faintly as though the water were breathing softly. Along the sides the varicoloured anthoid growths moved in the gentlest of watery breezes. The beauty of the submarine decorations of this pool was so magical that Guy found himself drawn from one pool to the next and eventually right into the middle of the wide area of rocks evacuated by the sea.

The early-morning sun shone through pearl-white cloud. It produced a glassy shadowless atmosphere among the pools. The bright, pure air had a shimmering, opalescent clarity which made the horizon seem close to hand, as if touchable. But most clearly magnified of all were the seeming horizon depths of the rock pools themselves as he gazed through their shining windows. So he went from pool to pool, dropping on to his knees and peering into each one as he came to it. If he dislodged some shingle or a stone by mistake, the whole interior world of the pool would retract itself from him. The image of his face, so alien to that life as it rose above the pool's rim, would seem in some ghostly way to obtrude its mirrorings into the water's depths and appear to be looking up at him and would slowly shiver and break into elongated fragments. Most of the time he simply peered and stared, not noticing the mirror image encased in the depths. He would hold his breath so that no stain of condensation or flicker of movement should obscure the pure translucency of the pool's window glass. Beyond he would see what appeared to be a paradise of underwater life. He imagined suddenly he was looking through windows that gave glimpses of some eternal, heavenly peace.

He looked down into one deep pool, fringed with seaweed. Its depths seemed endless. He gazed over the seaweed rim and there, silhouetted rather than illumined, he saw his head intrude over the reflection of the darkened ragged edge of the pool. It had greater translucency in its depths than he had thought. He saw his own silhouette, but he also saw what he was sure were eyes tilted upwards to him. He stared.

Was it his own face?

The eyes were open, he thought, but without brightness. Hair fringed the features like caressing seaweed. What at first had seemed dark sand at the pool's bottom was a mustard-coloured coat with a grey lining. Before he could stop himself he had gasped and the distant image began to break into fragments. Desperately, to stop himself from slipping, he plunged his hand into the pool and found purchase on a small shelf of rock just below the fringe of floating seaweed. The feel of its slimy surface beneath the water so shocked and appalled him that the boots tied round his neck slipped forward and tumbled into the pool. He grabbed one but the lace of the other broke loose and it dropped like a stone into the depths. There would be no likelihood of a new pair of boots for him, he knew that for sure. The boot for his right foot had to be retrieved or life wouldn't be worth living.

He waited for the ripples on the pool's surface to

subside before peering into it again. With a pricking sensation gathering at the nape of his neck he parted the seaweed fringe and peered keenly through the slightly moving water. There could be no doubt about the shape. A chill sweat broke out on his temples. It was a human form lying in the pool's depths. At first he thought it could be anyone, as if by thinking this he could persuade himself that he was not seeing what he least wanted to see. But the eyes were open and looking up at him. He could not mistake them. They were the eyes of Marie Valence.

He sprang back from the pool's edge, having forgotten all about his lost boot. The shock of what he'd seen made him give a spontaneous yelping cry. The sound roused sudden gulls' cries which were repeated and seemed to echo through the stillness. He was breathing in quivering bursts and shaking a little. A terror of the pool and what it contained seized hold of him. He jumped to his feet, but the instant he did so he knew the boot had somehow to be recovered. As for Marie Valence, if it *was* her he had seen down there, he knew he would have to do something about her, though it was a knowledge that seemed impotent to oppose the sudden terror exercised by the pool and the whole apparently empty world of rocks and dense pearly light surrounding him.

He thought how it had been at his mother's funeral, an empty, sunless, still morning like this one, but later in the year, and how he had stood there at the open graveside and felt that the surrounding emptiness of the graveyard and sky was simply a part of his own huge and devouring loneliness and that never again in his life would he feel able to think of himself as one of many, among the living, in the company of others. The memory coalesced with the excited, loving feeling he had for Marie and the urgency of his wanting to comfort her when she had said she was leaving. He realised he was standing now at Marie's graveside and the same tears he had shed for his mother burst out of his eyes now. They were disgraceful, silly, unworthy tears, he knew, but he could not help them. He brushed them out of his eyes. At that moment he found himself looking into another face.

A man's head, the hair plastered wetly to the skull, had risen out of a kind of narrow causeway among the rocks a few yards away. Guy recognised at once the Russian doctor with the long narrow face and the sideburns and the peering greenish eyes. As the whole figure came into view he saw he was wearing a damp-looking loose cloak with a rather crude opening at the neck, his strong bare arms poking through holes where there should have been sleeves. He came quickly across the rocks towards Guy and stopped within a yard of him.

'So what is it?'

Ashamed of his tears, though simultaneously startled by the doctor's appearance and quite unable to remember his name, Guy pointed abruptly at the pool and announced that his boot had fallen in. At once he knew how silly this sounded and was certainly no reason for his tears. He added:

'I think it's Marie. I think she's drowned.'

He knew his English voice sounded remarkably mature and authoritative even though he spoke the sentences very quickly. Apparently uncertain where he had seen Guy before, and screwing up his eyes, the doctor studied Guy's features closely and then leaned forward to look into the pool. He placed his head slowly below the level of the water, kept it there for a few moments, jumped back from the pool's edge and, to Guy's amazement, suddenly pulled the cloak off, lowered himself into the water naked and gleaming and swam swiftly downwards. Guy could see nothing but a flashing whiteness in the turbulence of the disturbed pool. Before he could be sure what was happening, the man's head reappeared. He had one arm round Marie's shoulders and was drawing her towards the pool's edge where, apparently able to find a footing on a ledge of rock, he rose slowly into a nearly upright position and brought the sodden, doll-like, obscene shape gradually, head first, in a supine position, on to a fairly level area. Then the dripping, naked man clambered out of the water and knelt down next to the corpse and gently, very gently, began brushing the hair and sand and seaweed away from the face with the tips of his fingers. As he did this his whole body heaved with the effort of gulping in breath and he seemed to be shaking and quivering.

'Masha, Masha, Masha,' he kept on muttering, followed by words Guy couldn't understand. 'Masha, Masha, Masha,' he said as if he were trying to wake her up. The heaving of his body gradually became a slow, rhythmic motion of keening and lamentation. 'Masha, Masha, Masha, *bozhe ty moy, chto ty sdelala, chto ty sdelala* . . .'

Guy had never seen any adult express emotion so openly. Even when his mother died nobody had shed more than a few discreet tears and he had been ashamed of the tears he had shed at her funeral. The doctor stopped heaving, stood up slowly and pulled on his cloak. It clung to his wet body and showed patches of damp at the shoulders and chest and stomach. He gave Guy a long solemn look.

'You know her?'

Guy nodded his head, trying not to look down.

'Look! Look!' the Russian commanded.

Guy made himself look down and he saw that the

brushing of the hair from the features revealed Marie not as dead but as a very pale, almost yellowish-ivory replica of the Marie he had known. Her eyes still stared upwards. The man touched Miles's jacket.

'Please.'

It took a moment for Guy to realise what he meant. Then he slipped it off. The man placed the jacket carefully and reverently over Marie's upturned staring face. They both lowered their heads in some kind of silent memorial. Then the man looked at him again.

'So you know Masha?'

'Not Masha. She's Marie. She was here last year.'

'We call her Masha.'

'Why?'

'She is Russian.'

It seemed all the explanation he would get. The man heaved his shoulders in a deep sigh.

'You know Fedya?'

'The man at Belinda House?'

It occurred to Guy that Fedya must be involved, but before he could speak the other said:

'It was a quarrel. We were talking. You remember?'

Guy said he remembered.

'A quarrel. Masha and Fedya. So . . .'

The doctor made a despairing, emptying gesture with his hands and shook his head several times. Guy supposed he was saying that Marie's death was due to a quarrel between her and Fedya.

'You mean the man you were talking to . . . you mean he killed her?'

The doctor closed his eyes. 'You will not understand,' was all he said slowly in his deep, accented voice. He was silent for several seconds and Guy felt awkward. He began to wonder whether the doctor himself might have had something to do with Marie's death.

'You know me,' said the doctor suddenly. 'I am

100

Zhenia Bazarov. I am doctor.'

'I know, I know . . . '

Guy's admission was disregarded as the doctor went on: 'I work for your English Dr Hodgson. He is good doctor but he loves money. Money to me is . . . ' A light dismissive handwave. 'Now Masha is dead because she had no money. Why?'

Guy said he didn't know and was about to say that he knew she needed money and was going away to sell some jewellery, when the doctor, looking solemnly into his face, announced: 'It is Russian business, Russian business. English people have no understanding.'

This silenced Guy for the time being.

'You believe,' the doctor said, still looking closely at Guy and without blinking his eyes, 'I am killing her? You believe it?'

Guy shook his head vigorously.

'So I will tell you. I am not killing her. Count Rostopchine, he, he . . .' the doctor struck his right fist into the palm of his left hand '. . . he kills Masha! He kills Masha!'

Guy was reminded that one of the Misses Bosanquet had said the man at Belinda House was employed by a Count. A dubious sort of connection was being made, it seemed, but because it was all 'Russian business' Guy felt uneasy about asking questions and doubted in any case whether he'd be able to make head or tail of the doctor's abrupt, rather mystifying remarks.

'So your name is?'

'Mine?'

'Who else? How many people are here?'

Guy had been so disconcerted by the sudden question that he even failed to notice the laconic tone in the doctor's voice. He said he was Guy Seddenham.

'And you have aunt?'

'Yes, Aunt Emily.'

'And sisters?'

'Yes, twin sisters. Jane and Edwina.'

'No mother?'

'My mother is dead.'

'So . . .' The doctor permitted his stern face to relax a moment into a sympathetic smile. 'I understand. My mother is also dead. My father is also dead. In my country if you do not agree with Tsar, with government, you must die. I am here alone, as you see. And now I am not being a person.' This cryptic remark was not immediately followed by any explanation. The doctor pulled the damp, sail-like material of the cloak away from his body. 'I am,' he said, still smiling, this time with a slightly amused, unassuming candour, 'I am collecting specimens of small, very small, sea animals. In my country everywhere is land. Here everywhere is sea. So . . .' And he spread out his arms towards the sea in a magnanimous and encompassing motion which suggested that it was all his, the sea and the sky and all things in them. 'And you? Why are you here?'

Guy realised that his presence deserved as much of an explanation as the doctor's and he told him.

'Yes, I can see,' the doctor agreed. 'You are pale. So you are better but you are not strong, I can see. So . . .' This must be a favourite word of his, Guy thought. 'So we cannot, cannot . . .' a word was being searched for in the doctor's English vocabulary '. . . cannot lift Masha, carry her? You understand?'

Guy nodded.

'So we go back to town,' the doctor said. 'So we tell? Who?'

Guy thought a moment. He had no real idea. But he said hesitantly, glancing upwards into the doctor's face:

'The policeman, I suppose.'

7

Mr William Ellis was told in due course. He was aroused by his wife who shook him awake, telling him a girl had come up from the esplanade saying that a woman had been found drowned and would the sergeant or the constable come at once. The sergeant had been given compassionate leave for two weeks to attend to personal matters in Southampton and all the responsibilities of policing the citizenry of Ventnor now rested with Mr Ellis, the town constable, and a couple of young lads of seventeen and eighteen who were designated his assistants. Mr Ellis climbed out of bed yawning and scratching his hair. He pulled on his old dressing gown and went down the narrow stairs of the constabulary house.

'What's this about a drowning?' he asked disagreeably, because drownings always appalled him, despite all the wounds and horrors he had witnessed in the Crimea. There was no worse sight, to his way of thinking, than a corpse turned fishy green by the action of the sea.

The girl said she had been sent up to tell him by Mrs Rees of Belinda House on the esplanade. A boy staying there had found a drowned woman among the rocks below West Hill. 'A foreign lady, sir, drownded, sir, please come down, sir.' Then there was something unclear about a foreign doctor.

'The doctor said she's drowned, is that what you mean, my dear?'

The girl's recollection was unclear, and what really

mattered was that the policeman, sir, should come as quick as he could before people started going on the rocks to see for themselves.

'Ah,' said Mr Ellis, 'now that's right sensible, that is.'

He had his wife rouse the two young assistants of his (they slept at the top of the constabulary house in the High Street) while he pulled on his uniform and drank a mug of his wife's strong tea. After straightening his uniform jacket before the mirror and carefully adjusting his peaked cap – to his wife's, if not his own, satisfaction – he summoned the two lads, who had armed themselves with a collapsible stretcher and other tackle, and told them to fall in behind him. Smartness, like respectability, was his watchword. The small group then marched down the steep, rutted lane from the High Street to the esplanade, led by the girl from Belinda House.

It was by now half-past eight, the sun had broken through the cloud layer and Sunday breakfasts were being served in all the guest houses. Through discreet curtains the constable and his party were observed – necks were strained and hushed words spoken – but since no one was quite sure what it all meant, the only followers he collected were two local boys who claimed to know all about the rocky area below West Hill, as well they might, Mr Ellis thought, since they were most likely those Captain Fenton had referred to as bathing there 'just as God made 'em'. The constable himself had never had occasion to visit the rocky area during the thirteen months he had been in Ventnor and was grateful to the boys for offering to help. It was hot, the heavy, dark material of his uniform made him sweat and the rocks proved slippery and full of pools. The boy at Belinda House who had first brought news of the drowning had not been permitted by his aunt to accompany the party on their melancholy trek, so Mr Ellis was pleased to be guided.

As for Guy, he had returned to bed on Aunt Emily's orders. His disobedience in going out without her permission at such an unholy hour of the morning was less serious in her eyes than the possibility that he could have done irreparable harm to his health by such behaviour. He had lost a boot, which was reprehensible, and he had returned in the company of that Russian doctor with the most disagreeable reputation (as the Misses Bosanquet at once pointed out), but, wholly compensating for such wayward conduct, he had acquired instant celebrity in Belinda House by claiming to have found a foreign lady drowned in a pool.

Meanwhile, the corpse was laid on the stretcher, draped with a sheet and conveyed slowly back across the rocks. Mr Ellis gave orders that it should be taken at once to the mortuary in the Infirmary. He could only judge by what he had seen, and what he had seen had persuaded him that the foreign lady had drowned herself, most likely as a result of a love affair and a broken heart. Her clothes did not leave the impression that she had been poor, but since no money had been found on her person and her pockets had been full of pebbles, suggesting that she had deliberately set about taking her life, he had to find out more about her, especially as there would be funeral costs. So he returned to Belinda House and asked to speak to the boy who had originally found her. Guy was brought down to the back parlour, by which time the constable was seated before an unlit fire, the collar of his jacket unbuttoned at the neck and beads of perspiration standing out on his temples as he gently fanned himself with his peaked cap.

'You are Master Guy ... Perhaps you'd be good

enough to spell your surname for me and I'll note it down.'

The surname was slowly copied down into the small notebook as were such details as the approximate time and circumstances of the discovery and the name of the deceased.

'So you knew her, did you?'

Guy explained how he had known her briefly the previous year and met her again this summer.

'So she was employed by Captain Fenton?'

'Yes, sir.'

'And this year?'

'Well, sir, what I heard the doctor say was . . . ' And he repeated the claim that Marie Valence had been killed by the Count.

'Well, I never did!' Mr Ellis exclaimed. 'And who might this Count be? A Russian?'

Guy said he thought so. All he knew for sure was that he lived at the Esplanade Hotel.

'Well, well, you've been most helpful, my boy.' And the little black notebook was closed with a snap. 'What a hot morning it is! You were fond of her, weren't you?'

Guy reddened slightly, muttered some kind of agreement and deliberately avoided the other's eyes.

'And the Russian doctor, he was fond of her, was he?'

Guy nodded.

'I'll have to speak to him. But I think that's all I need to know for the time being. Now you go back to bed and make a proper recovery from that cold.'

Aunt Emily had hovered just outside the parlour door during the constable's visit and demanded to be told everything as soon as he had gone. The twins, vowing that they would be on their best behaviour, were allowed to join her in listening to Guy's account of the questions he had been asked and the answers he had given. He took pride and a certain pleasure in telling his story with as many details as possible.

'So *she* was that woman in red! They were quarrelling, weren't they? That woman in red and that common fellow who's living here? Oh, I wouldn't be surprised if he didn't push her in that pool! Women like that always come to bad ends!'

Neither Guy nor the twins were really sure what she meant by that, but Guy protested at his aunt's dismissive tone. 'I was sorry for her and rather fond of her. She was always very nice to me.' This sounded lame and immediately elicited a sharp rebuke.

'Really, my dear Guy, no one can be *fond* of a woman like that! It's such a pity we couldn't have found a room at the Esplanade Hotel. There's bound to be a much nicer sort of people there.'

To which, of course, there was no answer. Guy was allowed to get dressed for lunch, but Aunt Emily insisted he should not accompany her and the twins on their Sunday afternoon walk. The walk, though, was curtailed by rain, which began falling heavily at about three o'clock, and all four of them then fell to playing cards in Aunt Emily's room, always making sure that she never lost more than two games in succession. Meanwhile, the constable, following what Guy had told him, decided to pay a visit to the Count who was living at the Esplanade Hotel among a much nicer sort of people.

Knowing the Russian habit of late rising, he had postponed his visit until near midday. The bells of the churches and chapels had ceased their ringing for the various morning services. The sun came in momentary gleams through increasing armadas of cloud flowing eastward. He walked down the esplanade, checked that the lady in question had not been seen in St Martin's

Villa since Thursday at the latest, and then only briefly, and made his way to the Esplanade Hotel where he learned from the manager that there was a Count Rostopchine occupying two rooms on the first floor. He went up the stairs. Just before he tapped on the floral design of the door's panelling he heard a loud bout of coughing from inside.

The door was opened by a fair-haired, rosy-cheeked young man wearing an obviously new suit cut in the English style. It was crumpled rather than ill-fitting, though the young man wore it with a slovenly and rather truculent air as though it were a uniform of which he felt ashamed. He showed the constable into an airy room overlooking the esplanade. All the constable saw at first was the back of a high wing chair, so high that it obscured its occupant completely from view. There was a brisk exchange of words in Russian between the occupant and the young man.

'Who is it?' a voice asked squeakily in accented English from the other side of the chair.

The constable explained.

'Come here, please. I am honoured, greatly honoured.'

When he came face to face with the Count, he could hardly help noticing the small skull with the neatly macassared hair, the trim moustache and the pallid complexion made paler by the unflatteringly harsh light from the sea. The Count was wearing a blue silk dressing gown with gold piping along the lapels and cuffs. He leaned forward to offer his right hand to the constable while with his left hand he held a pink handkerchief to his mouth. What struck the constable at once were the upturned, bird-like, shining eyes, and he recognised immediately the symptoms of illness that were so common among visitors to Ventnor. The handshake was limp and perfunctory and quickly over. Hardly, he thought, the handshake of a murderer.

'Very, very honoured to meet an English policeman,' said the Count. 'Please sit down.'

Mr Ellis had seen Russian officers in the Crimea who resembled the Count in their looks and their air of thin-lipped, unsmiling authority. He knew them and despised them. They had not done the fighting, so far as he had been able to see, and they had treated their subordinates worse than dogs. He sat down in a very upright way, his jaw jutting forward, and took out his notebook. The Count scrutinised him closely with narrowed eyes.

'So it is your uniform, yes?'

'Yes, sir.' Mr Ellis cleared his throat. 'I have one or two questions for you, sir.'

'You wish?' The Count indicated with his eyes that perhaps the constable would prefer to question him without the presence of the young man. 'I can ask him to . . .'

Having put two and two together, Mr Ellis thought it much better to question them both at the same time. The Count took dignified but silent offence on hearing this and crossed his legs.

'I believe, sir, you know a certain Russian lady by the name of Miss Valence, Marie Valence.' Mr Ellis pronounced the name as slowly and correctly as he could. 'That is correct, sir, isn't it?'

The Count withdrew his handkerchief, took in a slow, evidently painful breath and acknowledged that it was correct. He made a certain play of slowly, fussily, tucking the handkerchief back into his sleeve before he snapped his fingers. His young manservant jumped forward and offered cigarettes from a carved ivory box. Mr Ellis refused. The Count took one delicately and just

109

as delicately allowed the young man to touch the tip of it alight with a candle flame.

'She was a person of no consequence, as you English say.' His cigarette held between forefinger and thumb, he made little stabbing flourishes with it to accompany the pedantic phrasing. 'She and I were acquainted, but, well, not closely, you understand. I was her ... her master, shall I say, her teacher, her friend. She was free, completely free, you know.' The sentences emerged like practice exercises in an English phrasebook. 'So what is it you are pleased to learn about her?'

Mr Ellis watched the blue tobacco smoke curl in frolicsome wisps round the Count's face. 'I have to inform you, sir, that she is dead.'

There was a sudden freezing of his expression. 'Dead? How?'

Mr Ellis told what he knew. The Count looked straight at the constable but the more he heard, the less focused and intent were his bird-like eyes. After making a show of disbelief, he finally accepted that the news was true. He turned and spoke a few sharp words in Russian to his young manservant. The effect astonished Mr Ellis. It was only later that he realised how significant it was. The young man's mouth opened in a look matching disbelief with shock while the colour slowly drained from his face. Mr Ellis licked the tip of his pencil.

'What exactly were your relations with the deceased, sir?'

The Count's lips formed themselves into an ironical smile, but a cough overtook him before he coulld speak. A glass of water was brought. That was waved away and replaced by a glass of red wine. The Count tasted it and placed the glass carefully on a side table.

'I told you. We were acquainted. I paid for her room,

her food. But she was free, completely free.' The cigarette was waved in a loose flourish.

'When did you last see her?'

The Count consulted his manservant before answering. 'Tuesday, yes, Tuesday. For one week I have not been out, you understand. Such storms, such rain ... She came asking for money. Tuesday, yes.'

'And your servant, sir?'

'Oh, he does not see her!'

Mr Ellis glanced up and found the young manservant staring at him. He asked:

'Was there a quarrel?'

Pausing for short bouts of coughing, after the cigarette had been extinguished barely a quarter smoked, the Count explained that he and Marie Valence had had words but they had not quarrelled. He had simply refused to give her more money. As for Fedya, his manservant, it was of no consequence whether he'd quarrelled with her or not. Mr Ellis reflected on this phrase 'of no consequence' which had been used twice already during the short interview and recognised that it would always crop up when the whole truth proved embarrassing.

'Was the lady accustomed to take walks along the sands?'

This was dismissed. 'Perhaps she did, perhaps she did not.'

'Had the lady ever spoken of visiting the rocks below West Hill or the Undercliff?'

'No.'

The curt denial of the possibility made the constable feel it was the first true answer he had received so far. He raised his eyes and surveyed both faces.

'I have to ask myself, why should the lady be found in one of the deep pools? If she didn't make a habit of going there, she would hardly choose to go there in the middle of a storm, would she?'

The Count raised the handkerchief to his lips again, simultaneously nodding at the questions, but he did not speak.

'So I have to conclude that she may have wished to kill herself. If so, then I ask myself why. Do you know why she should wish to kill herself?'

The Count removed the handkerchief, parted his lips to speak and then closed them. It was clear meanwhile that the young man called Fedya simply had not understood, though his eyes remained fixed on Mr Ellis's face.

'Was she, do you know, enjoying close relations with anyone at the time of her death?' Such delicate phrasing seemed merely to puzzle his listener, so Mr Ellis asked bluntly: 'Had she any particular friends, sir, men friends, so far as you know?'

The Count emitted a brief, shuddering cough. He glanced quickly up at his manservant and then composed himself again by fussily drawing the lapels of his dressing gown more tightly across his chest.

'Many,' he said and pursed his lips.

Mr Ellis nodded, more to himself than in acknowledgement of what he had heard. He was beginning to realise that the truth would not be easily obtained.

'So she could've drowned herself out of unhappiness, sir?'

The Count raised an eyebrow in acquiescence and indifference.

'You see,' said Mr Ellis, adopting a sterner tone, 'it is my duty, sir, in the case of a death to establish conclusively that no foul play can be suspected. It is very unlikely, of course, that the lady in question would have been placed in that pool when she was already dead. I have to assume that she filled her pockets with stones and either slipped in or drowned herself quite deliberately. You understand what I'm saying?'

The Count said he did.

'Whichever way you look at it, sir, the circumstances are unhappy. You will appreciate that, being a Russian lady, it will be assumed that she drowned herself for some reason connected with other Russian visitors to Ventnor. There will be a certain suspicion, you understand. And it would not be good for the reputation of the esteemed Russian visitors to our seaside town if the poor lady were to receive no more than a pauper's burial, would it?'

The Count did not immediately realise the intent of the elaborate question, but the moment he understood he raised both hands in a gesture suggesting that heaven should forbid such an occurrence. He snapped his fingers, gave an order in Russian and a few seconds later a small metal box was placed in his hands by the obedient Fedya. The Count unlocked it. He offered Mr Ellis four sovereigns.

'That is very generous of you, sir. I will write you a receipt.'

The formalities over, he put away his notebook and stood up. The Count again extended his right hand.

'As you see, I am unwell, Constable. If it can be arranged, er, quietly . . . '

Mr Ellis explained that he would have to make certain other enquiries, but he hoped matters could be arranged as quietly as possible, as the Count requested. Although he was successful in concealing his distaste for the whole business, he was not successful in concealing his injured hand. The Count asked about it.

'I was wounded in the Crimea, sir, by a Russian bullet.'

113

'Ah, so we are old enemies!'

'If that is how you wish it,' said Mr Ellis, putting on his peaked cap and confronting the Count's small upturned face which was smiling quite broadly and with a certain sly triumph.

Mr Ellis returned to the constabulary house in the High Street for his midday meal. He had taken a strong dislike to Count Rostopchine. No doubt there would never be direct evidence of the Count's complicity, but Mr Ellis entertained the deepest suspicions of his contribution to the Russian lady's suicide, if that was what it was. On the present evidence it could hardly be anything else, he supposed, and after the meal he remained seated at the cleared table to write out his report of the morning's events. He ended his account by making it clear that his ignorance of the Russian language prevented him from ascertaining many details of the lady's personal habits and associates. It had grown colder, meanwhile, and begun to rain, so his wife lit the fire in the large cast-iron grate. He unlaced his boots, drank a mug of beer and stretched himself out in his deep armchair before the crackling fire, thinking it had been an unusually busy Sunday. The effort of it all had worn him out and he felt extremely tired. He quickly fell asleep. His wife did not wake him for fear of making him bad-tempered and it was nearly six o'clock in the evening when he found his shoulder being gently shaken by one of his young assistants. He blinked somewhat belligerently into the lad's anxious face.

'What is it, boy?'

The lad stammered out news more ominous than anything else he had heard that day. It turned out that another urgent message had come from Belinda House. Nothing specific was mentioned in the message, except that Dr Hodgson had been sent for and Mr Ellis was requested to come at once.

'Well, it never rains but it pours,' he remarked with a sigh. 'Thank you, boy. I'll put my boots on.'

The prospect of a quiet evening in front of the fire receded instantly as he leaned forward, pulled on his boots and relaced them. In silence he did up his jacket, put on his peaked cap and tied the supposedly waterproof cape at his neck. He had been right about one thing, he thought a little sadly: in Ventnor it never does rain but it really pours, as it was pouring down that evening after such a promising start to the day. In such a reflective, melancholy mood he stepped out into the rainy twilight and made his way through puddles along the High Street.

The doctor's pony and trap were standing outside Belinda House when he reached it. An oilskin cover on the trap glistened in the rain and the pony stood there looking a picture of misery. Beyond the esplanade wall and the bathing machines the white crests of pounding waves were clearly visible. Inside the house the constable found an air of despondency and alarm which almost matched the atmosphere outside. Mrs Rees appeared distraught. In hurried whispered sing-song she explained that her guests were having their evening meal and she didn't want them alarmed or disturbed in any way if it could be helped. If the Misses Bosanquet were to learn that the doctor had been summoned, they'd be bound to leave. As for what'd happened, it was all the fault of the Russians, she confided in a scarcely audible whisper through lips pressed close to the constable's wet left ear.

'Well, Mrs Rees, perhaps you'd be so good as to show me the way . . .'

Mrs Rees had been moving step by step backwards up

the stairs as she delivered her anxious whisperings and now fluttered busily ahead of him up to the first-floor landing. He was directed into a room immediately on the right at the very top of the stairs. It was a small, narrow room with one window at the end overlooking the next house, St Martin's Villa, and save for one oil lamp's illumination it was dark. But the illumination was quite sufficient to show why Mrs Rees had been so alarmed.

Dr Hodgson was seated on a chair beside the bed, bending over. Next to him on a little side table stood a bowl of water. At first Mr Ellis did not fully appreciate what had happened, but in a moment or so he realised that he was witnessing a scene reminiscent of some of the field stations in the Crimea. Count Rostopchine's young valet, the fellow known as Fedya whom he had seen only that morning in the Count's room at the Esplanade Hotel, was lying on the bed surrounded by evidence of blood – on the sheets, on the counterpane and on the pillow. Fresh, bright-red blood also stained the pieces of sheet which the doctor was using to bind the young man's wrists. A gash in the neck had spread a dark stain on to the pillow. Fedya lay there with closed eyes, looking more grey than white, and he appeared to be lifeless. He was naked to the waist, but this nakedness helped to reveal that he was still breathing. His chest rose and fell perceptibly but slowly. The bowl of water was being used to dampen the torn strips of sheet and wipe off some of the thicker oozings of blood, especially those coming from the neck wound. This water was growing a dark pink in colour against the white of the china bowl.

Mr Ellis did not need to ask what had happened. As soon as he entered, the doctor in greeting him had held up an ivory-handled cut-throat razor.

'Self-inflicted wounds,' he announced.

'How long ago?' Mr Ellis asked.

The doctor could only guess that the suicide attempt must have been made some time during the last couple of hours. The loss of blood was obviously considerable. He had only arrived a short while ago and had started trying to staunch the flow at once.

'His chances?'

The doctor shook his head. 'He's healthy, you can see that. But it's impossible to say. I'll get him to the Infirmary shortly. With your help, Mr Ellis.' And he busied himself with the wound at the neck, lifting Fedya's head gently to begin the process of bandaging.

Mr Ellis gazed down thoughtfully at the young man's ashen face. He had seen many young Russian faces similar to this one, and just as ashen, lying on the battlefields of the Crimea. He had seen others in the villages where he had been held captive and through which he had passed after his release. Ordinary Russian peasants like Fedya had come to his aid when he had been ill. Their simple, broad, sun-hardened features had always struck him as friendly. To think of them as the victims of suicide seemed unnatural and beyond all reasonable probability. So whatever had driven this young man to such a desperate act must have been the result of very strong emotion. At which point Mr Ellis put two and two together. He turned to Mrs Rees who had remained by the bedroom door averting her eyes from the sight of blood, but she said as if anticipating a question from him:

'We heard a groaning, Mr Ellis. One of the maids heard it. So I looked in. At once I knew, well . . . '

'You did exactly the right thing, Mrs Rees.'

'I thought of the doctor first, of course. Then I thought, well . . . '

Then he posed his question.

'Did he know the drowned woman?'

She nodded.

'Had they, er, quarrelled? Was that it?'

Mrs Rees now had a handkerchief pressed to her mouth. 'Yes, yes,' she whispered, 'I saw them quarrelling! Oh, they quarrelled all right! The scandal of it, though.' She caught her breath. 'And in my house!'

He told her not to upset herself. It was clear to him that this attempted suicide must be linked to the lady's drowning, though he would most certainly not be able to obtain corroboration of this from the young man in his present state and most likely not at all due to the language difficulty. It was equally clear to him that this attempted suicide would have to be hushed up. If the full force of the law were applied to it, there would be no knowing where the scandal might end. And he was as conscious as Mrs Rees of the dangers of scandal in a place as small as Ventnor.

'No, no,' he agreed softly, 'there'll not be a word about it,' trying to keep the words out of earshot of the doctor who had at that very moment begun tearing up more of the cotton sheets with a sharp rending sound. 'No, no, we'll move him as soon as Dr Hodgson's finished. I imagine his employer will . . .' The thought of the Count dismayed him for a moment until he recollected the four sovereigns still resting in his pocket.

'He's employed,' she whispered, 'by a Count. Shouldn't he be told?'

He assured her he would inform the Count himself as soon as possible.

'Oh, well,' she said, 'I'm so grateful. But if you'll excuse me . . .' And hurriedly she left the room, saying she had to look after her guests.

As the door closed, the doctor let Fedya's head rest

118

back on the blood-stained pillow and he began wiping his hands on some of the clean strips of sheet. Noting that Mr Ellis was now alone, he beckoned him over to the head of the bed, saying in a low voice:

'I didn't want to tell you while the landlady was here, but there's something I think I ought to mention to you, Constable. That locum of mine, the Russian doctor – you can't believe the trouble I've been having with him! He'd no sooner been given permission to examine the deceased – I'm referring to the woman found drowned this morning – than he'd . . . ' He cupped a hand to his mouth and whispered something in the constable's ear.

'Without authorisation, you mean?' asked a concerned Mr Ellis.

'I mean exactly that, Constable. Really, that fellow! Have you spoken to him yet about the drowning?'

'No, sir.'

'What with Captain Fenton complaining to me about his habit of swimming with no clothes on, and the way he keeps his room – it's unimaginable, you know, I couldn't've imagined anyone living like that – and now this, I think I've only one course left open to me. I think I'll have to dispense with his services.' He threw a wadge of cotton sheeting on to the floor with a flourish. 'But not a word about this to anyone. It's all in confidence for the present.'

'Of course, sir.'

8

On the following morning, a Monday, there was a certain amount of anxious whispering by the two Misses Bosanquet. They had been exceedingly alarmed by the comings and goings of the previous evening, which had not been concealed despite all Mrs Rees's efforts to explain the young man's state and the doctor's visit by hushed references to sudden illness. It was all, of course, a Russian matter, that went without saying, but the constable's presence was a lot less easy to explain. That hinted of scandal and criminal behaviour. The Misses Bosanquet, though they relished tittle-tattle, drew the line at scandal and criminal behaviour.

Shortly after breakfast a package wrapped in newspaper was delivered at Belinda House addressed to 'Master Guy, English Boy'. The handwriting was strong and quite legible but so unusual in the formation of the letters that it aroused Mrs Rees's extreme curiosity, a reaction shared by Mrs Emily Whitehouse. Since there was no other English boy named Guy living there, the package was clearly intended for Master Seddenham. He unwrapped it gingerly in Aunt Emily's presence because she expressed the fear that it might contain something nasty, not to say explosive, judging by the handwriting. When it turned out to contain a pair of brand-new black leather boots, accompanied by a note addressed simply to 'English Boy', this seemed something of an anticlimax. The note read:

I forgot. So here are new boots. Your friend Zhenia B.

'Who on earth is that?' asked Aunt Emily.

'The doctor,' Guy explained.

'First it's that hoity-toity young person with her cast-offs and now it's that loud-mouthed Russian with new boots. Really, Guy, you're associating with the strangest people! We are *not* paupers.'

But they were, to all intents and purposes, and Guy was grateful for the new boots. They were slightly too large for him, so that he had to pack them with some of the newspaper to make them fit snugly. Even Aunt Emily could not deny that they smartened his appearance and therefore made him more presentable. They also made him want to thank his benefactor at the earliest opportunity. He quite categorically refused to take charge of the twins that morning. They were left to Joan while he climbed the steep lane to the High Street and Belgrave Road.

It was a mild, calm morning of low cloud and fitful sunshine. Several family groups were walking slowly down the lane towards the esplanade and the beach. A baker's van drawn by two elderly horses creaked and shuddered in a slow, difficult ascent of the steeper part. Rain had washed away much of the surface soil and grit, leaving only the bigger, rougher stones and rocky ridges. Trying to avoid the van's wheels, ladies in the family groups expressed alarm at slipping and cried out for steadying arms. Last year, thought Guy, he might have been offering a steadying arm to his mother as they came down this same steep lane, because last year they had stayed for a time in one of the High Street houses before moving down to the Esplanade Hotel. The house had been on the other side of St Catherine's church and not far from Connaught House. He had no distance to go to play in the large upstairs nursery, where Miles and he had been joined not by Elizabeth, who rather scorned

121

Miles's games, but by Susan Hodgson from next door at Alto House. She had often taken part in their charades and helped move paper navies about the floor when Miles re-enacted Trafalgar or the siege of Sevastopol.

Guy thought of Susan again as he approached Alto House. The new and rather intriguing relationship with Elizabeth Fenton had driven all memories of Susan Hodgson from his mind during the past seven or eight days. He knew she had always been friendlier with Miles than with him. They had shared secrets and made little jokes which tended to emphasise Guy's role as an outsider. It had hardly ever seemed deliberate or malicious, but, just as he had now lost Miles as a friend and gained Elizabeth, so he now felt he had really become an outsider to Susan.

The new brass plate sparkled beside the open front door of Alto House. Just inside the tiled hallway a door on the left had 'Surgery' above it and pinned to it was a handwritten sheet giving the surgery times. Guy noted that on Mondays the morning surgery extended from 8 a.m. to 10 a.m. Unsure whether to introduce himself as a patient or a guest, since there were no doctors' names on the sheet, he hesitated. Suddenly Susan appeared on the stairs directly ahead of him, dressed in buttoned boots and a voluminous brown skirt and evidently ready to go out. Perhaps because he stood with his back to the light of the front door, or simply because at that moment she was preoccupied with a piece of paper she was scrutinising as she came down the stairs, she did not notice him until she had virtually reached the bottom step and was about to cross the hall. It was then that he said:

'Susan, do you remember me?'

And, in the moment of recognition, her pretty, slightly severe features and light-brown eyes formed a spontaneous smile and she exclaimed:

'It's Guy, isn't it? But you've grown so much!'

It was true in the sense that he was now taller than her, whereas last year he had always thought of her as taller than him. But he knew she did not really mean that. She implied by her exclamation and her smile that he interested her suddenly in a quite different way. He felt himself beginning to blush, though, knowing how curious she was, he also realised she had only to look closely at his clothes to see that his present circumstances were very different from last year's.

'Have you come to see me?' she asked in a tone which suggested that he could scarcely have come for any other reason.

'No, I've actually come to see the doctor.'

'Are you ill?'

'No, I . . .'

It dawned on him that to mention his new boots would be so humiliating he would probably have to fall down in a fit or give vent to a loud bout of coughing to excuse himself. He went quite red at the thought. She looked at him even more curiously.

'Father's gone out already on his rounds, I think. There's only our locum here now.'

Guy was about to admit that Dr Bazarov was the reason for his visit when the surgery door opened and the tall figure of the Russian doctor emerged. For a split second Guy feared he would spoil everything by mentioning the new boots. Instead, to his relief, the doctor placed a large protective hand on Guy's shoulder.

'Guido, my friend!'

It was an acknowledgement of friendship which apparently upset Susan Hodgson. On Sunday, as they had made their way back across the rocks, the doctor

123

had said he would call Guy 'Guido'. Guy assumed this might be the reason for Susan's sudden departure and tried to explain.

'Susan, I . . .' he began, only to be interrupted almost at once by Bazarov's sudden loud laugh and equally loud rejoinder:

'She is not my friend! You call me,' he called after her, 'smelly? I am smelly, yes?'

But Susan Hodgson did not look back or even acknowledge the question in any way.

'Sme-lly!' The word was repeated with amused, deliberate emphasis, as if it were being tested on the doctor's tongue. 'Sme-lly! Ha! So, Guido, are you doctor's patient?'

'No, I wanted to thank you for . . .'

'Ah, boots, yes! They are good?'

'Very good, thank you.'

'Good for going upstairs?'

Guy admitted they were, surprised though he was by the question, until he knew it was an invitation.

'No more patients, so upstairs we go. You must tell me, am I smelly or not smelly?' And the idea so amused the doctor that he broke into loud laughter again as they went up the stairs. 'In here, in here,' he instructed, quickly unlocking a door on the far side of the landing and ushering Guy in.

What Guy saw was a large bedroom with a bay window giving a view of the sea. One of the sashes was open, so the curtains stirred. There were half a dozen china bowls laid out against the skirting boards. Each contained several floating or semi-submerged sea-anemones with small stones, seaweed and sand in the bottom to create a miniature marine world. There was a washbasin in a marble-topped stand, a bed, a wardrobe and, set down against one wall, what appeared to be a shoulder yoke for carrying milk churns which had been adapted to carry two fair-sized medicine bottles. But, most intriguing of all, in the bay of the window stood a table with a large microscope and several books and instruments.

Guy had never before seen such a bedroom. It was true that it had an odd smell, though it was not immediately unpleasant to his nostrils. He thought it combined the sharp, salty smell of marine things with the odour of a smoking room. He was already familiar with the yoke and the medicine bottles, as he was with the long canvas cloak hanging on the back of the door. It was the table's contents which most excited his interest. Apart from the brightly gleaming microscope with its finely knurled knobs and rings for adjustments and the small glass plates laid ready for use, there was also a board with pins and cotton and several differently shaped scalpels neatly housed in an open box. There were also notebooks, writing materials and several impressive-looking scientific volumes, one of which was open at a coloured picture of sea anemones.

'Open your mouse, please.'

Guy had already noticed how difficult the doctor found it to pronounce the plain English 'th'. He giggled slightly as he was gently urged to sit down in an upright wooden chair.

'So why you laugh?'

Guy didn't try to explain. In any case, a glass spatula was being pressed down on his tongue.

'Wide, please.'

The doctor's breath was quite pure, Guy was relieved to find.

'Wider. Some inflammation. You sneeze, yes?'

'No, no, my cold's over. Honestly.'

'Honestly!' This apparently amused the doctor. 'I

must be sure, you see.'

'Why?'

'So you can smell!'

'Oh, I can smell!'

'So?'

Guy admitted he could smell something fishy and a smell of tobacco.

'So I am not smelly?'

'No, no, not really smelly.'

It was not the kind of atmosphere Guy liked, but it was not completely unpleasant.

'Miss Susan is wrong, you see. I am not smelly.'

'She . . .' Half in justification of her objections, Guy said: 'But all these bowls, why d'you have them in your bedroom?'

'My collection, my secrets.'

'What secrets?'

'Secrets of sea. I will show you.'

The doctor produced a board similar to the one on the table, but this one had been covered by a damp cloth. When the cloth was removed it revealed a sea anemone that had been neatly cut in half. The two halves were carefully pinned back or held with cotton. They exuded a slightly salty, fishy smell.

'You know it?'

Guy shook his head. He had no idea how he was intended to react. The doctor slowly, as if he were miming, picked up the volume that was open on the table and showed him the title-page. The heading read *Actinologia Britannica*. Guy knew enough Latin, learned chiefly from Mr Prendergast, to understand vaguely what it meant. He looked up into the greenish eyes and said brightly:

'*Acta*, that means seashore.'

'Yes, living creatures of seashore . . .'

'But they're flowers!' Guy protested.

'No, animals.' The doctor picked up a scalpel and pointed to the anemone already pinned to the board. 'I will show you. See it. It is named *peach-i-a hasta-ta*. And look here.'

Guy contemplated the shape of the anemone and more of Mr Prendergast's Latin came to his aid.

'*Hasta* is an arrow.'

'Yes, arrer.' Guy's attention was already being drawn to a page which the doctor was holding open for him. 'See. It is "arrer muzzlet"!'

'Arrer muzzlet' – the mysterious words reminded Guy of the sight of the two naked boys on his first visit to the area of rocks.

'Two local boys find it.'

'I think I saw them,' Guy said.

'They find three, four. I give penny for each one. So here you see is scientific description. Read it.'

Guy looked at the open page and read aloud quite slowly.

'"*THE ARROW MUZZLET*",' he read. '*Peachia hastata. Specific character:* column lengthened; conchula bearing from 12 to 20 lobes . . ." I don't understand any of it! What's it all mean?'

'It is scientific discovery.'

'What is?'

'No one discovers Arrow Muzzlet here in Ventnor before.'

'Is it important?'

'For me, yes.'

'Why?'

'I am scientist.'

'So what d'you do now? Now you've found it, I mean?'

'I must describe it.'

Guy could not be sure why. The object on the board looked rather pitiful and helpless in its dissected state.

'Who will want to know?'

The doctor tapped the front of the volume. 'Mr Gosse. He is scientist like me.'

'But it's only a sea anemone!'

'It has mouse like yours, Guido. I will show you.'

The doctor expertly placed the specimen below the microscope and Guy was instructed to look into it with one eye closed. Instantly, as if in a magic crystal, he saw to his intense surprise that what stared back at him looked very like a mouth, the mouth of the Arrow Muzzlet. It was white with deep-brown furrows. The shell-like shape had a pale salmon colour, the lobes pellucid, with an opaque white core. He gazed at it enthralled. The thrill of discovering such a 'secret', as the doctor called it, literally rose out of the miniature tunnel of the lens towards him. He let his eye feast on the rich marine colouring of the magnified mouth of this creature that was half flower, half animal.

Then, in the very process of studying it, he was reminded of looking down into the depths of the pool where he had seen the dead eyes of Marie Valence gazing back at him. He jerked himself away from the eyepiece of the microscope.

'So?'

'It's dead!'

'So?'

'I thought of Marie.'

'Ah!'

The doctor went to the window. He drew a case out of his breast pocket, extracted a small cigar and lit it. He blew the first stream of blue smoke directly at the windowpane where it formed a small temporary cloud before the breeze through the sash dispersed it.

'Why did she drown herself?' Guy asked.

'I told you, it is Russian business.'

'I'm sure she didn't have to.'

'You do not understand, Guido. You are English. We are all exiles. We have no home. I look now at your English sea, at your sky, and what I am really seeing is my own endless land. I feel sad.' He let more smoke gather in small tendrils round his face and he spoke through them, his eyes half closed as if in a trance. 'I am sad for Masha, but I am sad too for myself. I have no choice. I must stay here. Perhaps my eyes ... No, I have what we Russians call *toska, toska po rodine*! I close my eyes and I see my own land, my homeland, and I know I can never go back! Do you know what it means – never go back?'

Guy shook his head, but it was clear the doctor did not require an answer.

'It means I must be like your Robinson Crusoe. I must be alone. I must do my work here alone.'

'Robinson Crusoe wasn't alone,' Guy pointed out. 'He had Man Friday to help him.'

The doctor paused at this. Suddenly his sombre mood changed to something like his former exuberance. He swung round, the lighted cigar creating a miniature comet's tail of blue smoke through the air.

'Guido, that's why I do it!'

'Do what?'

'I buy you new boots, yes? So you will help me, yes? I want you to look into microscope' (he pronounced it with a short 'i', *mikroskop*) 'and write down what you are seeing. I will explain words. But you must write for me because my knowledge of English ... Well, I must describe scientific proof, you see. You will be Man Friday, yes?'

'Yes.'

'Good, good, good!' said the doctor and produced a large sheet of paper which he laid out excitedly on the table.

9

On the Monday afternoon the Captain ordered a carriage. It took him on a tour of Ventnor and returned by way of St Lawrence. As it followed the route along the clifftop, the carriage rocked with a soothing motion. An onshore breeze helped to make the tall covered vehicle sway a little more than usual and with the leather apron drawn only halfway up the window all the freshness of the salt air blew into the interior of the carriage without allowing strangers to see clearly who was inside. Captain Fenton enjoyed hiring this carriage for such outings. It was the only way he could take Molly out. His gout having worsened in the past week, especially with a recent sprain to his knee, he had also found it was the only way of travelling to see the sites for the new houses he was building in Ventnor. But his thoughts continually returned to the problem of his daughter Elizabeth.

'Why does she refuse to let Dr Hodgson see her? Why?'

He directed these questions to the interior of the carriage, but it was Molly, seated beside him, who answered:

'I think she knows, you know.'

'Knows what, my dear?'

'Knows about what happened.'

'Molly, dearest, I know you have persistently refused to tell me and I know I cannot force you. If she fell down and was hurt, surely you should have sent for the doctor. As for my condition at the time, well . . . Oh, I don't blame you, you know that.'

He patted her hand. Molly had become so withdrawn and frightened, that was the trouble, he thought. And she persistently refused to tell him why. He had been drunk, that was the fact of the matter, and he remembered very little about it. What he did remember was Hetherington, Hetherington in his angry mood that very morning. He tried to shake off the recollection by being jaunty.

'The building's going well, don't you think, my dear?'

'Yes.'

'Before the autumn we'll have another set of six houses. If my guess is right, we'll be able to let them before the winter. And perhaps then you and I . . .'

He squeezed her hand. Hetherington's warning rankled with him. If he were to have a chance of becoming mayor, he would have to remarry or ensure that nothing scandalous could attach to his reputation. In an unforgivably selfish way he had been relieved, even though saddened as well, by the news of Marie Valence's death. He was quite certain he had to refuse her, of course, absolutely no question about it . . . But it did not change the fact that, if he were to be mayor, he needed someone, preferably of course a wife, to act as his hostess, his lady mayoress, his moral support. He sighed at the thought.

'My life's not over yet, you know,' he said, patting Molly's hand again, but he had said the thought aloud as if he had been speaking to his beloved Amabel.

'No, it is not,' Molly agreed and she pressed his arm. Her look when he turned to her was one of utter devotion. 'You have much to live for, sir, you really have.'

131

Behind the passion of her words it was the 'sir' that hurt him, like the insertion of a needle. He knew in the depths of his heart that without his dear Amabel to act as hostess he would never be able to entertain at home. It was out of the question for Molly to act in that way, and how much could he depend on Elizabeth?

'We are funny people, we English,' he mused, 'so divided from one another by our class differences and so fond of one another as individuals. I've often thought . . . '

'It cannot be helped,' Molly said. She had been watching his face closely. 'Are you cold, sir?'

'No, I'm not at all cold. It's August, after all. See the paddle steamer . . . just rounding the point!'

Newly introduced on the sea-route to Ryde, the paddle steamer appeared gracefully swan-like in the slight swell, its thin, elegant funnel exuding a stream of smoke and its paddles making a creamy churning along the side of the hull. The Captain looked at his watch.

'Oh, it's half-past three. We must be getting back.'

But Molly seemed not to have heard him. She had turned away as he spoke and was staring not at the paddle steamer but at the rocks directly below the cliff. The wheels made a grinding noise in the shingle spread on the clifftop road and the carriage creaked as they moved from rut to rut. Above such noise could be heard the waves. The Captain watched Molly out of the corner of his eye, speculating. It was not that she was beautiful. He could well imagine that the majority of men in his social position would never give her a second look. She had a countrywoman's strength and freshness in her features, strong well-formed shoulders and a fine bosom. What was it that made him so susceptible to a woman's looks, her shapeliness, her physical appeal? Even more than a woman's sensuality, which could be judged from the look in her eyes or the way her fingers touched you, what he adored was her warm firm shape, the soft curves of her body, all the gentle, and yet assured, physical perfection of her womanhood. It hardly mattered if she were old or young, a woman's beauty was for him epitomised by her shapeliness, which had always seemed much better suited to the pleasures and rigours of life than a man's. That was why he loved women. During his years at sea he had always sought their company whenever he had been ashore, knowing of course it was not love, not the devoted love he had felt for Amabel, but it was as near to love as he could hope to find among the easy-going girls and fancy women of the dockside worlds of Africa and America. Molly had come to mean the solace of all the common women he had known in those ports. He had found that all his capacity for casual affairs had accumulated into this one, devoted love for her.

'What are you doing, my dear?'

To his astonishment, Molly had suddenly made the carriage stop and swiftly alighted. He was at first completely unable to react. The sharp twinges of gout tore at his leg like swordthrusts.

'My dear, what on earth?' he called after her, not even completing the question as the carriage door banged back against the coachwork and a breeze swirled round the interior of the carriage. She had gone quite determinedly towards the edge of the cliff. Her long black skirt flew flag-like about her legs and thighs and she held the shawl firmly round her shoulders, not looking back at him. In fact, she seemed to be looking down towards the rocks at the foot of the cliff.

'My dear,' he repeated, 'what are you doing?'

He was helpless at such a moment. Her strength was so much greater than his when the gout was bad. If his dependence on her was not total, it was real enough to oblige him to acknowledge that without her he felt bereft. Painfully he stepped down from the carriage, leaning heavily on his stick.

'I must have a word with her, William,' he explained to the coachman. 'My dear, what has possessed you?' he was saying to her, annoyed as well as anxious. 'Why are you staring down there like that?'

Molly suddenly turned to him and sought his arm for support. It was a gesture that conveyed all she needed to express at that moment. He interpreted it as love for him, gratitude, understanding, devotion, concern and even desire.

'Are you all right, my dear?'

She nodded. They went back to the carriage and again took their seats. As they started on their swaying way she said in an abstracted voice:

'Poor Jonquil.'

They were 'turns', these strange moods of hers, and he was used to them. More than once he had wondered about her sanity when she behaved so oddly. By chance he had once overheard someone saying she had been known as 'Batty Molly' in the past, though he had never cared to pry too closely into that past, nor to ask her whether Hetherington might be right: Were she and the constable connected in some way? And was there some other secret she had been keeping from him all these months?

The fear that the answers to such questions might not please him made him unwilling to ask them. She was irreplaceable, that he knew for sure. No matter what happened so far as his building projects or his hopes for the mayoralty were concerned, she, like his daughter Elizabeth, represented the central focus of his life.

'Of course,' he said, suddenly remembering, 'the

doctor said he'd come round at four o'clock! I'll ask him to see Elizabeth, what d'you think?'

Turgenev's friend Pavel Annenkov had arrived in Ventnor late the previous day. The rain had dampened the spirits of both men. There had also been a problem with the accommodation in Rock Cottage. Although it was comfortable enough for both of them to share, the landlady left a note in their room on the Monday morning requesting that Mr Tourgueneff's friend should refrain from smoking cigarettes. 'She's a Nonconformist,' Turgenev explained. 'But we must not pander to these Nonconformist whims.' And at midday, in the milder, drier weather, he went out in search of new accommodation.

His first stop was the Esplanade Hotel. The manager dropped a broad hint that he might shortly be in a position to offer two rooms. Unfortunately he could not guarantee that they would be available that day. He urged Turgenev to enquire at Belinda House, with which the hotel had an arrangement. Turgenev's enquiry met with an initially hesitant response from the landlady. When pressed, she agreed that two rooms were available. Both were on the first floor, one, overlooking the esplanade and the sea, was reasonably large (it had been occupied by the Misses Bosanquet), and the other, overlooking the adjacent house, was much smaller. He booked both of them.

Mrs Rees had vowed to herself that she would have no more Russian guests if she could help it, but in view of the poor summer and the fact that the only visitors who did not quibble over her prices were the Russians she relented. There was also no denying that the tall, impressive man with the magnificent near-white hair and deep-blue eyes was a most distinguished addition to

135

her clientele. His friend who came a little later and asked most respectfully if he might smoke cigarettes was clearly recognisable as a man of European culture and tastes. She was flattered to have such evidently important gentlemen as her guests and said as much to Mrs Emily Whitehouse.

'I do most sincerely hope you are right, Mrs Rees,' was Aunt Emily's slightly sceptical response as she seated herself at the table for dinner that evening. 'Only time will tell.'

The disappearance of the common young man and the hurried departure of the Misses Bosanquet had been upsetting, although it had left Aunt Emily herself in the privileged position of chief guest and Mrs Rees's sole confidante. The arrival of new Russians was naturally cause for some concern. More concern still was caused by her nephew's deplorable behaviour in associating with that quite disreputable man, the young Russian doctor with the appalling habits. There had been a most chilly atmosphere in the relations between her and Guy the whole day. It had started with the appearance of the new boots in the morning and been increased by his failure to return for lunch at one o'clock.

'It is all very well,' she said, flicking her napkin open and laying it in her lap, 'to send word you're occupied, but it is the height of rudeness, my boy, to make no appearance at lunch at all. So perhaps you would be good enough to explain exactly what you were doing.'

Guy, seated opposite her, felt defiant. 'I was helping the doctor with his scientific work.'

'What scientific work is that, pray?'

Guy began explaining about the doctor's interest in sea anemones and his discovery of a particular specimen in the pools below West Hill. He went on to explain that in return for the doctor's kindness in buying him a new pair of boots he had helped the doctor by looking in the microscope and trying to write down exactly what he saw. He had written everything out the way the doctor had instructed and the information had been sent off in a letter.

'I see.'

Aunt Emily felt a little out of her depth. She told Edwina not to fidget.

'What's a micro- ... micro- ...?' asked Edwina. Guy explained.

'This, er, specimen,' Aunt Emily asked, 'what's it called?'

'The Arrow Muzzlet.'

The name was hard to believe. 'The Arrow what?'

'Muzzlet.'

'It sounds like a kind of gun. But if it's Russian, that's not entirely surprising.'

Guy pointed out that it was not Russian and it was not a gun.

'If it's only just an *anemone*,' said Edwina scathingly, 'we've found *hundreds* of them! They're everywhere, just everywhere!'

Jane agreed.

'There will be no more discussion of this,' ordered Aunt Emily. 'And please, Edwina and Jane, both of you, do stop looking round!'

The two Russian gentlemen had been speaking quietly together at the table which that morning had been occupied by the Misses Bosanquet. Their conversation was earnest, not loud as it had been when the doctor and Fedya had been there, and, somewhat to Mrs Rees's discomfort, it had been accompanied by the uncorking of a wine bottle which had not been purchased on the premises. She did not cater for such tastes herself, but she did not want to offend her new guests by imposing restrictions. The two men sipped the wine during the meal.

Wiping her mouth, Aunt Emily announced unduly loudly:

'No father should abandon his children in the way yours has done. And I say this despite the fact that he is my brother.'

She deposited such wisdom into a special niche of silence that had taken shape in the granite hush of the dining room. It was as if her sharp voice had been deliberately intended to put an end to the men's subdued foreign talk. The rest of the meal passed uneasily in silences and whisperings until she announced to the fidgety twins:

'Yes, you may both get down, dears, if you are finished. Now go and tell Joan that you may play quietly in your bedroom. *Quietly*, mind you. I will be up in due course.'

Guy could tell that his aunt was not so much offended by the presence of the new arrivals as intrigued by them. He had also discerned in her attitude towards his relationship with Zhenia a certain covert envy as well as coolness. Her mention during the meal of the need to go back to Lambeth had been rather half-hearted as a threat to their holiday, whose future, Guy knew, depended as much on the receipt of news from their father as on Aunt Emily finding good reason for staying until the weekend as she had arranged in the first place. In the absence of the Misses Bosanquet, who were never a strong inducement, Guy placed his hopes now on the recent arrivals.

'You will join me at cards this evening, Guy,' Aunt Emily instructed. She remained disapproving and aloof even though he suspected she had already forgiven him for failing to appear for lunch. He knew that if he were

138

really to assert his independence – all the greater, it seemed, since he'd made friends with Zhenia – she would not be able to stop him, but he did not want to offend her if he could help it. At that moment she exclaimed, her expression quite changed:

'Oh, how charming!'

On his way out of the dining room Turgenev had bowed to her politely as he passed her table. She suddenly looked quite rosy and fiddled busily with her napkin.

'You can tell he is a gentleman,' she declared in a whisper. 'I must ask Mrs Rees to introduce us. In half an hour, then, Guy. In the back parlour.'

She rose in her stately way and swished quietly out into the hall. He followed after a minute or so, unwilling to climb the stairs at once to the small top-floor room where he had been obliged to spend so much time during his illness. The day occupied in peering into a microscope and then writing out the unusual names had left him stimulated and restless. His aunt and the twins now seemed dull. The friendship with Zhenia had blossomed so suddenly and his help as a Man Friday had meant they had worked so closely together that he felt he had literally been initiated into a new world. It was a *Russian* world, a world of science, of novel interests and a certain crazy unfamiliar earnestness that appealed to him because it was boyish and fresh but also often plain silly. Yet it seemed an easy enough world to enter. He thought it would be just as easy to make friends with one of the new arrivals as it had been to make friends with Zhenia. After all, the Russians were known to be a friendly people.

He climbed the stairs and found himself beside the door to what had been Fedya's room. With the intention of saying something about his aunt wanting to be introduced, he tapped on the door. Immediately he was alarmed. The very act of tapping made the door open inwards. It revealed that the room was unoccupied but filled with the new arrival's things, a smart leather travelling trunk in one corner, shoes beside the bed and a large wide-brimmed sunhat cast down on the coverlet. None of these things attracted his attention as much as the vista revealed beyond.

What instantly drew his eyes to it in fixed amazement was the view through the window at the end of the room. There, perhaps scarcely ten feet away across the space between Belinda House and St Martin's Villa, was the open sash window to Marie's room and the room's interior was clearly lit by the slanting rays of the sunset. He understood instantly what he had never understood before. The bareness of the room opposite reminded him of his first sight of Marie standing naked in the window. He remembered the little crucifix hanging between her breasts, the one she had made him kiss, and he knew now that she had been showing herself to Fedya. She had loved him, he thought, and then they had quarrelled. The recollection of her upturned eyes made him close the door hurriedly.

At that moment he heard foreign voices raised in heated discussion. Then a voice began reading. He turned and ran up the next flight of stairs out of earshot.

In the room where the Misses Bosanquet had spent so much time watching the comings and goings on the esplanade, Annenkov wearing pince-nez was seated at the table reading aloud the words which Turgenev had just written on a sheet of ruled music paper.

'We firmly rely on a reasonable welcome from all sections of our people,' he read. 'Good, good ... And also on the sympathy and protection of our government. Good ... We represent ourselves to our government as people ready to assist in the cause of promoting popular education; we wish to bring order and organisation to the disorganised social forces which are often unknown to our government ... Strong, eh? All right, all right ... We submit both them and ourselves to our government's constant control. By extending literacy to those very people whom our government is emancipating, we are promoting its own cause ... Good, good ... We are also emancipating them from another servitude – from the servitude of ignorance. Well put, well put!'

Turgenev watched his friend reading and when the latter unclipped his pince-nez after reading the passage he lightly thumped the table.

'We *must* have the support of the government!' he insisted. 'It's essential!'

Annenkov waved the pince-nez in the air and shook his head. 'They'll laugh it to scorn! You know they will! "A half-hearted liberal attempt to influence the government ..." Think what Herzen will say about it! Think what your so-called nihilists will say about it! As for the Rostopchines of this world, God help us!'

'Oh, I know we'll be attacked!' Turgenev agreed. 'They'll attack us from the left and from the right and from the centre! They'll be sure to attack us from the sides! But we *must* do something. When the mass of our people are liberated from serfdom, they'll be sure to listen to fanatics so long as we don't do something to liberate them from ignorance! That's why we must act and act now!'

'Very well, very well, let's consult Rostovtzoff and Kruze.' Annenkov was prepared to concede that much, but in a much harsher tone he added: 'As for that Rostopchine, I swear to you I'll never mention his name again!'

'I forgot to tell you,' said Turgenev, beginning to smile. 'He's gone. The rooms are vacant in the hotel. Do you want to move?'

'No, no. Let's stay here.'

Ostentatiously, with a laugh, Annenkov lit a cigarette.

10

On Tuesday morning Aunt Emily insisted that Guy take charge of the twins and there was no refusing her. She had again muttered threats about leaving before the week was out and therefore her plan to go round the Ventnor shops that morning accompanied by Joan had to be acceded to. Against his will and better judgement Guy was persuaded by the twins to show them where he had found the drowned lady.

A strong wind blew over the entire area of rocks and pools. The tide was coming in, raising feathery spouts of water like steam from locomotive funnels at each bursting of a wave among the tall rocks. The foam-laced sea looked majestic and menacing, but its noise was far more impressive. In the area just below the cliffs it made a roaring that reminded Guy of a description of the guns at Sevastopol. In his mind's eye he imagined the sea as the allied armies triumphantly assaulting the Russian redoubts. In fact, it bore little resemblance to his imaginings. As the sea flowed among the pools and swelled the weed-curtains on their surfaces they seemed both enlarged and distressed, as if their still and secret inner lives were being beset by revolutions and earthquakes. He looked from one to another and all the pools seemed to merge into so much unsettled, swelling water.

No, it was impossible – he couldn't tell which of the pools had contained Marie's body. The waves burst in among the rocks so violently and suddenly that he and the twins literally had to jump back to avoid being drenched by flying spray. The twins, barefoot like him from having waded through the freshwater stream, waved their unlaced shoes about as they asked which pool it was, but their shouts and cries sounded to his ears like desecrations in a place he considered sacred to the memory of Marie Valence and he ignored them.

'Oh, you're not *trying*!' Edwina reproached him.

'Oh, the waves are such a nuisance!' was Jane's exclamation.

He told them to keep away from the waves. They needed no telling, knowing as well as he did the penalty for having wet clothes.

'Guy, look! Look!' cried Edwina. 'It's the hoity-toity one!'

Her piercing voice broke through the wave-roar, annoying him and confusing him. Turning, he saw Elizabeth Fenton on the far side of the freshwater stream. She was waving to them. He scrambled back across the rocks in her direction, followed by the twins, and when they were in earshot they heard her sing out:

'Hello, Edwina! Hello, Jane! How are you?'

All three waded through the broad area of freshwater calling back greetings. Guy was uncertain why he felt such excitement at seeing Elizabeth again. The twins in any case had grown bored with the rocks and were glad to be back on the sand.

'We were beginning to get wet,' he explained a little breathlessly.

'Did you get the jacket?' she asked without fussing about preliminaries. 'I brought it round.'

'Oh, yes,' he said, but conscious of his tight velvet jacket, now quite dampened by spray, he started explaining that his aunt disapproved of charity.

'Yes, yes, I understand,' she said. 'It was silly of me

really. Oh, aren't the waves big!'

Her auburn hair was tucked beneath a scarf wrapped over her head as protection against the wind. A few loose strands and curls were blown across her forehead and cheeks. They drew Guy's attention to the pallor of her face. Her blue eyes looked at him intently.

'What are you doing here this morning?' she asked.

'I'd promised to show the twins where I found . . .'

'Where you found what?'

'Where he found the drowned lady!' piped Edwina. Caustically she added: 'And he didn't know which pool it was!'

'I don't think it really matters,' Elizabeth remarked calmly. She drew the scarf more tightly round her cheeks. 'I think she deserved to be killed!'

'Killed!'

Guy's shocked cry seemed to surprise her. She tried uncertainly to maintain both the sweetness of her smile and her composure.

'Yes, she was killed.'

'How d'you know that?'

'Dr Hodgson told Father yesterday.'

The reply struck Guy as so incredible he was lost for anything to say. At that moment the roaring of the waves was so loud that words were unnecessary, but Elizabeth thought he had said something because when he next heard her she was saying:

'The Russian doctor did an . . . I can't remember what the word was. A topsy or something.'

'A topsy?' asked a puzzled Jane. 'What's a topsy?'

'I don't know exactly. Doctors do it.' She was giving herself an air of adult superiority under this questioning and trying to look sure of herself. Guy's mistrustful and aggressive scrutiny of her face had begun to upset her.

145

'They cut open people and find out what went wrong.'

This drew cries of amazement and shock from the twins.

'So what happened?' asked Guy.

'She hadn't drowned.'

The twins made a long 'O-o-o-o!' sound and Elizabeth turned away. By now the incoming waves were beginning to douse them with spray again. Guy was filled with disbelief. He simply did not believe Marie had not drowned and said so. Elizabeth spoke directly into his ear just above the noise of the waves so the twins should not hear:

'She was going to have a baby.'

'I don't believe you!' he shouted.

She darted a brilliant sideways glance at him, which showed the whites of her eyes, and told him he must believe her. At that moment he felt one of the twins pluck at his sleeve.

'Guy, look!'

All of them looked up. Against a sky full of racing clouds they saw the figure of Mr Ellis above them, on the clifftop. He could be recognised by his uniform, although he was too far off to be recognised by his face. He looked doll-like and stiff, as though fixed to the rim of green turf above the outcroppings of rock and stone on the cliff-face, and the fact that he was so still while the long grass and bushes nearby flowed so vigorously in the strong wind made his appearance seem particularly sinister. He appeared to be looking down on them in a kind of judgement.

'It's just the policeman,' Guy said. His lips were dry as he spoke, aware that if the policeman were suspicious about the cause of Marie's death he would be part of that suspicion, as would Zhenia. He shivered at the thought. Then the whole impression was dispersed. The doll-like figure waved at them. In relief, even with some joy, they all waved busily back.

'Yes, it's nice Mr Ellis,' said Elizabeth, waving. 'We're very lucky to have him as constable, Father says. Now I must hurry back. Will you be coming to see us, Guy, now you're better?'

He gestured encompassingly at the twins while grinning with pleasure at her question. 'Yes, I'd like to, only . . .'

'I think you're very good, how you look after them.' She smiled quickly and nervously. The twins had already become interested in the way the incoming waves mingled with the freshwater stream. 'I'd imagined you'd be here this morning, you know. Please, Guy, come and see me. Now that Miles is away and Susan Hodgson is so busy I feel quite alone. I know I have my father to look after, but he's not been well. And he's very moody. He has an attack of gout. All these recent happenings have been very upsetting. He even wanted me to be present this afternoon at that woman's funeral. I said no, absolutely no.'

'This afternoon. What time?'

Guy's interest startled her. She frowned at his rather commanding way of asking and he tried to conceal his interest by beginning to apologise, when she announced:

'Three o'clock. In the new churchyard. I don't expect there'll be anyone there.'

And she turned from him as briskly as she could in view of the runnels of water underfoot and began jumping with light short steps from one spit of hard sand to the next, away from him.

The new churchyard was nothing but a small sloping field adjoining the old churchyard. It was here, in the

147

second of two newly dug graves, that Marie Valence was to be buried. An elderly verger informed Guy and Dr Bazarov, who were the only two mourners, that the rector had given permission for the burial, though there was to be no service or ceremony of committal. The coffin was brought on the back of a farm cart. It was lowered into the grave by two of the undertaker's men helped by two grave-diggers and then the latter began shovelling the sticky reddish soil back into the open grave-mouth. Sunlight like bits of bright copperware flashed over the unmown field-grass as it was swayed and smoothed by the wind. The sounds of the shovelling were just as scattered and dispersed. Each person, so Guy felt, was separated by the wind, just as the sounds were separated from each other and the falling shovelfuls of earth finally separated him from Marie.

It took barely thirty minutes. Zhenia carried a small wreath which he placed on the pile of bare earth. There was no other decoration on the grave. The men put their ropes and shovels in the back of the cart and rode solemnly away, one of them having lit a pipe. At the entrance to the new churchyard, by a makeshift wooden gate, stood Mr Ellis. He had observed the burial from a distance and now came forward to speak to the doctor.

'The Captain sends his regrets, sir. He had wanted to be present. He was the lady's employer last year. But he has a bad attack of gout, you see, sir, and so he couldn't come.'

The doctor said he understood.

'I had to make sure, you see, sir,' said Mr Ellis, 'that the sum of money put aside for the burial was used for that purpose in a seemly and respectable way. The Captain was very insistent. A pity there were not more of your countrymen, sir, don't you think?'

148

'It was Russian business,' said Zhenia pithily.

'Yes, sir.'

'She was poor woman needing money. Russian aristocracy is not interested.'

'I see, sir.' The constable nodded and scratched his beard. 'About the matter of the poor young fellow who was taken to the Infirmary on Sunday. Will you want to do an autopsy now that he, er . . .?'

'No.'

The constable touched the peak of his cap in a kind of salute. 'Yes, sir. In that case we must assume there is only one answer to the whole business. A very sad business, of course. I am sorry, sir, by the way, about Dr Hodgson's decision. He is entirely within his rights, as I'm sure you understand, but I'm sorry. I thought you should know.'

Mr Ellis gave a nod in Guy's direction, more in acknowledgement of his presence than in token of any respect, and walked sedately away beneath the yew trees of the old churchyard. Zhenia heaved his shoulders, sighing, but made no effort to follow the constable's example. Instead he deliberately sat down on a large tombstone which was partly covered in ivy. He looked so depressed that at first Guy hesitated to say anything.

'Forgive me, I am tired,' the doctor said. 'I had many patients.'

In the silence that followed Guy asked:

'Is it true she was killed?'

'Who told you?'

He explained about Elizabeth.

'Perhaps she was killed.'

'Was it Fedya?'

'No.'

The wind played with the doctor's long hair. He

149

raised his face and looked straight at Guy. His eyes were narowed, as if the empty windy brightness of the afternoon and the flashes of sunlight were dazzling.

'Then what happened to him?'

There was a pause of several seconds.

'He wanted to end his life.'

'What did he do?'

'Cut himself.' He indicated where by drawing a finger graphically across his wrists and neck. 'He lost much blood.' The words danced about in the wind. 'Too much. He died . . . early today. He told me . . . he told me . . . he was not killing Masha. He loved Masha . . . loved her very much. Do you know what it means?'

'What?'

'To love very much?'

'It means . . .' Guy paused over his answer, thinking he would say how much he had felt for Marie, but the other interrupted him.

'It means she is pregnant. Masha was pregnant. *E basta!*'

'How d'you know?'

'I am doctor! She asked me to . . . to perform abortion. I said no. So she needed money.' Bazarov shrugged his shoulders. 'A simple, simple story. She needed money in order to . . . in order to pay for abortion.'

'What is that?'

'To remove foetus, remove baby! Cut it out, kill it!'

Guy was shocked by the quick, dismissive way the words were spoken quite as much as by the words themselves. Then the doctor shouted in a ringing voice:

'So why must I take her baby from her? Why?'

Guy felt he was being scolded. He stirred shingle pebbles about with his right boot.

'So she drowned herself?'

Instead of agreeing with him, the doctor laughed.

'Perhaps.'

'You mean she didn't?'

Rocking slowly backwards and forwards where he was sitting, Bazarov folded his arms and looked down at the shingle path.

'Masha goes to pool, yes? She puts stones in pockets, yes?'

Guy nodded. 'Yes.'

'She jumps in water, yes? And she hits her head. Masha had bad cut on head, you see. So?'

'So she drowns,' said Guy.

There was a slow shaking of the head. 'No.'

'Why not?'

'I know secret, you see.'

'What?'

'A big secret, Guido, my English friend.'

'What secret?'

'I perform autopsy. It is against law. But I find in Masha's lungs . . . I find in Masha's lungs *no trace of sea-water*! So Masha does not drown. It is proof!'

Guy saw at once that this must be proof. He stared at the sitting figure of his friend who was in turn looking back at him from beneath his brows with his usual rather severe, fixed expression.

'Have you told the policeman?'

Bazarov slowly shook his head.

'Why not?'

'Dr Hodgson said no.'

'But if you have proof,' Guy protested. 'If you're sure she was killed, the policeman must be told!'

'*I* have proof! I, Zhenia Bazarov, have proof!' He pointed at himself. 'Dr Hodgson denies proof. He says no. He also says I must leave his house.'

'Why?'

'Too smelly. Too scientific. Not interested in money. Not interested in law. Not swimming in correct costume . . .' The recital was made in a laconic imitation of the way Dr Hodgson might have listed his faults, accompanied by a sad smile. 'You see, Guido, I have no home. I am exile and I am not being a person.'

Again it was that strange expression. Guy found it silly.

'We are all people. Even . . .' He was going to say that even those buried around them had been people, but it seemed silly to say such a thing.

'People are like trees in forests,' said Bazarov dismissively. 'No scientist will concern himself with each tree separately. Human beings are all alike.'

He stood up.

'So where are you living?' Guy asked.

'Moral diseases . . .' Bazarov strode along the path '. . . moral diseases are product of poor education, of rubbish in people's heads! Change society and people are different! One human example is sufficient to judge all human examples!'

The words were almost being shouted. They had stopped beneath a yew tree. The churchyard was empty and the sunlight had vanished. Deep emerald shadows had formed in the long grass among the headstones and the whole scene seemed momentarily dark and chill.

'So tell me who killed her?' Guy felt Zhenia was deliberately evading the real issue.

'Masha? Who killed Masha?' Bazarov spoke indifferently. 'She was victim of society. She was not needed.'

'Oh, she was! I know she was!'

A curious glance from the greenish eyes. 'What you know about it, Guido? You love her, eh?'

'I know she . . .'

It was on the tip of his tongue to tell of his feelings for

Marie. Instead he looked away in embarrassment.

'So what you know about love, Guido, eh?' The question was full of mockery. 'Love – it is romantic nonsense! So much of life is wasted because of love!'

'No, she showed me what love could mean! She . . .'

Scornful humour greeted this.

'She did not need love! She needed money! Count Rostopchine . . .' the name was spoken with extreme bitterness '. . . he gave no money, Fedya had no money! Russian business, Guido! And she did not want child!' Zhenia looked sternly into Guy's face. 'You must not be romantic!'

Abruptly he swung round and strode off along the path between the graves. He left the distinct impression that he felt this young English Guido was no more than a foolish boy. In a matter of moments the tall figure had disappeared among the tree shadows and was then lost to sight beyond the buttress of the church tower. Guy felt resentful and hurt and embittered. It was incredible to him that someone who took such care over a sea anemone should be so hard-hearted about Marie and not even trouble to find out whether or not she had been killed. But then, he thought, none of the other Russians in Ventnor seemed to be interested. No one seemed to be interested so far as he could see. The policeman was not, nor was Captain Fenton. As for Elizabeth, she could not even bring herself to mention Marie's name.

Suddenly it occurred to him that he was the only one who cared. At that moment he made a vow. He vowed to himself and the windy afternoon that he would find out how she had died. No matter how much it cost him. No matter how difficult it was. A gust of wind equally suddenly set a yew tree creaking sharply like a thunder-crack above his head. In the same instant, almost like lightning, sunlight lit up the graveyard.

Part III

11

It was a 'Russian business', there could be little doubt about that. Mr Ellis had decided as much as soon as he had learned that the drowned lady was Russian. All the other evidence pointed the same way. She had drowned herself, poor woman, most likely as a result of an unhappy love affair with the young chap called Fedya. It was known that they had quarrelled. It was also known from the evidence supplied by the young Russian doctor that Miss Valence had been pregnant. It was not hard to put two and two together.

Two other pieces of evidence from the same source did raise doubts, Mr Ellis admitted, but they were suspect in more senses than one. The first piece of evidence was the blow to Miss Valence's head. It was consistent with her having fallen heavily backwards and it could have been sustained as she fell in the pool. Supposing she had in fact struck her head before actually entering the water, she might – the constable emphasised the word in his mind – she *might* have been dead before her immersion, in which case the second piece of evidence about the lack of sea-water in her lungs could be explained. In any case, both pieces of evidence had come from the young doctor's unauthorised autopsy and could be considered suspect in the sense that he himself might not be entirely blameless. 'For all I know,' Dr Hodgson had exclaimed, 'he might've been destroying evidence of his own guilt! There was no authorisation, no corroboration! I mean, I couldn't trust someone like that, could I? I couldn't have him under my roof a moment longer, not after that!'

Dr Hodgson's heated words had settled the matter more or less. Ever since the young Russian doctor's arrival in Ventnor only three weeks before there had been rumours about him. His naked sea-bathing, of course, his odd habit of carrying medicine bottles yoked over his shoulders, his strange canvas garment had all aroused interest. Now there were suggestions of criminality. Not that Mr Ellis himself entertained any suspicions of that kind. He was personally rather fond of the young Russian doctor. He approved of the way he had shown an unusual readiness to offer medical treatment free of charge to some of the poorest families in town. Truth to tell, he found him pleasanter than Dr Hodgson and was distressed by his recent banishment from Alto House. Still, there were other matters apart from the Russian doctor's eccentric behaviour which required to be cleared up before Mr Ellis could feel sure it was all a 'Russian business' and no longer his concern.

For one thing, Count Rostopchine had paid his bill and left the Esplanade Hotel without giving a forwarding address. Then there had been the death of Fedya. Mr Ellis supposed the two were connected. After all, the Count would want to avoid more scandal, though Mr Ellis doubted very much whether the Count himself was directly involved in Marie Valence's death as had been suggested. On the other hand, one circumstance of her death remained puzzling. He thought it over a great deal and on the Tuesday morning tested his hypothesis by taking a short walk along the clifftop. Could she have thrown herself down from there? The answer was no. The pool in which she had been found was too far from the cliff bottom. What Mr Ellis did notice was a sort of narrow causeway among the tall rocks. He saw that if she had followed this narrow causeway down towards the sea she would have passed close to the pool. No doubt that was precisely what she had done. His discovery put to rest any queries about why it had been that pool and not some other. He had been so pleased about this that he had waved to the children standing on the sand below him and been gratified to see them wave back.

One other small problem nagged at him. Why had no other members of the Russian colony in Ventnor attended her burial or offered any suggestions as to why she had taken her own life? Mr Ellis spent a day mulling this question over. Finally, on the Wednesday evening, he decided to bring his enquiries to an end by raising the matter with the Russians. It did not take him long to discover that the leading member of the Russian colony was a famous writer staying at Rock Cottage. A discreet enquiry brought him the news that the Russian gentleman and his friend were no longer there, having moved down to Belinda House at the beginning of the week. So Mr Ellis made his way down the steep lane from Belgrave Road to the esplanade.

It was shortly after dinner-time. Mrs Rees was delighted to see him, which made a nice change after the sombre whisperings of his last visit. She spoke enthusiastically of her new Russian guests. They were so distinguished and so refined, she confided, and what is more the taller of them, the gentleman with the silver hair, had become especially friendly with her guest, Mrs Whitehouse. Mr Ellis was shown into the back parlour. A tall gentleman with a large, impressive head of silver hair, a light-coloured beard, broad face and candid, bright blue eyes, rose politely and shook his hand, introducing himself as 'Ivan Turgenev'. Also in the room, seated at a small card table, were Mrs Emily Whitehouse and her nephew Guy Seddenham. Mr Ellis

159

explained that he wished to ask the Russian gentleman no more than two or three questions about the deceased Russian lady and he apologised for interrupting the card game.

'Oh, I am being beaten hollow! It will be a relief not to go on playing!' cried Mrs Whitehouse. 'If I may be permitted to stay while you ask your questions, Constable, I would deem it a great privilege.'

'Of course, ma'am.'

The notebook was produced and the tip of the pencil licked. It was noticeable that Turgenev smiled faintly and his eyes lit up with amusement at the decorum and efficiency of this red-cheeked English policeman. As for the questions, they were not unexpected. How long had he been in Ventnor? When had he met the deceased? What did he know about her? Could he perhaps suggest which members of the Russian colony she had been used to meeting most frequently? Turgenev answered them all in good English in an attractively accented, slightly high-pitched voice.

'And now, sir, a final question. I have to ask you whether you can remember when you last saw her and whether it was with anyone.'

Turgenev looked thoughtful. 'Yes, I saw her for the last time . . .' he contemplated the ceiling for a moment or so '. . . on Thursday. Yes, it was Thursday. I remember a strong wind. It was about half-past twelve in the afternoon. I saw her cross the road and begin talking to the young doctor, the nihilist.'

'Pardon, sir?'

'Ni-hil-ist.' Turgenev laughed. 'Of course, in England you do not have them, I think! She was talking to the young Russian doctor.'

'So that is the last time you saw her, sir?'

'Yes. Except . . .' Turgenev placed his hands loosely

together and gazed at each of his listeners in turn. He cleared his throat. When he began speaking again, his voice seemed to have acquired a different timbre and to be that of an orator speaking in high but exact tones out of some immense, engulfing stillness. 'I was unable to sleep that night. Suddenly I thought I heard the sound of a violin string being plucked very weakly and piteously. I raised my head. The moon was low in the sky and looked me straight in the eyes. Its light lay white as chalk on the floor.... The strange sound came again clearly. I leaned on one elbow. My heart was seized by a slight fear. A moment passed, then another ... I leaned back on the pillow, thinking of the state one can get into when one is wakeful. A bit later I fell asleep, or I thought I did. I had a strange dream. I dreamt I was lying in my bedroom, on my bed, I wasn't sleeping and I couldn't even close my eyes. There was that sound again. I turned over. The line of moonlight on the floor began gently to rise up and straighten out and become slightly rounded at the top ... There stood in front of me, as if through a mist, the motionless figure of a woman all in white.... I wanted to see her features – and then I suddenly began shivering because the air had gone cold around me. And then I realised I wasn't lying on my bed but sitting up, and where I thought the phantom had stood was the moonlight shining in a long white line across the floor.'

All three of his listeners were transfixed by the story. For one instant at least the silence filling the parlour seemed to extend beyond Belinda House to the whole of the esplanade and the whole of Ventnor. Aunt Emily, who had held a small silk handkerchief to her mouth during the telling of the story, now sighed and said breathily:

'You are a poet, sir, a true poet.'

161

'Thank you.'

Mr Ellis uneasily moved in his chair. 'About the, er, doctor, sir . . .'

'It confirms it all, doesn't it?' declared Aunt Emily excitedly.

'What, ma'am?'

'The phantom, the apparition. . . . It confirms her spirit was restless, don't you see?'

'It might suggest that, ma'am. Sir, about the doctor, you used this word. Could you please explain its meaning?'

'Ni-hil-ist? It is from the Latin *nihil*, meaning nothing. A ni-hil-ist believes in nothing.' When his listeners appeared not to understand him, Turgenev added, lowering his voice: 'In Russia we call them by that name, except that we really mean they do not believe in the established system, in existing laws. They believe only in science. For the sake of science they wish to change society. Here in England you might regard them as . . . as . . . as *revolutionaries.*'

Aunt Emily gave a gasp.

'Do you mean, sir,' Mr Ellis asked, 'that the doctor is a revolutionary?'

'Not precisely . . .'

Before Turgenev could do more by way of elaboration than make a two-handed gesture which suggested the ineluctable role of Fate in human affairs, Mrs Emily Whitehouse spoke up firmly in agreement.

'From what I have seen and heard of that young man, Constable, I would say he had the manners of a revolutionary! I haven't the slightest hesitation in saying that! When he was here last week, sitting in the dining room . . .'

Her account of Bazarov's visit to Belinda House was listened to in polite silence. It only remained for Guy to be summoned to her aid in corroborating what had happened for him to become the centre of attention.

'I only know he's a scientist,' was his rather limp defence of his friend when Mr Ellis asked him. The latter meanwhile wrote busily in his notebook. To Guy it suddenly appeared obvious that Aunt Emily's hostility towards Bazarov had found receptive ears. 'I didn't mean . . .'

'Please don't interrupt the constable when he's writing,' admonished his aunt.

'A serious charge, you know,' commented Mr Ellis, closing his notebook.

In a diffident voice, smiling tentatively and leaning slightly forward, Turgenev asked:

'Ellis? Ellis?'

'Beg your pardon, sir?'

'Your name is Ellis, is it?'

Mr Ellis frowned and straightened his back with a slight air of defiance.

'It is, sir.'

'I am asking because your English names are often so difficult. Is your name like the girl's name?'

'No, Ellis, sir.'

'It does sound very like Alice, doesn't it!' Aunt Emily exclaimed. 'How right you are! Alice, Ellis, I can hardly tell the . . . Oh, where on earth is the boy off to?'

Guy slipped out of the room at that moment.

He slipped out into a windy dusk. Trees were flowing in the wind, their leaves beating hard as birds' wings against a streaky tin-coloured sky. The sea smelt strong. Its noisy explosions of waves and deeper rumblings as of huge armies gathering unseen in the far dark brought an urgent and rising panic to his heart and lungs. He had been shocked by the haunting effect of Turgenev's dream. It had made him aware that Marie's spirit was

163

indeed restless and might indeed haunt him as it had seemed to haunt the speaker, but equally pressing had been the sense that Zhenia Bazarov was now in some kind of new danger as a result of Turgenev's use of the word 'nihilist' to describe him. Whether or not it meant that the doctor was a revolutionary seemed to matter less than the probability that he would now be suspected of darker deeds. He was the last person to be seen with her, it seemed, and there could be no doubt that he was the one to drag her from the bottom of the pool. Though these could be innocent enough facts in themselves, they could easily be made to appear suspicious to suspicious minds. Guy felt that they menaced his friend and were part of a mounting sea of menaces surrounding him also in the night air.

Not having seen Zhenia that day, he did not know where to find him. He knew he would have to go to Alto House first. It would mean encountering Susan Hodgson again, perhaps, or even Dr Hodgson himself, but he hoped he would be able to discover his friend's whereabouts simply by asking one of the maids. As it turned out, it was Susan who answered the door, Wednesday being the maids' night off, and though she did not appear too upset at seeing him again she was disconcerted by his queries about the doctor.

'We couldn't stand his smelly things, all his horrid specimens, as he called them! Such behaviour, Guy, you can't imagine!'

But he could imagine. He could imagine very well what she meant and sympathise up to a point. What he couldn't understand was her abruptly dismissive 'Oh, one of the inns, I think!' when he asked where Bazarov had gone. She stood at the top of the steps of Alto House and pointed along the High Street with a flourish.

'Ask in one of the inns!'

There were half-a-dozen drinking places in Ventnor, so Miles had told him. Though he had been inside none of them, last year Miles had taken him to one where fishermen gathered, the Anchor, in order to negotiate with a fellow called Joe Cockerell for the hire of a boat. Recalling that it was somewhere along the High Street, Guy hurried under dim oil lamps hung at infrequent intervals and eventually found its sign swinging in the wind. The place was full. By squeezing and pushing he reached the bar where, apparently, his windswept appearance rather than his attempts to make himself heard above the hubbub brought him the publican's attention. It was obvious he was under-age and not one of the usual clientele, but his pleas to be taken to the Russian doctor were received sympathetically. There had been other enquiries about his whereabouts, it seemed. A boy was sent from the back of the bar to scout round several other places in the High Street. Five minutes later he returned with the news that the doctor was in the Hoe and Turnip.

This was a tavern at the other end of the High Street and tucked away down an alley. Steps led down into a public bar that was less full of patrons than the Anchor but much stuffier. The drinkers also looked shabbier. Some appeared to be wearing nothing more elegant than sacking round their shoulders. The boy led Guy quickly through the public bar and along a passageway at the back. A simple wooden door on a latch opened into a tiny room lit by two candles. Bazarov was sitting with his back to the wall, his face shining with perspiration and his eyes glazed and excited. With him were two men. One quite young, hardly older than Guy himself, had a moustache and a healthy pink face. The other was an older man, with a thick beard and spectacles. Both were seated on benches round the wall and in front of them was a table on which stood a large tankard, wine glasses, a bottle, a loaf of bread and an open portfolio with papers. These papers were being scrutinised when Guy was shown in.

'Guido! Guido! My assistant!' cried Bazarov. 'See, here are two friends of Mr Gosse!'

'Holdsworth,' said the bearded older man, introducing himself. 'Have a seat, young fellow. This is my son James, also a . . .'

'Have seat, yes!' Bazarov echoed. 'More drinks, gentlemen!'

Mr Holdsworth senior politely declined the invitation, evidently finding it a trifle improper, while Bazarov drank from the tankard, wiped his mouth with the back of his hand and then munched on a piece of bread which he tore from the loaf on the table. His behaviour was so strange, even by his eccentric standards, that Guy did not at first appreciate what had happened to his friend. He quickly realised it was the ale in the tankard that caused Zhenia's excessive exuberance.

'Your letter, Guido, friend of my heart! Your letter brings our friends! Discovery of arrer muzzlet, you see . . .'

'Such an odd name!' remarked Mr Holdsworth senior.

'It means I am famous! And you are famous! We are all famous!'

And he drank again, thumping the tankard back on the table.

'Yes, the famous Arrow Muzzlet!' the older Holdsworth echoed in a precise, schoolmasterish voice. 'What does it mean exactly, I wonder? Gosse calls it that in his *Actinologia*. I looked it up as soon as I received the

166

letter. A local name, I suppose.'

'Local boys,' exclaimed Bazarov as soon as he heard the word 'local', 'local boys find 'em!'

'What's he saying?' the older Holdsworth asked. His son James was trying to restrain giggles.

'I saw them myself,' said Guy. 'There were two local boys . . .'

'Local boys, yes!' Bazarov was becoming irrepressible. 'We find example of *peach-i-a*, *peach-iiii-aaaa*, *peach-iii-aaa has-has-has* . . .'

'Yes, yes, yes,' said the older Holdsworth through Bazarov's hissings.

'Apologies, gentlemen!' said Bazarov in a slurred way.

'No, no, we understand . . .'

'Difficult, diff-i-cult words . . .'

'Yes, yes, yes. Well, young fellow,' said the older Holdsworth, 'you are the one who wrote the letter, are you?'

Guy agreed he was.

'And you were the one, I understand from our Russian friend here, who actually studied the details in the microscope?'

Again Guy agreed.

'Most admirable,' said Mr Holdsworth. 'You have helped in a material way to further a piece of valuable biological research. I feel you should be aware of the service you have done to the cause of scientific knowledge. Not all scientific knowledge may seem at first sight of immediate value to mankind. We who seek out the secrets of the sea are only just beginning our voyage of discovery, as it were. Our friend here has merely set sail into unknown regions. But it is from the sea that all life came, as we all know, and so it is in the simplest of the sea's creatures that we may be able to

167

find the beginnings of life on this planet.'

'Amen,' said James Holdsworth piously, as if his father had been uttering a prayer. The word led to a short pause filled by sounds of distant voices from the adjacent public bar. Guy screwed up his courage and said:

'I have some serious news, Zhenia.'

Bazarov did not immediately take this in. Instead it was the older Holdsworth who responded with:

'In what connection?'

'In connection with the death of Marie Valence.'

Bazarov's expression changed. He looked fierce. 'What news?'

Guy explained what he had heard at Belinda House. The bearded Mr Holdsworth looked startled and his pink-faced son began looking nervously from one face to another round the table. Suddenly Bazarov slammed his fist down, making the wine glasses jump about.

'So I am ni-hil-ist! I am destroyer! I am called murderer, yes?'

'No, no,' Guy began protesting, 'nobody actually said so!'

'You know what I am telling our friends?'

'It is scarcely credible,' muttered the older Holdsworth, shaking his head.

'I am telling our friends,' said Bazarov fiercely, his eyes fixed on Guy, 'perhaps I am famous, perhaps not, it makes no difference! What is making difference is I am what I am! I am called nihilist, yes? So what is nihilist?'

The fierceness of his manner quite alarmed Guy. The younger Holdsworth interrupted with a rapid contribution of his own.

'Before you came he had been talking about this. I thought he'd had a bit too much to drink.'

The remark, being addressed to Guy, seemed to be made without regard to Bazarov's presence at all, but the latter apparently did not resent this behaviour and launched into a further slightly inebriated peroration.

'So I am nihilist, so I am not being a person, you see! I deny my own name, I destroy my own identity! I refuse ... refuse, you understand? ... refuse to acknowledge my fame and my name as possession! We live in age of possessions, yes? What we possess is what we are. It is our position in society. When we were in graveyard, remember?'

Guy nodded.

'In graveyard what is remaining? Only name is remaining. Am I right? Am I right?'

Both Holdsworths nodded obediently, though they looked a little unsure of themselves in the presence of this fierce and rather drunk Russian.

'I am right, gentlemen! I defy you, I defy everyone to overcome possessiveness of names. We must all ...' Bazarov wiped his mouth on his sleeve '... we must all free ourselves of possession by name. We must abolish fame and honour and respect, all possessiveness of a person's good name in society. We must simply *be – be*, I repeat, as I am trying to be here in your little English town, be good, be helpful, be loving, but be nihilist, not possessing name, a naked person, simply working to find secrets, for good of mankind. It is what I believe, gentlemen! It is my credo! It is my ni–hil–ism!'

'Yes, yes, yes, so you've insisted,' agreed the older Holdsworth, but the triumphant way in which Bazarov ended his speech seemed to alarm as well as impress him and he leaned across the table to collect up the papers which had spilled out of the portfolio, saying in a puzzled, diffident way: 'I have the greatest respect for your sentiments, sir. They are noble and quite befitting a scientist. But you will have to excuse us. We mustn't miss the coach to Ryde.'

'More drinks!' shouted an exuberant Bazarov.

This time the Holdsworths ignored him. The older Holdsworth, removing his spectacles and wiping them with a handkerchief, explained briefly to Guy that they had come from Torquay, where they had been collecting specimens for a number of years for the famous Mr Gosse, Fellow of the Royal Society. They had sought to encourage an interest in such matters wherever they could and now, to their intense surprise and gratification, they had come across this Russian gentleman who had made a genuine discovery of the first order. 'And the most important thing of all,' he concluded, 'is that we've been able to confirm it as a discovery of the *peachia hastata* or Arrow Muzzlet. Very remarkable, very remarkable.'

The Holdsworths politely withdrew. Bazarov had another tankard of ale brought to him from the public bar and leaned back expansively against the wall, his strong neck fully extended.

'So?' he asked Guy when they were alone. 'What am I to do, Guido, my friend?'

Guy asked him where he was living now.

'I am living here. I have room upstairs. What I am doing now is working for science. *Mikroskop*, specimens, bottles, all are upstairs. But what do I do about your policeman?'

Guy pointed out that if Zhenia had been the last person to see Marie alive, according to the testimony of Turgenev, the famous Russian writer, and the first, after Guy himself, to see her dead, might not there be some connection? Bazarov drew his lips together and gave a soft, low whistle. As he did so he relaxed his rigid pose. He leaned over the table and peered in the candlelight into Guy's face.

'I do not like policemen. So I do not tell your policeman what I know. But I tell you, Guido. So listen

170

carefully.' He drank some of the beer and licked the froth from his lips. 'True, Masha comes to me. Perhaps Turgenev sees her. What I know is she comes to my room. She begs me to take away baby, understand? I say no.' He sighed, breathing beery breath towards Guy. 'If I had said yes, perhaps she is living now and Fedya is living now. But I say no. I ask her what she will do. She says she is going again to next house.'

'Which house?'

'House of Captain Fenton. Where she was living last year.'

'Connaught House?'

'Yes.'

'Why?'

'Guido, Guido, not so excited!'

'So she went?'

'Yes, she went.' Bazarov's tone changed. 'It was dark, but someone saw her.'

'Who?'

'Dr Hodgson.' Bazarov's green eyes looked unblinkingly through the candlelight. 'You know what it means?'

'I think so . . .'

'It means Dr Hodgson sees her at Alto House and he sees her again in Infirmary. After autopsy. He was angry, very angry. He says I am destroying evidence. He says I, I, Zhenia Bazarov, medical doctor, I am guilty!'

Bazarov flung his arms up in the air and shook his head in disbelief and evident amazement. His eyes continued their almost unblinking scrutiny of Guy's face. But he said nothing more.

'So that's why you had to leave the doctor's house?'

Bazarov nodded. There was a long silence. Guy realised how much evidence seemed to be piling up

171

against his friend. The only fact in his favour, although it was little consolation, was Fedya's death after his suicide attempt. So long as it was assumed that his death was a suicide, like Marie's, due to a lovers' quarrel, Zhenia's discovery that she might have died earlier would not matter.

'But I *am* guilty,' Bazarov suddenly said.

'No, you can't be!'

'In my heart, Guido, in my soul I am guilty!'

His thin face with the broad forehead had a skull-like appearance, white as bone, in the upward flickering light of the candle. For the first time since knowing him Guy was aware how completely self-absorbed the other could be.

'I am guilty, Guido, because I didn't help. I am guilty, guilty, yes, I know it!'

'No, you're not, you couldn't be . . .'

Guy knew he could not speak with conviction. Zhenia's sudden melancholy had so altered his mood that he seemed locked inside himself, quite as remote from Guy's logic as he was from the noises of the bar next door or the sound of the wind outside. Then, with a little shock, a frisson touching his spine lightly, Guy felt in his presence, in this tiny stuffy room, a brief intimation of death. He sensed that the guilt which consumed his friend was due not only to his memory of Marie but to all those little extinctions, second by second, that comprise our lives and tick away all memory and all love. He shivered and felt frightened.

'Thank you for telling me,' he murmured.

Bazarov remained in his trance. Guy crept out of the dark, tiny parlour, latching the door quietly behind him. He had to test the truth of what he had just been told.

12

After he had rung the bell, he waited. The blank appearance of the front of Connaught House gave an impression of emptiness but he knew the house could not be empty. Behind him, with a great noise of hoofbeats and the sharp, clangorous grinding of wheels on cobblestones, the night coach for Ryde passed along Belgrave Road. Though its lanterns were lit, he could not see into its interior and had to imagine the two Holdsworths being swayed from side to side as the big vehicle rolled on its way. He tugged once more at the bell-pull and even before its interior ringing was finished, the front door was swung open. The woman who stood there looked familiar, but he could not be sure exactly where he had seen her.

'Who is it you want?' She asked the question abruptly and then leaned out into the darkness, looking beyond Guy. 'So it's started raining, has it?'

'Yes.'

'Who did you want to see?'

'I would like to see Miss Elizabeth.'

Though there was a light burning in the hallway, it was by the flickering light of the little glass oil lamp which she raised up to shoulder-level that she now studied his face.

''Tis Miss Elizabeth, yes?'

The repeating of the name brought to Guy's notice the woman's country accent. He recognised her as the woman who had been in charge of the donkey rides. Trying to smile against the brightness of the light shining in his face, he stammered out:

'She invited me to come and see her. She said she felt quite alone now that Miles wasn't here.'

The woman's handsome, peach-coloured face, whose expression had been so concentrated at first, now showed signs of a rather child-like, vulnerable smile and she stood aside for him to enter the house.

'If she said you should come, then you are welcome, I'm sure. She is the mistress now. If you will come into the drawing room, sir. What name shall I say?'

Guy told her. It had to be repeated, but she nodded her understanding and silently led him across the hall. The drawing room turned out to be colder than Guy had remembered it from last year. Even the previous summer it was hardly ever used. Now it had an unaired, fusty smell and in the dimness of the single oil lamp which the woman carried into the room the large furniture, the heavy curtains and the pictures seemed more museum-like than ever. Guy remembered Miles telling him that it had been their mother's favourite room and they wanted to keep it exactly as it was.

'Please wait here and I will tell Miss Elizabeth.'

The woman lit a candle and went off with it. He heard her footsteps going slowly up the stairs. Two large windows overlooking the back garden and the whole of Ventnor bay now showed, with the curtains undrawn, an apparently totally black darkness that reflected the gleam of the lamp and the dim interior illumination and Guy himself. But he could discern through this reflection the shape of the garden wall and a tree and in the outer distance, very dimly, the massive flickering of wave-crests on the sea. Rain fell soundlessly against the panes. The droplets went down the outer glass like little silver tears.

'Guy,' said Elizabeth's musical voice behind him, 'how nice of you to come and see me.'

174

How mannered she was! Guy thought. He recalled the woman's remark, 'She is the mistress now' and he felt Elizabeth had assumed the role defiantly, as though this room of all the rooms in the house needed to have her authority imposed upon its embalmed, museum-like stillness.

'Good evening,' he said and bowed slightly, 'I hope I'm not disturbing you.'

'No, dear Guy, of course you're not. Oh, your hair has rain on it!'

She came quite close to him, right into the circle of the light, and he saw the brilliance of her shining eyes and the look of genuine pleasure on her face. Her closeness deeply excited him. For an instant he had the impression she was about to raise her hand and touch his hair.

'Yes, but it's not very heavy.'

'It's been such a terrible August and we'd so hoped it would be nice. My father says we need good summers for the town's future.'

'Who,' he asked quietly, 'is the person who opened the door? I don't think I remember her from last year.'

'Molly, you mean? She is our housekeeper.'

Being so close, he looked directly into her eyes. She looked back in the same direct way, her eyelashes making a slight quivering. The communion of their eyes sharply increased their excitement at their closeness. The conversational manner which they had both adopted seemed quite inappropriate and they were lost for words for a moment.

'Does she . . .?'

He was going to ask about the donkeys when the Captain appeared through the double doors at one side of the drawing room saying loudly and rather brusquely:

175

'I heard a voice in here. Ah, so it's you! Good heavens, Guy, isn't it?'

'Guy Seddenham, sir.'

'You're enjoying your holiday, are you?'

'Well, sir . . .'

'Ah, the weather. We told you about Miles, didn't we?'

'Yes, sir.'

'Excuse my not chatting just at the moment. I have a lot on my mind.' Then to Elizabeth: 'Where is that other decanter, my dear, I wonder?' It was not that he enquired commandingly. His voice was very slightly aggrieved, like the voice of someone whose immediate concerns were more important than the domestic cares surrounding him. Guy noticed he was leaning on a stick as he stood in the doorway. 'I have papers to go through for tomorrow and I would prefer to study them in peace and quiet.'

'Of course, Father,' said Elizabeth. 'The decanter is probably where I asked Molly to put it.'

So saying, she strode towards her father, who moved back to let her pass, and went over to some part of the Captain's 'cabin' invisible to Guy from where he was standing. He heard the Captain say 'Thank you, my dear,' and then Elizabeth reappeared, closed the double doors behind her and came up to Guy again, who recognised then why she should be regarded as the mistress of this household.

'I think we'd better go up to my room,' she whispered. 'It will then not disturb Father. If you do not think it is too forward of a young lady to invite you into her room?'

'Of course I don't,' he whispered back.

She squeezed his arm and picked up the oil lamp. That lightly squeezing pressure on his arm and the noise of her dress beside him alerted his whole body to her. They went out into the darkness of the hall and up the stairs, she still whispering to him words that seemed to run like fingers all over his skin:

'It is so nice of you to come, so very nice. Father has been disagreeable lately. We haven't even been talking to each other. And I love having people to talk to! How I miss Miles! He and I used to talk and talk and talk . . . Oh, your jacket's quite wet! Are all your clothes wet?'

'Not very.'

'I'm sure they must be. Poor Guy!'

He fell easily into the role of her obedient escort, though he resented her artless way of patronising him. Sensing as much, she added as they reached the landing:

'I really think you must come and try on some of my brother's clothes. They're simply not being used and I don't think Miles'll want them.'

He said nothing to this, except that once inside her bedroom, which was well lighted and cosy with a fire burning in the grate, he felt so hurt by her grand manner that he deliberately changed the subject.

'I went to the funeral yesterday afternoon.'

'You did? Come in and take off that jacket. We'll dry it in front of the fire.'

'It wasn't really a funeral, it was just a burial.'

'Was it? Look, I'll hang it over the back of this chair.'

'I learned something else, too.'

'That's right. It won't take away too much of the heat.'

'I learned she came here, Elizabeth.'

'You did? Now what about the other things?'

'They're all right, thank you,' he said. 'Did she come here?'

'Do please sit down, Guy dear. Who are you talking about?'

'You know who I'm talking about.'

'If you're talking about Marie, I have no wish to discuss her.'

'She came here, Elizabeth, and I think you know she did.'

Elizabeth took her place in an upright upholstered armchair and clasped her hands together. She began to assume the severity of her room. 'Guy dear, I'm finding this disagreeable.'

'You told me the day before yesterday you thought she'd been killed. Don't you want to find out who killed her?'

'It is not my business.'

'It is the business of anyone who has a conscience,' he said, not anticipating how priggish it sounded.

'I do not have a bad conscience, Guy. If she came here, she came here. I cannot see what business it is of mine, or what business it is of yours.'

They were silent. He looked into the busily crackling flames.

'If she came here after dark,' he said.

'No, she came here in the afternoon.'

The admission made her blush. They both knew that she had been caught out by this remark.

'And she didn't come here again after dark?' he asked.

She was silent and looked away into the fire. Her hands were clasped so tightly he could see the whites of her knuckles. 'What if she did?' she whispered.

'It would be,' he said quietly, 'the last place she was seen alive.'

'What do you mean?'

'I mean what I say, Elizabeth.'

Then he looked up and his eye was attracted by something he saw on the mantelpiece. It made him jump to his feet. He felt the heat of the fire against his forelegs as he stared at the object on the mantelpiece.

'Guy, what is it?'

'Where did you find this?' he asked in an unsteady, incredulous voice and held the object towards her. She took it.

'Downstairs.'

'Whereabouts downstairs?'

'Oh, I don't remember!' She was irritated by his questioning. 'Why does it matter where?'

'She wore one like it.'

'Lots of Russian people wear them. I think it may have been brought in from the street. You can see the chain is broken.'

He would have liked to ask for it back but she hastily stuffed it out of sight in a pocket of her dress.

'You see, if it was hers, it'd mean she'd been here, wouldn't it?'

'It mightn't mean anything of the kind.' She seemed to want to dismiss the whole thing. 'Why can't we just talk about something else?'

'If Marie came here,' he said, looking at the slight pinkness which had arisen on Elizabeth's pale face, 'and she was killed, as you said she was, why shouldn't she have been killed here?'

He knew it was insulting, though he tried to make the question sound as light-hearted as possible. She grew red with annoyance.

'Guy, what *are* you saying? That's quite silly. Who would kill her here?'

Put like that, he knew what he had said was unpardonably silly and it was now his turn to blush. She went relentlessly on.

'She was found in a deep pool, wasn't she? You found her yourself. What on earth makes you think anyone from here had anything to do with that? I mean . . .'

He waited for her to explain what she meant and she proceeded to be quite logical.

'I mean, Father has gout and Molly's got bad feet.'

It was enough. He knew he had been guilty of quite groundless suspicions. Worse, he had spoiled the pleasure of talking to Elizabeth. That had become the most unexpected and keenly anticipated of pleasures during this rainy holiday.

'I am very sorry,' he said.

She gave him a composed, grudging smile in return.

'You do not need to be sorry. You were fond of that person, I suppose. Miles was, too.' She stood up. 'I'll fetch the clothes.'

Resenting more strongly than ever her attitude towards Marie and her readiness to treat him as an object of charity, Guy also sprang to his feet, explaining that he had to return to Belinda House because his aunt would be waiting to play more evening games of cards. She was obviously rather impressed by his loyalty to his aunt, unable though she was to conceal her annoyance at his decision to leave so soon.

'Yes, I see. What about tomorrow night then?'

He said he could come after dinner.

'Dear Guy,' she said, 'I'll let you know. I'll have to sort them through, you see.'

Grandly holding the oil lamp aloft, she went sedately ahead of him down the stairs. He wondered at her show of composure and superiority. By the front door, excited again by her closeness as she held the door open, he felt a spontaneous impulse to kiss her For a moment he hesitated, seeing the bright and knowing look in her eyes. Then he bent forward and kissed her on the lips. Her startled raising of a hand to her mouth had a gesture of farewell about it and he quickly ran down the steps into the rainy night.

180

It had happened so suddenly he didn't have time to feel amazed by his behaviour until he was halfway down the steep lane to the esplanade. To his astonishment he found he was exhilarated, not ashamed. A flood of tender, elated feeling for Elizabeth literally made his heart race. He walked on air. From little pool to pool of lantern light he descended the lane through what scarcely seemed to be darkness at all. Everything around him seemed clearly visible, just as the sea and the voices of fishermen ascending from the shore sounded sharp and distinct. Particularly loud was the scraping sound made by a wooden sledge loaded with fish which two of the men were hauling up the steep uneven slope.

He found Aunt Emily playing patience in the back parlour. Mrs Rees was with her, but as soon as Guy returned she left and Aunt Emily insisted on playing four quick games in succession, all of which she won easily. She studied Guy dubiously at the end of the final game.

'You really haven't been trying, Guy. Your mind hasn't been on the cards at all.'

He pleaded tiredness. She wondered whether his high colour and the brightness of his eyes might not be the signs of another cold, in which case the best place for him was bed. He agreed and they ascended the stairs together.

In his high room he undressed, blew out the candle and stood naked before the small window. Despite the rain it was a warm night. His body felt hot, but not with a fever. He felt hot with excitement. He recalled the conversation with Elizabeth and the suspicion that she was not telling him the whole truth. Then he remembered what he had seen on her mantelpiece. A chill feeling ran down his spine. He peered as far down as he could into the blackness which filled the area between

181

the side of Belinda House and St Martin's Villa next door but he could not see the window where Marie had been on the day of his arrival. It was pitch dark.

That very moment there was a flash of light. It came from the horizon and showed him the shapes of the houses and a momentary glimmer of that closed window. He flinched from it. The whole sky had been lit up by what he instantly realised was a lightning flash, because within a few seconds there resounded the reverberation of distant thunder. The lightning was repeated, a flickering illumination that silhouetted chimneypots and sloped roofs, and the soft rain began to fall with slightly more insistence. Somewhere a couple of dogs started barking.

13

Mrs Emily Whitehouse told everyone she met there was one thing she could not abide – apart from fidgety children, lateness at meal-times, impoliteness from servants, the neglect of cold symptoms, the impertinence of those who disagreed with her and noisy foreigners – and it was thunderstorms at night. She took less exception to them during the day, but at night she could not abide them. Her night had consequently been spent in fearful anticipation of every conceivable kind of disaster and by morning she decided she had had enough. They would leave Ventnor by the Ryde coach that evening.

She announced her decision at breakfast. Guy and the twins protested that they ought to be allowed to stay the full two weeks as arranged. She was adamant and she instructed Guy to accompany her to the post office. The time had come to send a telegram to Charles Augustus.

He did as he was told. The telegram was despatched at half-past ten and he spent the rest of the morning until lunch-time looking after the twins. Since the weather was unusually warm and sticky and he had not slept well, he left them to their seaweed games and found a small dry crevice among the rocks where the sound of the sea and cloudy sunlight lulled him into drowsiness and a whirlpool of dreams. They were maddening, unnerving, terrifying deeps of nightmare into which he seemed to fall as if he were drowning. He awoke in a sweat to find his face spattered with a light rain.

Thinking he was late for lunch, he raced across the

sand towards the esplanade, only to discover that the twins had already returned to Belinda House because of the rain and that it was in any case only half-past twelve. Lunch was an occasion of silences and resentments. The twins were particularly upset at the prospect of the holiday ending so soon. Aunt Emily presided with raised chin and pursed lips. To Guy, who had begun to interpret her moods, she seemed contrite rather than complacent at having spoilt their holiday, but he knew she would not change her mind.

Shortly after lunch two things happened that changed everything for the better. The first was the arrival of a small wax-sealed note addressed to him. He did not recognise the copperplate handwriting. It happened that Aunt Emily was resting and so the note did not give rise to awkward questions. He took it up to his room and tore open the seal. It was quite short.

Dear Guy,
    It would be a very great pleasure if you would consent to pay me a visit at seven this evening. I have sorted my brother's clothes and there will be the leisure for you to examine them if you care to.
                              Your fond friend,
                                  Elizabeth

He stared at the impeccable handwriting and felt both excited and annoyed. He was annoyed with her for using the pretext of charity, but on rereading the note several times he noticed that what had mattered most to her was the 'very great pleasure' and this excited him. Her candour in referring to herself as a fond friend gave him a matching pleasure. He felt ready to rush to Connaught House at once and would have done so had

184

not something even more exciting occurred literally within minutes.

Elizabeth's note was still in his hand when Edwina burst into his room and announced that Aunt Emily wished to see him downstairs. She had some 'very special news', Edwina declared. Guy thrust the note in the pocket of his tight trousers and followed her down to Aunt Emily's room on the floor below. He had naturally expected that his aunt would be resting. In fact she had put on a grey silk dressing gown and was standing in the middle of the room with a piece of yellow paper in her hand. This she held out to Guy as soon as he entered.

'Mrs Rees said it arrived at the Esplanade Hotel this morning and was only brought along here after lunch. It's from your father.'

Guy took the piece of paper and read:

ALL IS WELL. MONEY ORDER DESPATCH C/O ESPLANADE HOTEL. ARRIVING SOON. SINCEREST LOVE. TOM.

It was almost beyond belief! Those, of course, were the words Aunt Emily used as her face broke into a delighted smile. The twins whooped and danced with joy. Immediately all four of them started discussing what was to be done when the money arrived and what it all meant. To the twins and Guy it was obvious that their father would be coming at the weekend, which meant that their holiday would be prolonged till then. To Aunt Emily it simply meant that her brother, whom she always reproached for unpunctuality, had at least arrived in England, but she doubted very much whether he would be coming down to Ventnor. This declaration of doubt brought a swift end to the first flush of their excitement. The twins were sent off to be with Joan

185

and, more soberly, Aunt Emily and Guy discussed whether to remain in Ventnor and await more news or return at once to London. It seemed on the whole wiser to remain where they were for the time being, since the rooms were paid for until Sunday, and there was always the possibility that the arrival of the telegram at the Esplanade Hotel was a sign that Tom Seddenham had not consulted Charles Augustus and assumed they were staying there as they had done last year.

'So impetuous,' sighed Aunt Emily. 'It was always your father's weakness.'

Guy had never thought of his father as impetuous. He had heard him described as vague and even indecisive, characteristics which he identified in himself and even felt a little ashamed of, but to be impetuous meant, to him, to be bold and courageous and he liked the idea that he could be thought bold and courageous like his father. The happiness of anticipating his father's arrival and the money order which they so badly needed made him feel bold enough to confide in his aunt how much he wanted to become a doctor. She patted his arm and said she was sure it would be possible now and went on to talk about new clothes for them all and trips by carriage if the weather improved, perhaps to Ryde or Newport. Then she realised that another telegram had to be despatched, so Guy was sent urgently with money to have another message sent to Charles Augustus cancelling the first. ' He will think I have gone quite out of my mind!' she cried. 'Still, it isn't every day you get a telegram, is it?' Apart from the fact that thunder occasionally rumbled in the distance and Mrs Rees assured them there would be bound to be another storm that night, Aunt Emily was in a mood for conversation and engaged Guy in talk until dinner-time.

It was partway through dinner when he noticed the

hands of the marble clock in the dining room already pointing to fifteen minutes after seven and with a shock recalled Elizabeth's note in his pocket. He had to wait until the meal was over before leaving. A very fine rain, barely visible in the twilight, quickly wetted his hair and jacket as he hurried up the steep lane to the High Street and Belgrave Road. He was excited now just as much by the prospect of giving Elizabeth his good news as by the thought of seeing her again. It seemed sensible for him to assume that the pleasure expressed in her note meant she had not been offended by the kiss and genuinely wanted to see him.

Again, apart from a glow of light in a basement window, the front of Connaught House was unlit. He tugged at the bell-pull and waited. Expecting to see the woman called Molly, he was surprised to find the front door drawn cautiously open and then Elizabeth's voice enquired softly through the opening who it was.

'It's me, Guy.'

'You're late,' she whispered as she let him in. 'I asked you to come at seven.'

He apologised, explaining about the telegram. Her tone had not exactly been scolding so much as disappointed and she acknowledged what he said with a light laugh.

'Oh, what good news, Guy. But now,' she said commandingly, 'you must come upstairs and get dry.' She raised the candle to study his face and hair. 'Father left about twenty minutes ago. He's gone to a meeting of the Watch Committee. So now we can be together.'

He wondered exactly what she meant, echoing the words to himself. There was something strange in her behaviour, he felt. In the darkness of the hall, lit only by her oil lamp and a single candle fixed beside the long mirror, he could see the brilliance of her eyes even

187

though her features were a pale blur. The rustle of her dress sounded quite loud, but it was the scent she wore which surprised him most. It was sweet and musky and familiar, and the artificiality of it in association with her rustling movements excited and intrigued him.

'You haven't been listening,' he protested in a soft voice, a little breathless from running through the rain. Again she appeared not to notice his words as she led him up the stairs with the oil lamp held aloft.

'I'm very glad your father's coming back, of course I am. We can talk all about it up in the warmth of my room.'

He was comforted by the darkness of the house and its quietness. It seemed perfectly natural for him to be accompanying her upstairs to her bedroom. She was lonely and bored, after all, and he did not consider he was doing anything wrong. On the other hand, if he had told Aunt Emily he was being invited by Elizabeth Fenton to go up to her bedroom, he was sure he would have been given an instant lesson in the rights and wrongs of such behaviour. Elizabeth's rather surreptitious manner made it seem that she was herself doubtful about the propriety and wisdom of what she was doing, and the little wafts of seductive perfume did not help to lessen the dangers.

'Are you alone in the house?' he asked.

'No, Dora's downstairs. Molly's out, but she'll be back.' She held out her hand as soon as the bedroom door was closed. 'We'll do what we did yesterday. Take off your jacket and let's dry it.'

The bright fire made the room uncomfortably hot for him and he was glad to remove his jacket.

'Come on, come on,' she chivvied, and he released the wet jacket into her grasp. She put it over the back of the chair in front of the fire and then seized a towel from the shadows. 'Guy dear, come and kneel down here,' she commanded, 'and let me dry your hair.'

He had supposed in the dark of the hall that she was wearing a dress. Now he saw it was a pink silk gown tied at the front with ribbons. It flowed right down to the floor and created a pretty swishing sound as she walked, but its voluminousness was not sufficient to conceal the shape of her figure beneath it, nor did it entirely hide a sensuous white triangle of skin at the nape of her neck or a delicate line of cleavage at her bosom. As she approached him holding the towel, her almost straight brows and the drawn-back auburn hair seemed to be those of a woman, not of a girl. All that contradicted such maturity were her eyes in their unusual brightness and the full pinkness of her lips. These lips, slightly parted, seemed to him deliciously inviting and innocent and fresh and lacking all the assumed confidence of her perfume.

'Kneel down. Here, by this little stool.'

He was unsure how to react to such an odd request. He had never knelt in front of anyone in his life though he had seen pictures of men kneeling in front of Queen Victoria. She gave him no time to reflect on the matter, for she sat down on the stool with a hissing of silk and in a cloud of that dangerous perfume and he simultaneously dropped to his knees beside her. She began vigorously rubbing the towel over his hair.

'You've got lovely hair, Guy dear. Last year you didn't grow it so long, did you? Oh, your shirt's wet!'

He knew his shirt was wet at the neck, but the sudden closeness of Elizabeth concerned him far more deeply. What she was wearing, as well as her behaviour, seemed deliberately intended to entice him. He assumed she wanted to be kissed. He raised his head, looked into her slightly surprised eyes, and kissed her just as he had

189

kissed her the previous evening. Her lips were hot and dry. She started back from him. He continued to study her closely, still breathing quite hard and quivering in excitement at his boldness. Her lips remained open without emitting a sound. She allowed him to lean forward again, put his arms round her and draw her gently towards him. This time the pressure of his lips on hers met no resistance. She yielded softly to his embrace for the long instant of the kiss. He felt the same instantaneous sexual arousal in the closeness to Elizabeth as he had felt in the closeness of Marie. Then she pushed against him and he released her. She looked boldly at him, her hands holding the towel having fallen to her sides, and she smiled with an uncharacteristically teasing shyness.

'Why did you kiss me like that? Last night I . . .'

'Didn't you want to be kissed?'

She flung the towel away. 'I don't know.'

He suspected she had wanted it and the flimsy gown and the perfume and the warm room were all deliberate enticements.

'You know you're very pretty,' he said. He felt he had to take the initiative, perhaps impetuously, and he stood up. She had also risen and now quickly turned away, an embarrassed pinkness delicately colouring her cheeks. She was evidently aware for the first time of the feelings she had aroused in him.

'I thought,' she said, trying hard to recover control of the situation, 'you'd like to try on the clothes. I fetched them out of Miles's room.' She indicated a neat pile of clothes on top of the chest-of-drawers. 'Of course, if your father's coming back I suppose you'll have plenty of money now.'

'Yes,' he said.

She ran the tip of her tongue round her lips. There was a pause. She seemed to hesitate between giving up the idea of the clothes as superfluous and a strong impulse to say something quite open and frank. He watched her raise a finger to her mouth, frown and then look at him sideways.

'If I'm pretty,' she asked, taking in a breath, 'do you think I'm just a little girl?'

He thought it was too childish a question for him to answer and gave a shrug of the shoulders.

'Don't you think I should be treated as a woman?' Her eyes held a teasing challenge in them. She opened her palms to the glow of the fire. 'Father does. He doesn't believe I can understand what went on between him and . . . and that woman.'

He noticed the straightness of her mouth, just as it had been when he had asked her about the time of Marie's funeral. Immediately he recognised something else about her. The perfume she wore was the same as Marie's. Yet it was her words that now astonished him.

'What went on? Between your father and . . .'

It seemed impossible. Her words came between them like a barrier of air.

'That woman,' she repeated.

'Do you mean Marie?'

'I'm not going to say her name!' She turned away from him as she spoke and started shaking her clasped hands up and down in a gesture that was both stubborn and despairing.

'Do you mean Marie and your father . . .'

'Yes, yes, yes, yes, I do mean that! Nobody knows it, Guy dear, but it's been preying on my mind and I must tell someone!'

Both of them were startled by a thunderclap overhead, followed by a succession of diminishing rumbles. She covered her ears.

'Tell me,' he said.

She resumed her gestures with her clasped hands. 'I

191

suppose there'll be another storm like last night's. Yes, I'll tell you. She came here last year to teach us French. Well, of course, you know that. At first I liked her. Miles liked her, too. Then I began to suspect she was trying to turn Miles against me. I suppose I'm touchy. People say I am. The long and short of it is . . .' She walked backwards and forwards, three or four steps each way, and gave him the strong impression she had rehearsed what she was going to say. 'I began to hate her. But I didn't hate her because of Miles. I hated her because of the memory of my mother. You see, I'd always believed Father would remain true to her and would never think of another woman for the rest of his life. Can you understand that, Guy?'

He understood it perfectly. He thought of his own father and he felt sure he would remain true to his mother. There would never be another woman in his father's life.

'I do,' he said.

'Then perhaps you'll understand how I felt when I realised . . . when I realised my father and that woman were . . . were . . .'

Perhaps, he thought, she simply did not know what word to use. She had her back to him and he felt an uprush of pity for her mixed with a sudden strong recollection of Marie and his feeling for her.

'Lovers,' he said softly. 'They were lovers, you mean?'

'Yes.' She burst into tears but went on speaking. 'Yes. I found out. I found out and couldn't believe. I didn't want to believe. It was late last summer. After you'd left. It lasted a short time, I think. Then Marie – oh, I said I wouldn't, I said I wouldn't!'

She started sobbing and as she searched for a handkerchief in the folds of the silken gown something dropped to the floor. Guy, who had been about to comfort her, saw what it was and stood still. His eyes searched the shelf of the mantelpiece where he had last seen it. It was not there. It was lying on the floor face downwards and there was a name engraved on the back of it. About to stoop to pick it up, he noticed that Elizabeth had also seen it. Her crying stopped. She stood looking down at the floor with the handkerchief clutched in her hand.

They both stood quite still. The fire hissed and crackled into the stillness and the sash windows rattled very faintly in their frames as the wind from the sea struck them. There was a brief flash of lightning which drew their eyes instantly towards the outer blackness. It was followed by a noise of thunder, but faint and unreal.

'You found it downstairs, didn't you?'

She nodded dumbly. He stared closely at her. She darted a glance in his direction but then busied herself with wiping her eyes and blowing her nose. He looked down again at the object on the floor and then back to her.

'I can understand – that you didn't want to believe, I mean. But just think ...' he paused, recalling what she had said when he was last in this room '... Marie's dead, Fedya's dead, and if she came back here late on Thursday night ...'

She nodded her head again, this time more vigorously, and then clenched her hand into a fist round the handkerchief.

'Tell me,' he said.

'Yes, she did come back.' She heaved a sigh, wiping her eyes. 'The first time she came she wanted money. The second time it was late and I don't know what she wanted. I heard my father talking loudly down below. I couldn't hear exactly. I was up here, you see, and the sounds weren't distinct. Then there was silence. After a time I heard the front door close. It made a very loud noise. I supposed she'd banged it shut when she left.'

'You don't remember anything else?'

She shook her head.

'You found this on Friday morning – downstairs?'

'Yes.'

'Where?'

'By the drawing-room door.' She looked at Guy with curiosity. Her tear-reddened eyes betrayed that same slightly provocative, challenging interest which they had shown before. 'Why are you so interested in this? You said she wore it. How do you know that? I never saw her wearing it.'

He stooped and picked up the object by its broken chain, looked at it, both the back and the front. Then, surprising himself with his own boldness, he put out his hand and untied the top ribbon of her gown.

'Guy!' she exclaimed.

The garment loosened very easily. It eased an inch or so along the shoulder and revealed her white skin and the swelling of her bosom. He untied the next ribbon. Before the gown could slip lower she put her hands up to hold it.

'Guy, what are you doing?'

Then he gently lifted her hands away. The silk gown came right away from her shoulders and hung loosely down from her arms. Her bare bosom with the fine rosy nipples had an innocently sensuous look that aroused and awed him. It was proof, if any were needed, that she was a woman and lovelier than he had imagined. He held the little crucifix to the white skin of her chest, between her breasts. Her mouth opened, but she

194

seemed so astonished by what he had done that she did not say a word.

'She wore it here,' he said. 'I think it was the most precious of her possessions and I don't think she'd have given it to anyone. If it was lying on the floor, it must've been pulled off. Who pulled it off? I'd like to know that very much.'

Suddenly she drew the gown back across her bosom and turned sharply away from him. 'I'd like to know how *you* know, Guy. How do *you* know she wore it there?'

He resisted the impulse to tell her, much though he wanted to. It was not shyness or shame that made him hesitate, it was simply that he wanted to know something else.

'That perfume,' he said, 'who gave it to you?'

'Molly.'

'Molly!'

The exclamation made her turn round and look at him. He smiled.

'It belonged to Marie,' he said.

'It didn't!'

'Yes, it did. I know that for sure.'

'Guy, how do *you* know this? How do you know all these things about her?' She started doing up the bows, her eyelids fluttering. 'All I know is Molly gave me a little bottle of perfume. She said she'd found it. I had to break the seal on it, so I don't see how it could've belonged to her.'

'Probably it was left over from last year. When she was here. If you say Molly found it...'

'Yes, she found it in...'

They both knew then. If it had been found in the Captain's bedroom, it was further proof of her own

195

assertions. She looked up at him from under her brows, still engaged in retying the ribbons. He saw she had gone pale.

'It means she knows, doesn't it?'

He had not thought of that before, but now it seemed clear.

'You must ask her. Oh no, no, no ... please, Guy, no!'

Her hand was over her mouth in sudden horror. She had been taken in by Molly, he thought, by her father, perhaps even by Miles. She was wearing the perfume of the woman she hated. She had not realised as much as he had, but she had realised enough, he thought. The flimsy gown and his whole visit had been designed as a distraction, for her as well as for him. Perhaps she had wanted, he thought, to avert his attention from what he'd seen on the last visit, if it hadn't been for the accident of it falling on the floor, he might have been. Now he looked down at the little crucifix in his hand and he knew it was all the proof he needed.

'Guy, please, give it me!' she cried, reaching for it.

He grabbed his jacket from the back of the chair. 'I've got to find her,' he said.

He dashed out of the bedroom and on to the landing and began groping his way down the dark stairs.

14

The warm rain spun round him in the darkness as he slammed the front door behind him. He could see a faint light far down the High Street, beyond the church, but close by him, apart from one slit of light in Alto house, he could see only dim shapes of houses silhouetted against a grey sky. Leaves rustled busily just beside him and he remembered that this was a tall hedge. Beyond the rustling sounds was another noise, like animals moving. Then the door of Connaught House opened and he heard Elizabeth shouting:

'Molly, Molly, are you there?'

In that instant Guy was sure she would be coming out into the road. Nothing happened. He waited, thinking she would have to spend a few moments getting used to the darkness.

'Guy!'

Elizabeth's voice was shouting – uncertainly, he felt, even imploringly. Then again:

'Guy, please!'

And then there was a muffled sound, in which he thought he caught the word 'God!' Afterwards the front door banged again, by which time Guy had instinctively begun feeling his way along the hedge, running his hands through the leaves, and he heard nothing more. His eyes were growing accustomed to the night.

It was suddenly obvious to him why she had been shouting. It almost made him stop in his tracks. He was beyond the hedge by now and approaching the church. If it had not been for the thought of the gravestones, barely visible through the rain-filled air, he would have turned back. As it was, he knew exactly what he had to do. He began running along the cobbles through the semi-darkness, momentarily aided by a flash of lightning which lit up the whole High Street.

He ran the length of it. The alley leading to the Hoe and Turnip was lit by a lantern. In the room at the back there was also some kind of light and without even stopping to knock he unlatched the door and went in. Bazarov was sitting at the end of the table, his back against the peeling whitewashed wall, and he was talking vigorously to someone who looked very much like a pirate with a dirty woollen cap pulled over wiry black hair and a weatherbeaten bearded face. Guy recognised him from last year. He was the Joe Cockerell from whom Miles had hired a boat. The moment Guy entered, Bazarov stopped what he was saying, stood up and ostentatiously enfolded him in a dramatic embrace so that all breath was forced from his lungs for a moment, to which was added the greater embarrassment of being kissed on both cheeks.

'Guido, friend! You are stranger here! Why you no come sooner?'

Guy tried to explain through his gasps, but Joe Cockerell interrupted with:

'Well, sir, I'll be off 'ome now. An interestin' talk, sir. Like you says . . .' Already on his feet, he upended his mug and finished his beer.

'Remember what I say, Dzhoe,' said Bazarov, who now leaned across the table and wagged a finger. 'Co-operative work! You must all work in co-operative!'

'Yes, sir.'

'When all people work in co-operative, no more rich, no more poor. It will be freedom, Dzhoe!'

198

Joe Cockerell looked doubtful. 'Yes, sir, well, sir, I must thank you for attendin' to my 'and. 'Tis a lot better.' He raised his left hand and demonstrated the white cotton bandage. 'I'll come agin tomorrer.'

'Freedom from tyranny! We must have freedom from tyranny!'

It seemed that Zhenia's exhortations were a necessary part of his medical treatment and that any pretext, even that of Guy's arrival, could be used as a means of escape for his patients. Dressed as he was in the loose canvas garment which he wore for sorties to the shore, Bazarov had an austere, priest-like imperviousness about him. In the dim confinement of such a monkish cell, Guy was so struck by the likeness that it seemed only right for him to reveal that he was holding the little crucifix. He held it out and asked what name was engraved on the back.

Bazarov took it, turned it over, stooped down to the couple of candles burning in tin holders on the table and scrutinised it. Guy saw that his long hair had damp ends to it and he realised he must have only recently returned from the sea. The table itself was littered with clay beer mugs, a small bowl, scissors, jars and strips of cloth, all evidence of a primitive and makeshift doctor's consultancy. Bazarov straightened up, saying softly:

'Where you find it, Guido?'

His tone had changed. In place of his former brash manner he was now suddenly solemn, as if the feel of the crucifix as much as the name on it conveyed the need to treat it with the utmost care. The greenish eyes gazed piercingly at Guy; they seemed at first to be scolding him for having offered up for scrutiny so personal an object, but then it appeared more likely that they were simply saddened. Guy was reluctant to say anything about Connaught House in the presence of a stranger.

'It was given to me, Zhenia.'

Joe Cockerell said: 'Them's what you Russians wear, isn't it? A pretty thing. Well, sir, shall I pay tomorrer?'

'Pay?' In a preoccupied way Bazarov slowly reseated himself against the wall. 'No, no, Dzhoe, no need to pay. You come tomorrow. I must see your hand tomorrow.'

Effusively, if a little uneasily, Joe thanked the doctor and left the room with a clattering of boots on the stone floor. As soon as the door closed, Guy asked:

'Zhenia, is it?'

The latter nodded. 'It's her name on it, yes.' He handed the crucifix back.

'Don't you understand what it means?'

'It is religious object. Not important.'

'Not important!' Guy was speechless for several seconds. He stared at Bazarov while the latter lit a small cigar from one of the candles and stretched himself back against the wall lethargically. He completed his leisurely movement by placing his hands behind his head.

'If . . . *if* Marie went to Connaught House late on Thursday night,' Guy said, 'and was killed there, that would explain two things. The first thing is this crucifix. I know she wore it – here.' He pointed to his chest. 'I know she wouldn't let it go unless, well, unless she couldn't help it. It was very precious. Zhenia, you've got to believe me!'

Bazarov grinned, his eyes closed. 'I believe, Guido. But I'm tired, tired . . .' The blue smoke made fronds round his face.

'And the second thing is, it'd explain, wouldn't it, why you didn't find any seawater in Marie's lungs. Don't you see that?'

'I'm tired, Guido.'

'Supposing she was killed at Connaught House,' Guy went on, 'well, it'd mean you couldn't be guilty and

200

you said . . .'

'What?'

'You said you were. I know you couldn't be, but you blamed yourself, didn't you?'

It sounded petulant. Bazarov suddenly opened his eyes and took the cigar out of his mouth. His face had a stern, set expression which Guy interpreted as meaning not so much irritation as set purpose. In any case, it was intimidating.

'So,' he said, 'you tell me what happened.' He replaced the cigar and closed his eyes.

'I'm guessing they wanted to conceal Marie's body so they pull it, drag it, you know . . .'

As he spoke Guy knew he was making it all up. How could the Captain with his gout do anything like that, even with the help of the woman called Molly? The idea was nonsense. He felt he was making a complete fool of himself. There seemed to be no way of explaining how, if Marie had died at Connaught House, her body could have been found in one of the deep tidal pools below West Cliff. He stopped, bit his lip and wished he were somewhere else, anywhere save in the presence of the intimidating Bazarov. His suspicions about the woman called Molly appeared to be no more substantial than the blue cigar smoke.

'You know Molly Ford?' Bazarov suddenly asked. His eyes remained closed.

'Molly Ford's her name, is it? I know her, yes. She's the donkey woman. You see, I thought she might've used her donkeys . . .'

'She had foot infection,' was Bazarov's laconic comment. He now opened his eyes and yawned. 'I treated her. She is better. But she did it, Guido. You are right.'

At first Guy thought he had misheard.

201

'Right?'

'Now you have proof. Now I understand.'

'What?'

'Look, I show you my proof also.'

Bazarov stood up, stubbed out the cigar and, grinning broadly, placed an arm round Guy's shoulder.

'I will show you what she used.'

He swept Guy out of the room and into the alley, talking still as they went out into the warm thundery darkness and the light rain.

'I also ask myself, Guido, if Masha does not kill herself, how is she lying in pool? Is it very strong person? No. Is it by sea? No. So if it is by land somehow she reaches deep pool by herself, yes? No.'

The thunder sounded as if it were several rooms away and was no more than an indistinct background noise to the sound of their boots on the cobblestones and Bazarov's loud questions.

'So it is now I begin to understand. You have your proof and I show you my proof.'

They went hurriedly side by side towards St Catherine's church, past the stone wall of the graveyard, beneath the overhanging yew trees which sent down a steady shower of raindrops and beside the high thick hedge whose leaves rustled wetly. When the two tall adjacent silhouettes of Alto House and Connaught House loomed nearly opposite them, and just beyond a wide cobbled area where the coach horses were changed, Bazarov whispered:

'In here.'

He opened a small wicket gate. A low wooden structure was visible in the darkness. Noises of animals making sudden, anxious movements could be heard at the same instant as a shaft of light spread out from the interior and a woman's voice asked sharply:

'Who's there?'

It was Molly's voice, Guy realised.

'You are Molly Ford?' asked Bazarov.

'Ah, so it's you, Doctor. Who's that with you?'

At first sight of Guy and the tall figure of Bazarov, Molly shrank away. She held up a lantern which showed not only her face, but the faces of the four donkeys in their stalls and the saddles hung on the wooden walls and the gnarled wooden uprights supporting the straw roof. The far side was open to the field, a blackness into which silver raindrops now blew.

'Don't you frighten 'em,' she commanded. 'They're fearful o' the thunder!'

Clearly startled though she was, Molly's handsome face seemed darkly impassive in the poor light. Her eyes were narrowed and her lips slightly parted. She appeared as much defiant towards these strangers as she was protective towards the animals and was not prepared to allow anyone to intrude.

To Guy, on seeing her, it hardly seemed likely that she had planned and executed a callous killing as he had supposed. But an object caught his eye. Indeed, he could scarcely avoid seeing it. It was a rectangular wooden trough filled with hay and sacking and it stood in the centre of the wooden structure. What caught his attention was the fact that it had crude shafts attached to one end. Suddenly he knew exactly what could have happened.

'Zhenia, I see!' he exclaimed.

'So you see my proof, yes?' said Bazarov.

They both looked at Molly. She gave them peering glances as she held up the lantern with a crooked arm.

'We wanted to ask you about the donkeys,' Guy said. 'They obey you, don't they?'

'Yes. Of course.' She nodded, beginning to smile, and looked round at the faces of the donkeys. Gently patting one of them, she seemed to fall into a momentary daydream and the smile slowly vanished from her face. It had perhaps dawned on her that her visitors were not really interested in her donkeys at all. 'So what is it you want?'

'You know,' said Guy quite loudly, above the shifting noises of the donkeys and a rustling wind in the straw roof, 'you know about Marie Valence, don't you? You know she's dead?'

Whether she did not understand the name or had simply misheard him, she appeared to ignore his presence and his question entirely. Instead she leaned against the donkey's side and began whispering something. Bazarov spoke over this whispering, in a rather brusque and incongruous way which clearly disturbed the donkeys who shuffled about in alarm:

'We have proof, Molly Ford. We know what you do. You kill Masha and put her body in ... in ...' He kicked the trough with the hay and sacking in it. 'What is it, Guido? No, it is unimportant. I see you, Molly Ford, I see you. You bring hay ... hay, is it? ... yes, hay, you bring hay for animals in it, yes? I see you bringing hay for animals!'

Then Guy understood better still what could have happened. If she had been used to using this sledge for bringing fodder to the donkeys, she could easily have used it to carry Marie's body down to the shore. But he also realised that Molly Ford would not admit anything of the kind to the doctor, at least not so long as he used such a bullying tone. He peered round the donkey's flank to see exactly what she was doing. To his astonishment he saw she was smiling and muttering to herself. Seeing this, Guy held out the little crucifix towards her.

'This was hers. This was Marie's.'

He held the crucifix by the broken chain so that it was

204

in a direct line of vision between his eyes and hers. It was easy for him to tell what effect it had. Though she might never have seen it before, the shape of the crucifix evidently awed her.

'Miss Elizabeth found it last Friday. Marie wasn't drowned, you know. The doctor'll tell you that.'

Bazarov's deep voice said in agreement: 'It is true.'

'She was dead before she was put in that pool.' Guy licked his lips, still speaking loudly. 'I think she died where this crucifix was found. And it was found by the door of the drawing room.'

Molly began to look frightened. She ran her hands in a distracted way along the donkey's coat.

'I don't know nothing,' she whispered.

Guy sensed, though, that she felt trapped, but it was not an adult trapped so much as a child who would escape into fantasy. In a self-justifying, slightly plaintive tone she muttered:

'Can Jonquil here tell 'em, eh?'

Letting the hand holding the crucifix fall to his side, Guy thought it was probably only the donkey which might really know the truth. And the donkey would never speak. As for Molly, she had simply to say nothing at all and no one would ever know. Her supposed simplemindedness would be her protection. Marie's death would then remain forever a case of accidental drowning. Everyone would accept that as the most likely solution.

'I think someone hit Marie,' he whispered. 'That's what I think.' She turned her head half towards him, concentrating. 'Perhaps you or the Captain. And she was killed. And you had to hide what happened. And you dragged Marie along the floor and the chain broke.' He spoke with pauses between the whispers to see whether she was really listening and to test the sense of what he was saying to himself. 'And then you got one of these . . .' he pointed at the donkeys, whose strange, wise, elongated faces looked softly at him out of a warm darkness '. . . you got one of these and you . . .'

But he did not finish. She appeared transfixed by what he had been saying. Her eyes were no longer pinched into slits but almost completely open and staring. It had all been guesses on his part and he had never imagined she would react so seriously to his inventions. He began to feel frightened. She evidently believed him and her expression could not conceal the shock of her reaction. She leaned towards him with a fierce, accusing whisper:

''Ow d'you know? 'Ow d'you know?'

The questions were both taunts and admissions, challenges and avowals, as though she were talking to Guy and herself at the same time. Her eyes did not seem to focus on Guy's face. She stared into the air between them, to the point where the crucifix had been hanging. Her leaning face had a numb, beaten look. Suddenly she thrust out her hand:

'Let me see it!'

He let her have the crucifix. She turned it over slowly and awkwardly in her hand and Guy noticed she was shaking. Her boots made a brief scuffling movement in the straw underfoot. There was a slight ruffling of the straw over their heads as the wind blew smoothly over it. Otherwise her scrutiny of the crucifix was accompanied by silence, save for one sound that Guy could not at first interpret and when he did it came as a sharp shock. The rapid clicking sound which filled the immediate surrounding stillness came from the chattering of her teeth. She started shaking her head.

'N-n-n-no-o-o!'

* * *

206

In that instant there was a lightning flash followed almost at once by an explosion of thunder overhead. Molly's wailing cry was drowned in a violent clattering which in its turn was quickly augmented by the donkeys' wild uneven braying. The lantern went out and in the deafening blackness Guy was suddenly buffeted by some large object and thrown down into the wet straw. It took him a moment or so to realise that all four donkeys had broken out of their stalls. Molly began shrieking. This was followed by a sound of rapid hoofbeats out on the cobblestones.

In a daze Guy scrambled to his feet. A further flash of lightning showed him the entrance to the wooden structure and by the time the next thunderclap resounded he was through the wicket gate and saw all four animals heading for the steep lane. Molly had clutched one of them and was desperately clinging to it. She succeeded in swinging herself on to the animal's back and then she seemed to abandon herself to its frenzied pursuit of its companions. Guy dashed after her across the cobblestones.

The front door of Connaught House opened at that moment. Elizabeth was there in a coat and hat, holding a lantern. She shouted something he could not hear, then rushed down the steps calling out his name, but he hardly paused in his running. All he heard her say for certain was 'Get Mr Ellis!' by which time he was already busy with his own pursuit of rider and donkey into the dark tunnel-like slope of the lane to the esplanade, guided only by the pools of lantern light and feeble light from cottage windows. It was just sufficient for his plunging feet. He was jarred and shaken by his boots' striking against ruts and stones, but all the time his eyes were fixed on the fleeting shapes below him. The upcoming rush of the steep lane echoed with the distant clatter of hooves. At each footfall, though, that sound seemed to grow toy-like and miniature in the increasing noise of the approaching sea. He glimpsed a stone wall, heard a dog run yelping away and yet never for a moment doubted the strength in his legs and his ability to reach the bottom of the lane. It surprised him how soon he was there. Suddenly he saw rider and donkey clearly outlined by the lights of the Esplanade Hotel. The other animals had apparently raced towards the sand. He saw Molly slow up, or perhaps the donkey itself hesitated, for he found himself quite close. He rushed along the esplanade towards her.

'Give it me back!' he shouted.

To his astonishment a voice just behind him called out: 'Molly, stop!'

He saw Elizabeth running towards him. Molly, now firmly seated on the donkey, made an effort to control the animal, calling out, 'Jonquil, Jonquil, calm now, dear, calm now!' but the braying of her companions from the shore suddenly impelled her forward and the donkey raced with spurts of sand from her flying hooves down the slope between beached boats and bathing machines and huts and out of sight. A couple of men came out of the hotel to ask what the noise was all about.

'The donkeys've run away!' Elizabeth cried. 'They're scared by the thunder!'

Guy did not bother to argue with her or explain why he had run down the lane. For all he knew Molly had already thrown away the crucifix, his one piece of proof. That wasn't why he had felt the need to run. It was because he was now convinced of Molly's guilt. Her effort to deny his words was all the proof he needed.

'Oh, Guy, she'll be killed!' Elizabeth shouted.

He gave her one glance, saw her pretty, scared face and bright eyes shining in the rain and said:

'I know she did it, you know.'

She looked back, her mouth open, but said nothing. It seemed to be a silent acknowledgement that he was right. Immediately he turned and ran down the slope beyond the esplanade, following after Molly on the donkey and knowing now for certain she should not be allowed to escape.

The noise of the sea came up towards him like an approaching railway locomotive, in a ponderous, unstoppable, unceasing roar. Glimpsing the strange silhouette of a shape on a donkey against the white of the waves, he felt the sharp cooling wind directly off the sea slap him in the face and he heard the powerful resonance of the waves as they burst and crashed on the shingle. At which point as he ran, the soft sand offering suction to his feet like a toothless mouth, a slow-motion tedium overcame him, his effort of running seeming to be drowned beneath a dragging weight as tremendous as the sea's powerful outward undertow as it rolled sand and shingle together in the ebbing of each wave. The slowness accentuated each movement: the lifting of one leg after another proceeded by gradual, infinitely slow stages. He saw, in the intermittent whiteness of wave-crests and a frothy lacework on wavebacks, the shape of animal and rider partly submerged, entering, disappearing, reappearing, flashing darkly, vanishing, causing jets of spray momentarily out of the churning sea, shuttered instantly from him by the darkness. Equally he recognised, as if this were some delirium, like the unconnected bits of dream and reality which he had experienced in his illness, that he was no longer in control of himself, that everything he did was dictated by the inconstancy of the sea itself. His lungs pumped

209

and ached and he wrenched the exhausted muscles of his legs again and again in trying to increase the pace of his slow-motion progress. And all he could think was that Molly should not be allowed to escape.

Then to his horror he was in the sea. Water came up as high as his thighs and he found himself pulled under by the weight of it. A huge wave poured its full force over him and torrents of water washed past him. Shivering, his teeth chattering, he was just as suddenly released. He saw the lines upon lines of high waves making their way towards him, wearing their white epaulettes of foam. He sprang back, stood up and with the return of his determination and strength began to run, seeing the donkey again, though now riderless. Before he could be sure whether it was Jonquil he stumbled on Molly. She was clambering to her feet, as sodden as he was. He tried to grab her but she thrust him aside with a strength that astonished him and shrieked out 'Jonquil! Jonquil!' He glanced behind and saw that Elizabeth had followed with her lantern at some distance. She was not close enough to help and in any case Molly was already on her feet and running up the sand in the direction of the rocks, her voice wailing 'Jonqui-i-il' with a frantic, plaintive urgency. The donkey seemed at that point to be lost from sight in the greater darkness of the rocks below the Undercliff and even Molly's running figure, visible in silhouette against the sand's paleness, quickly merged with the rock shadow. Both were gone in an instant.

Guy stopped, thinking he would see them again because his eyes were now quite accustomed to the dark. There was much activity behind him as men's voices called to each other through the night air. They were rounding up the other animals which showed less determination than the runaway Jonquil. Guy assumed Molly was simply trying to do the same thing.

Suddenly breathless and hatless, Elizabeth ran up to him, the storm lantern casting a weird network of shadows on the sand and shingle.

'I can't see them,' he said.

'You've been . . . in the sea,' she gasped. 'You were running so fast . . . I couldn't . . . I couldn't keep up!'

'Where've they gone?' he asked as if she had not spoken.

She followed his eyes, breathing hard, and for several moments said nothing more. The line of tall rocks were a solid black shadow against the skyline, with a silver streak of light below them where the freshwater stream glimmered and momentary splinters and bud-bursts of pale ivory discernible above, where waves broke and shot up spray.

'The causeway,' she gasped out.

He opened his mouth to agree but suddenly much more than agreement was needed. He realised something else. Jonquil *had* spoken after all! The donkey had gone into the causeway, just as she must have done the night Marie had been killed! That was why Molly had tried so urgently to stop her! He instantly began running as hard as he could up the sandy shore, knowing where the crevice was just under the cliff itself, which led into the narrow causeway through the rocks. Elizabeth followed just behind him.

They splashed through the stream, the water rising up to his knees, but the lantern showed the hoofmarks and the signs of Molly's footsteps on the sand spits between the runnels and both sets of marks seemed to vanish into the sheer face of the dark rock at one point. It was only when Elizabeth held up the lantern that they saw the crevice.

'I'll go in,' he said.

'We'll both go.'

She looked at him solemnly and firmly as she spoke.

He knew they were both frightened but neither would admit it. The crevice was dark and echoing. As soon as they were in its cramped wet space they heard the magnified, growling noise of the sea a short way further along and Guy's shadow stretching ahead down the shaft of rock seemed to meet the vaster blackness of the sea's presence almost at once. It was like entering a tunnel scarcely wider than his shoulders but filled underfoot with pools and slimy surfaces on which he slipped and slithered. They went slowly down the uneven gradient, holding on to whatever they could find.

He thought at first he must have been wrong about the donkey entering such a place. Until he remembered that he and Bazarov had clambered up it with the medicine bottles after finding Marie's body. And then he heard the wailing voice of Molly echoing in distorted, plangent appeal above the huge noise of the sea. They could see nothing still, but he went on down the causeway, remembering that it opened out further down into a plateau of rocks and pools. At least that was what he remembered, except that as they came to it now both of them saw that the sea was bursting over the open area and there, dimly visible, were Molly already half submerged and the donkey apparently swimming with only its head and tall ears above water. As soon as the light of the lantern fanned out across the mass of churning waves the animal seemed to be attracted to it and scrambled in ungainly panic on to a shelf of adjacent rock and came charging at them. Elizabeth screamed as the donkey, slithering frantically and shedding gouts of water, knocked her to one side and then went rushing up the causeway in a flying mass of pebbles and splashes. It dashed the lantern from her hands and extinguished the light, leaving them in darkness. Guy held Elizabeth tight in that instant, straining his eyes to see Molly's shape against the heaving layers of incoming tide.

Then the sea rushed at them with its own much greater force. It rose to their waists and chests and almost swept them off their feet. Elizabeth cried out and the cry gave him strength to heave her towards the rocks out of the sea's reach. Helped by the returning rush of the tide, she managed to find a foothold while he found himself automatically swimming in panicky breaststroke in a frantic effort to stay afloat. Through the noise of water in his ears he heard a quite distinct scream for help, but the tide seemed to be sweeping him along and any second he felt he would be carried under or knocked unconscious by the force of waves breaking against the rocks. Then the scream was right next to him. He saw Molly's face awash with the sea and swathed in strands of hair. She was washed towards him and he grabbed her as if she had been driven into his arms. She made a faint-hearted effort to struggle free but it was no time before she simply let him carry her and surrendered to the vigour of his pumping legs and the bouncy, uprushing pressure of the waves which gave them buoyancy. It lasted only a moment. He caught sight of an arm reaching down and realised Molly's weight had been taken from him. Another weight then pressed down on him and he was tumbled about in the millrace of the tide.

He grabbed hold of seaweed, forlornly hoping it would give him a firm handhold. The water sank away from him momentarily. He shouted. Then the sea rushed against his face again and swept over him and darkened everything. He had not taken in enough breath and he told himself that next time he must not shout but simply breathe in. It took ages for the water to recede. But he held on and the next time his mouth rose above water just long enough for him to gulp in air before the tide came back and almost dislodged him and buried him again beneath its darkening, swirling weight. He knew he would never have the courage to leave go of the seaweed. It was the only thing in the world that kept him alive. Time and again, it seemed, he was raised up just enough to breathe in a lungful of air, to keep holding on, only to be submerged again.

His fingers began to give up. He could feel the sea's force pulling him away when suddenly he was lifted under the armpits and pulled free. He had no strength left to resist. Someone was holding him, that he knew for sure, and the tide was lifting them both and he was turned over on his back and being held by the head and he saw lights which were not stars directly above him and then hands reached down and seized his hands and he was being hauled up. But at that moment voices started shouting. They were shouting loudly near and far as he sank into unconsciousness. He understood nothing at all until much later he knew he was being carried up the causeway on a stretcher and there was a loud noise of metal-shod boots crunching on shingle.

15

Through one of those periodic strokes of good fortune which affect the English climate as if bearing witness to the hand of God in men's affairs, the weather changed. For a moment. A sunlight truly suited to the luxuriance of August poured down on Ventnor the next morning. The noisy tide of the previous night had smoothed the sand to the firmness and lustre of well-polished mahogany. Everything had a glitter to it. The gulls' cries were practically the only sound to fill Ventnor bay as the tide receded and the only activity from the calm morning sea was the bright-eyed sparkle of its blue surface.

For Mr Ellis, despite appearances, it was a morning of sadness. He had learned certain things from Master Seddenham which he would have preferred never to have known, since they concerned Connaught House and someone dear to him. He had his faint suspicions, of course, but now it seemed there was no doubt. It could no longer be considered a 'Russian business'. Now it had to be considered a very English and a very local matter and much closer to his own heart than he had imagined.

It was also a tragedy, of that he had no doubt. He had been summoned from attending the meeting of the Watch Committee in St Catherine's church rooms by the young Russian doctor. Bazarov had burst in with a story about the donkeys and the murder of the Russian lady, Miss Valence. The sergeant was fortunately in attendance, so Mr Ellis and his two assistants were deputed to look into the matter. On the doctor's insistence, they accompanied him to the shore where evidence of the misfortune over the donkeys was clear enough. All four of them were being rounded up and the word was that Molly Ford and Miss Fenton were somewhere in the rocks below the Undercliff. Led by the doctor, they hurried across the sand. Their lanterns soon showed an alarmed Miss Fenton running towards them. She cried out that the boy Guy Seddenham was near to drowning. The doctor raced ahead down the narrow causeway, stripped off his cloak and boots and plunged naked into the boiling sea – in a manner, Mr Ellis reflected, which could well have attracted the attention of the Misses Bosanquet, the two maiden ladies who had laid a complaint against him for such unseemly behaviour. But what might have caused offence to maiden ladies suddenly caused shock and bewilderment to all the anxious onlookers.

The boy was rescued. The doctor swam through the raging sea and brought him back to where the constable's two assistants grabbed hold of him and hauled him to safety. At which moment he seemed more dead than alive. But the rapidly rising tide thrust its way fiercely over the rocks and seemed to seize the naked swimmer in its grip and sweep him away from outstretched hands and virtually swamp him. They saw his head rise and an arm break the surface and then nothing was visible in the swirling millrace of waves and foam.

At first none of them had believed it. They had strained their eyes and shouted and fanned the yellow rays of the lanterns over the tidewashed rocks but there had been no sight or sound of the young doctor. For fifteen or twenty minutes they had waited, moving progressively back as the sea advanced, and it was only

216

when Mr Ellis announced that there was not much likelihood now, giving expression to a fear none of them wanted to utter, that they all retreated back up the causeway with the boy laid on a stretcher and Mr Ellis himself carrying the doctor's cloak and boots. The news spread quickly enough that the Russian doctor was feared drowned.

The reaction to the tragedy surprised Mr Ellis. He realised he had not been resident long enough in Ventnor to appreciate exactly how the local people would receive such news. They always behaved politely to visitors, but in their hearts they considered them to be intruders and the strange Russian doctor was no exception to this rule. True, he had helped some of the poorer families and even made friends with one of the fishermen, Joe Cockerell, and his two sons. Joe had put to sea with both boys at first light in search of any sign of the missing doctor, but they had found nothing. That was almost the sole expression of practical concern among the local people. The doctor had been foreign and eccentric and intimidating and no one had known him very well during his three weeks' residence. Save for Mr Ellis himself and the boy, Guy Seddenham. The doctor had no friends, it seemed, in the Russian colony, nor among the upper classes of Ventnor society. It was painfully clear to Mr Ellis that the doctor had been a stranger among them and it was as a stranger that he would be mourned.

'You could have done no more!' Aunt Emily exclaimed to Guy as they stood in the bright morning sunlight. 'You rescued that poor woman and it was a most courageous act.'

This was part of the story which had spread quickly through Ventnor. Mrs Emily Whitehouse was not one to discourage it. Her pride in Guy was unshakable. He'd been brought back to Belinda House soaked and exhausted. Though his concern for the doctor's whereabouts was understandable, his outburst of grief on being brought home seemed exaggerated. 'Poor boy, it is *not* your fault,' she insisted. 'You cannot blame yourself.' What mattered was that the woman called Molly had been rescued – she was 'the donkey woman,' so the twins subsequently told her – and Guy was safe. With their father due to return so soon, Aunt Emily was especially anxious that Guy and the twins should be in the best of health for his arrival. She was also anxious that Guy should have a new set of clothes. This accounted for the fact that they had just paid a visit to the tailor in the High Street after negotiating the money order which had arrived that morning. But Guy's low spirits had not been altered by this treat and she tried another tack, realising he had been brooding on the death of his Russian friend.

'I think we have been so fortunate to have so distinguished a man as an acquaintance, don't you?' She had her parasol open and gave it the merest hint of an excited twirl. 'I'd been thinking we might move to the Esplanade Hotel now the manager tells me he has a vacancy, but I don't see the need now. With Mr Tourgueneff at Belinda House, why should we go to the Esplanade Hotel? He is so entertaining. I have entirely revised my opinion of the Russians. They are a most civilised and understanding people.' She dabbed a handkerchief to her temples – not that it was hot, strictly speaking, but the sunlight suggested heat and it was August and there were matters to be contemplated. 'Read the telegram again, Guy dear.'

This was the second telegram from his father and it had arrived shortly before they left Belinda House. They had been to the Esplanade Hotel to ensure that accommodation could be made available for Thomas Seddenham, Esquire.

'ARRIVING SUNDAY AFTERNOON,' Guy read. 'MOST URGENTLY REQUIRE TWO ROOMS. FONDEST LOVE. TOM.'

'He does not say when exactly, does he?' Aunt Emily complained. 'That's so like him.' She paused and looked hesitantly at her nephew. 'Guy dear, how much do you think we ought to tell him about, er, you know – about what happened last night?'

Guy said nothing immediately. The numbness of his sense of shock remained so complete that he could hardly believe he was standing in bright sunlight and looking through misty eyes at the sparkling sand and sea. All he had been able to do since recovering consciousness was blame himself. He blamed himself for causing all the events of the previous twenty-four hours and most of all for the death of his friend. Still, he had slept very soundly despite blaming himself and there was some comfort to be gained from the thought that no one else seemed ready to blame him. And at the very back of his mind he was even ready to believe that he might have committed an act of heroism in rescuing Molly, though it had been quite unintentional. Yet he had lost his one piece of proof, Marie's small wooden crucifix, and to that extent he had failed. The rest, including his father's return, was overwhelmed by his general feeling of desolation.

'No,' he murmured.

'It is entirely as you wish, Guy dear. I was wondering . . .'

Guy waited for his aunt to complete her thought aloud, but she was distracted by the loud crying of a gull. A sea breeze had sprung up and shook her parasol.

'Where are they?'

'The twins? Down there.'

'Of course. My eyesight plays such tricks . . .'

They were doing no more than they usually did when they came across lengths of seaweed on wet sand. The shore was streaked with them after the previous tide. On this occasion a small dog had joined the twins' fun. Guy was ordered to see that they behaved less exuberantly. Aunt Emily herself meanwhile returned in a stately way to Belinda House, feeling thankful that she had been out while there was still some promise of sunshine.

'Ah, how pleasant it is out!' she cried with an exaggerated show of enthusiasm, meeting Turgenev in the hallway of Belinda House. 'I see that you are ready to go out. It's been such a pleasant morning.'

The tall man bowed to her and explained that he hoped a stroll in the fresh sea air would help to get rid of a cold. Aunt Emily doubted this very much.

'Bed is the only place for a cold,' she said emphatically and was about to explain the fatal dangers of neglecting a cold when Turgenev smiled in his sweet way, briefly wiped his nose with a large white handkerchief which disappeared afterwards up his sleeve with a flourish and said:

'I have a request, Mrs Whitehouse. On this map I see this place. How do you pronounce the name?'

'That's Bournemouth.'

The two of them studied the map of the Isle of Wight and the coastline of Hampshire which had been fixed to the wall next to the hatstand. Mrs Rees, seeing them, also approached.

'Not Bunmouss?'

'No, Bourne-, Bourne-mouth.' Aunt Emily articulated the name as clearly as she could.

'Bonmuss?'

'No, B-o-u-rne-mouth.'

'What is it, Mrs Whitehouse?'

'I am trying to explain how the name Bournemouth is pronounced, Mrs Rees. It is a very hard word for foreigners to master.'

'Oh, Bowen-, Bowen-mouth, is it?' came the sing-song voice. 'Bowenmouth is how we call it.'

'I think it must be closer to Bo-urne-, Bo-urne-mouth,' Aunt Emily insisted.

'Bornmouse?'

'No, no, Bowenmouth. Th-th-th. That's how it should be.'

'I think closer to Bo-u-rne-mouth.'

'Bunmoss?'

'No, Bo-wen-mouth. See?'

'Bonemouf?'

'Bournemouth.'

'Bjornmouse?'

'That's it! That's it!'

Mrs Rees applauded.

'Bjornmouse,' Turgenev repeated to himself doubt-fully.

'I am sure you will be able to find it,' said Aunt Emily, more out of a practical concern for his reaching it than out of a deep conviction that his pronunciation would guarantee such an outcome.

'I am most grateful,' he said, bowing. 'I hope to visit it on Monday.'

He was assured by Mrs Rees that he could catch a boat. When she had gone off about her business in Belinda House, Aunt Emily, feeling a little hot and bothered by the effort of English-language instruction, was ready to go up to her room for a rest, but Turgenev detained her for one further question. He asked where her nephew was.

'Guy?' she responded in surprise. 'Oh, he's out on the

221

sand watching over Jane and Edwina.'

'I wish to have a word with him. Thank you very much.'

They parted smilingly. Turgenev walked out on to the esplanade, into the bright sunshine and the gulls' cries, and he soon saw what he was looking for. The two little girls were making their own names out of lengths of seaweed. The letters J and A and N were easily visible on one clear stretch of sand and an E and a D elsewhere, but a little black-and-white dog – a terrier, Turgenev thought – was enjoying pulling bits off a W, running about with a length of pale-green seaweed hanging from its mouth and being chased by an infuriated Edwina. Guy had seated himself on a rock and Turgenev approached him there.

'I am interested in knowing,' he began, looking into the boy's dark brown eyes upturned towards him, 'if it is true about what happened last night.'

Guy stood up. 'Last night, sir?'

Turgenev explained briefly what he knew about the young doctor's disappearance, how he had apparently been swept away by the tide after rescuing Guy. 'Is it true?'

Guy nodded. 'It was all my fault, sir. He shouldn't have drowned, not for my sake.'

But as he said it he suddenly felt relieved of the weight of self-blame. The large bearded face was leaning towards him, the eyes pouched in warm, compassionate friendliness.

'How was it your fault?'

'I was sure Marie hadn't died by drowning. I was sure she'd been put in the pool where we found her. But now ...' Guy felt an ache in his throat and looked away. 'It doesn't matter any more.' Suddenly he added: 'He loved

222

the sea, sir. He wasn't a revolutionary. He was a scientist and discovered sea anemones – down there, in the rock pools. Mr Holdsworth came from Torquay about it.'

Guy had spoken a trifle too insistently, as though trying to make an impression. He thought he would never be understood. Turgenev smiled.

'I am glad you think so well of him. You will always remember him, will you?'

'Always.'

Their conversation was interrupted by the barking of the little black-and-white terrier. It had seized some more seaweed and been chased away and then returned and was now being chased away a second time. Guy called to the twins but they had run off along the sand.

'Such pretty girls!' Turgenev exclaimed.

Guy stared at the bright sea. A dazzle more brilliant than the light-blue sparkle filled his eyes. He felt the rims of his eyes pricked by tears.

'I will remember him because he loved truth. He found out that Marie hadn't drowned, he found out about her baby. No one will believe it now, of course.' Guy swallowed quickly. 'We had some proof, you see. Or I thought it was proof. Zhenia believed me . . .'

'Zhenia?'

'The doctor, sir. Dr Bazarov.'

'Ah!'

'He believed me. Oh, you wouldn't understand, sir!'

'Proof?' asked Turgenev quietly.

Guy realised he had been understood. He also realised how little value words had in themselves. They were swallowed up by all the millions of succeeding words spoken by people to hide the truths of the past, like the successive six-inch-high waves that danced up the sand, broke into lines of creamy foam, receded and surrendered the damp sand to the next upcoming line of waves.

'It was something she wore. A Russian crucifix. We thought it was proof, sir.'

Turgenev raised his eyes from scrutiny of Guy's face and looked out to sea. An expression of deeply reflective sadness dwelt on his features. As strands of silver hair were blown across his forehead he seemed to Guy to have acquired the impermeable look of some object from nature, a fretted rock, a giant stone facing violent seas. There was a pause and then Turgenev asked:

'You loved her?'

It was not the question, nor the accent, but the assumption of deep and sensitive understanding that pierced his heart. He felt he had been looked into and explored by the tender scalpel of those words.

'Yes.'

'Then that is proof.'

Turgenev said it simply, a smile on his lips. He bowed. Guy was aware suddenly that he had been allowed the privilege of the emotion. For love was an inestimable privilege, granted only sparingly. It came often with mysterious swiftness and in inexplicable ways. It had been granted to him, as it were, by the grace of those words and he knew then, with a painful, wounding certainty, that he would love Marie as he had loved his mother and the two memories would never leave him for the rest of his life.

Turgenev turned away from him and walked slowly along the sand. The light wind brought feathery white tips to the crests of the waves. Cloud shadow passed slowly over the sea's surface and the shore and the roofs of the town. In the High Street Constable Ellis, smart in his tight, belted uniform with buttons gleaming, walked thoughtfully in the direction of Belgrave Road. He politely saluted townspeople, patted the heads of children, exchanged a few words with tradesmen and exuded a confident, avuncular goodwill that his apple-red cheeks and sparkling eyes amply justified. He was possessed by a modest but assured conviction that justice was on his side, even if it were not always seen to be done exactly in accord with his wishes. This sunny morning he felt very strongly that no one would be able to hide from its ubiquitous eye.

In feeling this, he included himself. He recognised that his half-sister's perilous foray into the area of rocks after the crazed donkey had been provoked by a guilty conscience. If he were to believe what he had since learned by questioning the boy, Guy Seddenham, and Miss Elizabeth Fenton, then he knew the reasons for that guilty conscience. He also knew what, of course, he had always sought to conceal: that the woman known as 'Batty Molly' was his half-sister, for whose sake he had taken the Queen's shilling and fought in the Crimea and been wounded and captured. But she, meanwhile, had contracted a wretched marriage with a butcher in Southampton who had forced her to hump carcasses in the slaughterhouse and physically maltreated her. So much so that he had done irreparable harm to her hearing with his continuous cuffings and blows. Until she had finally rounded on him and driven a butcher's knife into his stomach and run away to Ventnor in her ragged, reeking clothes and sought out her half-brother as she had always told herself she never would. And he had welcomed her and given her the first comfort she had known from a man in all the five years of her marriage.

Mr Ellis simply could not believe Molly was capable of committing murder, whether her victim was her husband (who had not died) or Marie Valence (who apparently had not drowned). When he had accompanied her back to Connaught House hysterically sobbing and unable to give a coherent account of what had happened, he concluded she knew something but was so fearful of the past that she dared not speak of it. No more than he dared speak about the relationship between them. Sooner or later, perhaps, like the bright morning sunshine, justice would seek them all out and their secrets would be revealed. At the very moment of recognising this, Mr Ellis felt a sudden and grateful release. He realised he had very little to conceal and nothing to be ashamed of. It was all a matter of reputations – and what did reputations matter in the end, he thought, when there were so many more precious things in life?

Meanwhile, at Connaught House, suspicions had overnight become awful truths. When Molly was brought back in a hysterical, sodden condition and at once put to bed, it was to Elizabeth that she eventually confessed all, not to Mr Ellis. He had only been told what Elizabeth saw fit to tell him. It was later that Elizabeth had confronted her father, on his return from the meeting of the Watch Committee. Her accusations came as a profound shock to him. At first he tried to deny them, but eventually the directness of her blue accusing eyes made him confess. All night he had sat in his 'cabin' drinking. It was into this atmosphere of readiness to make full confession that the constable stepped when the door of Connaught House was opened to him by a tearful Dora.

He took off his peaked cap and tucked it under his arm. He knew exactly where he was expected to go. The museum-like drawing room was as tidy and lifeless as ever. He passed through it and approached the double

226

doors leading to the Captain's 'cabin'. One of the doors was ajar. He gently pushed it open and saw the Captain slumped in his chair behind the desk. His face was pale, with grey cheeks that darkened along the jaw-line. His eyes were red-rimmed and moist. He sat with one leg stiffly extended, which caused him to appear slumped, though his left hand was firmly gripped round the knob of an upright walking stick. It alone gave his posture less an appearance of weakness and acquiescence as of rigid and somewhat despairing dignity. The tightness of the gripping fingers suggested a prolonged effort of will.

'Ah, Mr Ellis! Forgive me for not getting up. As you can see, I've . . .'

His right hand indicated the unstoppered decanter and the glass on his desk. The smoke-laden air of the room and the stale port-wine smell told their own story. It was the set line of his mouth which told most. It was set in the rictus of a self-conscious, half-embarrassed, half-inebriated smile. The two men looked directly and unswervingly into each other's eyes.

'I have to ask you some questions, sir,' said Mr Ellis, 'about the circumstances surrounding the death of Miss Marie Valence. May I sit down?'

A hand-wave directed him to the usual chair. The notebook appeared. Mr Ellis often felt a natural hostility towards his superior, but he had learned in the course of the past year that Captain Fenton had a shrewdness of insight into human affairs which a subordinate could deeply appreciate.

'Yes,' said the Captain slowly, breathing in sharply through his nostrils, 'I'd expected this. I knew you'd have to question me. You will have to understand that if I'd not been so affected by . . .' Here his hand shook, in an indefinite way, towards the objects on his desk and his eyes rose to the portrait of his late wife above the mantelpiece. He breathed in and out again heavily. 'I was at sea more than twenty years, you know, and I learned I couldn't do without the solace and joy of female company. I had a loving wife, that is true, but I needed more than that. It was a very shaming thing . . .'

'Yes, sir.'

'So don't ask me questions. Just let me speak.'

It was the gathering defiance in the Captain's voice, the vocal recognition that the substance of the confession mattered more than the propriety of it, that impressed and silenced his listener. The voice was not speaking exactly to Mr Ellis, in any case, but more in the direction of the window and the sunlit vista of Ventnor Bay, with a hoarse, unoiled rasping.

'The bottle, Mr Ellis, has its own solace and joy. It suppressed my shame, pickled it, don't you know. Lately it's brought something else – unconsciousness is one way of describing it, I suppose. Stupor, bestial stupor, that's what it was.' A heavy sigh. The Captain's hand, shaking a little, reached out for the wineglass. 'Then my wife died. I looked for comfort and I found it first in the young lady whose name you've just mentioned. But it was a short-lived, unworthy comfort. That was a year ago.' He turned the stem of the glass slowly between forefinger and thumb, watching the ruby liquid quiver within its upturned translucent cone of fine crystal. 'I then had a stroke of good fortune which literally transformed my life. I think you know what I mean.'

He did not raise his eyes. He contemplated the redness of the wine and its reflection, a curious blushing sparkle on the bright surface of the silver salver.

'I am not ashamed to admit to you that I love the woman called Molly Ford. I love her dearly, with all my heart. I cherish her, despite all her strangeness. I would marry her if only . . .' He looked up solemnly. 'I have a certain social position, you know. Yet after what she's done for me . . .'

There ensued a silence which Mr Ellis was wise enough not to interrupt. The bells of St Catherine's began ringing peal upon peal. The resonant, blunt clouds of sound shaded the background silence. When he began speaking again through the distant noise, the Captain's rasping voice sounded more intimate and confiding.

'I will tell you what happened. I am in duty bound to.' He drank and put down the glass. 'Miss Valence came here a week ago asking for money. My daughter wouldn't hear of it and she left. I don't think my daughter had any clear idea at that time what had happened last year – between Miss Valence . . .' Several sharp taps came from the upright walking stick. 'I was inebriated, Mr Ellis, that is all I can say in my own defence. I was near enough in a stupor. Well, she came back after dark the same day. She was shown in here and she sat where you're sitting now. She told me she was with child and needed money badly. That was her story.' Here the Captain paused and pursed his lips tightly. His eyes strayed to a point equidistant between the window and Mr Ellis. 'I didn't believe it. I knew she was here in Ventnor as a companion to the Russian Count. Oh, she admitted that! But she talked about the need to be free, the need for . . . ah, yes, I remember, *la liberation,* the emancipation of women, of the Russian serfs . . . The long and the short of it was she wanted money. If I didn't let her have money she'd denounce me, she'd blackmail me. After all, hadn't we been lovers? she said. And at that I lost my temper! I worked myself into a rage, a blind rage . . .'

Instead of continuing on such a high note, the Captain's voice died suddenly. The recollection of what had followed evidently gave him a shock. There was quite a long pause.

'The boy, Guy Seddenham,' interposed Mr Ellis, 'mentioned a crucifix. . . .'

At the mention of this the Captain's expression tautened and his eyes travelled slowly towards the constable's face. Without looking down, without so much as blinking his eyes, his right hand gently drew open the desk drawer, felt for something and then lifted from it a small silver chain. There dangled at the end a small wooden crucifix. The Captain held it up.

'You are referring to this, Mr Ellis?'

The constable had honestly not supposed that the 'proof', as the boy had called it, would ever be offered to him so readily. He had nothing save the boy's description of it on which to base his identification of it, but the slanted crosspiece on the stave was sufficiently unusual to make the object fit. The constable also recognised why the boy had been reluctant to describe his 'proof' when he had first mentioned it. The crucifix appeared so small and intimate an object, even with a certain crudeness in the carving, which left the impression that it would hardly be worn outside clothing. As it swung in the air he could see letters carved on the back.

'Yes, sir.'

The Captain let it drop on the surface of the desk where his hand clenched itself round it and covered it entirely from view, except for a few links of the little silver chain.

'You will know as well as I do that this means nothing. You will bear witness that I've shown it to you. There has been no attempt to conceal it.'

Mr Ellis did not respond to these remarks. His only

230

sure intuition was that he had to allow the Captain to speak at his own pace and on his own terms. If the crucifix was 'proof', then it would be worth nothing without the Captain's testimony and that could only be obtained by allowing him to give it freely.

'I find it hard to remember,' said the Captain. 'I was in a rage, that I do know. And then she did something unexpected. She unbuttoned the front of her dress and held this out to me and asked me never to forget her, saying she didn't want me to be angry with her, reminding me we'd been more than friends. . . .' The walking stick gave several sharp, emphatic taps. 'I lost my balance in that instant, Mr Ellis, believe it or not as you wish, and . . . and I tried to grab hold of it, because you see, it reminded me of my shame. I did grab it and I pulled. The chain broke so easily it might've been the tiniest thread and . . . and I over-balanced against her, both trying to steady myself and to thrust her from me, and I fell, I fell heavily, wrenching my left leg. But as I did so I must've pushed her so hard she struck her head against some marble projection on that fireplace behind you. Because I remember seeing her eyes looking up at me. And that's all I can remember. My leg gave under my weight and I fell . . .'

For some reason the bells ceased their pealing at almost the same instant. In the pause Mr Ellis was attracted by another very slight sound. He had never noticed it before. It was the quiet but busy ticking of a brass carriage clock on the mantelpiece, just below the portrait of the late Amabel Fenton. The very smallness and ordinariness of this regular ticking made him aware of a similar smallness and ordinariness in the Captain's account of what had happened during Marie Valence's last visit.

'You will appreciate it was dark. The oil lamp on the

231

sideboard was the sole light. I'd done something of which I wasn't fully conscious at the time. It was only last night as I sat here that I began to put it all together piece by piece in my memory and even now I'm not sure. Can you understand that, Mr Ellis?' But no reply was expected or given and the Captain went slowly on. 'Molly'd come in, hearing my raging, and she'd seen it all happen. She knew of course about Miss Valence and myself. As I've now discovered, she thought I'd killed her. Perhaps with this.' He tapped the walking stick again. 'All I can recall clearly is gaining consciousness and finding Marie gone. I assumed she'd left of her own accord. What I didn't know, and only learned last night after Molly'd told my daughter, was that she'd dragged Marie's body into the hall and had then, by some means of her own devising, carried the body out of the house and placed it in that sledge contraption and taken it down to the rocks.' The Captain then heaved a deep sigh. 'She did it all for me, you know. She did it out of love. How many crimes are committed in the name of love, Mr Ellis, eh?'

The constable was prepared to be patient so long as the Captain continued with his confession, but such philosophical questions were not to his taste; and he said so. For the first time since he had begun speaking the Captain smiled at this reminder of his duty.

'You are quite right, I must keep to the point.' Here he banged his clenched right hand lightly on the surface of the desk. 'When I last saw it, she had it on,' he said in a soft, wistful voice.

Mr Ellis was deeply puzzled. 'What are you referring to, sir?'

'She told me she wore it in memory of her parents. It was the most precious of all her possessions. Only her lovers were permitted to know of its existence. Or

232

perhaps I should say ...' the Captain stopped and directed intent, thoughtful eyes at the constable '... perhaps I should say only those who sinned with her were granted that privilege.'

To Mr Ellis these words provoked an uncomfortable question about the boy who was the source of his information. How could he possibly have known *that much* about the so-called 'proof' now lying in the Captain's open palm?

'I see, sir, what you're referring to, but ...'

The Captain raised an eyebrow. 'I'm referring to sin, Constable. A sin against the Holy Ghost. My sin and Molly's sin.' He was shaking his head in bewilderment. 'It was the cause of her guilty conscience, wasn't it? If she hadn't been shown it by the boy, would she have told you what she'd done? Would she have told anyone? She tried to conceal a death, didn't she? If my daughter Elizabeth hadn't found it lying about the next day and taken it to her room, suspecting something, you know, but not knowing exactly what, and if she hadn't found it again out on the cobblestones last night where Molly'd flung it, would I be any the wiser, or would you?'

And he held up the little wooden crucifix. It dangled in the air, the silver chain glinting.

'You take it, Mr Ellis,' he said quietly, 'because it must be on your conscience as well, I think.'

At that moment the constable knew, from the look in the Captain's eyes, that his relationship with Molly, his half-sister, was no longer a secret. The dryness of his lips as he opened his mouth to speak told him that much; Mr Ellis moistened them a little with his tongue.

'You mean?'

'Molly told my daughter that she is related to you, that you'd insisted she keep it a secret. Surely that's on your conscience, isn't it?' There was no recrimination in the Captain's words, only weariness. 'It seems she thought she'd killed her husband. And I didn't even know she'd been married! Did you know that?'

Mr Ellis nodded. He recognised that the Captain, knowing what he knew now, need never have confessed. He could have used this secret knowledge to ensure that the constable never knew anything. Marie Valence's death would then have been no more than an accidental drowning and no autopsy evidence would ever have proved otherwise.

'I'd always wondered why she came here. I'd supposed that such happiness had come to me by chance. But I know better now, don't I? I know you didn't want her to tell me. It would've been to your discredit and to mine, wouldn't it? You preferred it to remain secret. So what about all the things I've just told you?'

The full burden of dispensing justice now fell on Mr Ellis. He stared back at the little crucifix dangling from the Captain's hand and knew in that instant the true extent of his cowardice.

'I think, sir, it would be best if nothing were said at all.'

They were not the words of a coward, but of someone well-versed in the compromises of life. The Captain's expression did not change. He did no more than move his outstretched hand a little further across the desk, dangling the crucifix close to the constable's ample chest.

'Take it, Mr Ellis. It has done its work here.'

16

It was Sunday. The two weeks spent in Ventnor, Turgenev reflected, had shown him, as if the teeming rain and high winds were an orchestration of his thoughts, that human efforts to change the world were mostly vain endeavours undertaken in the name of vain ideals. His initiative for a society to spread literacy and primary education in his own country had been accompanied by a growing sense of its futility. Even if he obtained official approval for it (unlikely enough, as he well knew), he would be in danger of compromising himself and his own generation of the intelligentsia by appearing not only to co-operate with, but also to serve, the Russian government. What would his free and independent voice as a writer be worth then? He would be confined to the role of government ideologue and apologist for all the caprices of those in power. May that day never come for Russian literature! If Russian literature should ever lose its free and independent spirit, in what circles of hell would Russian writers then be forced to live out their futile and tormented lives?

The raindrops running down the outside of the window were reminders, not metaphors. Tears though they might seem to be, they were chiefly reminders of the last two rainy weeks in this quiet seaside place. Here, he reflected, they had been able to discuss the freedom of Russia without constraint or fear, yet the weather had celebrated not their vain hopes but the dismal facts of two certain deaths and another almost a certainty. When he looked out on the grey, featureless sea on this grey, top-hatted Sunday, he was over-whelmed by a sense that what the future needed was some dark, wild, huge figure, seemingly sprung from the earth, full of strength and anger and honesty. When he thought of that, he found himself inadvertently considering the fate of the young Russian doctor who had apparently been drowned. What was his name? Ah, yes, Bazarov!

Annenkov's voice interrupted him. 'You never told me what that English policeman wanted yesterday.'

Turgenev put down his knife and wiped his mouth with his napkin. They were breakfasting together in Annenkov's room overlooking the esplanade.

'A very extraordinary thing, when I come to think of it. Yet it is typical and rather touching. You didn't meet her, of course.'

Such oblique, somewhat coquettish references to examples or persons were a feature of Turgenev's conversation when he did not like to be taxed directly on a subject. Annenkov recognised the symptoms and yet also knew enough to realise that a certain touchiness might be appropriate.

'Oh, it's a pity it happened!' At which Turgenev glanced up, faintly surprised at his friend's exclamation. 'Yes,' said Annenkov, 'a great pity! Our national reputation's suffered in the past week – in a local sense, I mean. We can be thankful Rostopchine made no fuss. Though I was genuinely sorry about his manservant.'

The manservant referred to was, of course, Fedya, whose body had been sent back to Russia in a sealed casket paid for by money raised among leading members of the Russian colony. The cause of his death had not been enquired into very closely.

'Ah, but you're wrong!'

The exclamation was this time from Turgenev. He

236

crumpled the starched napkin in his large hand.

'Well, tell me then.'

'The English policeman informed me,' said Turgenev, and in saying it he gave a slight shrug of his shoulders, 'pressing me to treat it as confidential, you understand.' He spread his hands. 'Who am I to disobey the full force of English law? So I warn you, my dear friend, if he hears you telling anyone else, Queen Victoria herself will be displeased.'

'I understand she is not often amused.'

'After so many confinements would you still be amused? No, then let me defy the full force of English law. . . . The English policeman informed me that Mademoiselle Valence's death had been conclusively explained. It turns out it was an "English" matter.'

'Typical and rather touching – weren't they your words?'

'Ah!'

The brown tea, for which he had never acquired a real taste, sent up wisps of steam from the large round breakfast cup. Turgenev stirred in some sugar but added no milk. It was apparently unheard of to take lemon with your tea in Ventnor. He raised the steaming cup and tasted it.

'I was referring to an intimate matter, you see. It turns out that Marie, who spoke in the name of our younger "scientific" generation, always wore an Orthodox crucifix.' He took several further sips of the hot tea, blinking a little at his friend opposite. 'That I found touching. Yet it's also rather typical, don't you think? The belief in science is much the same as religious belief. So she wore this crucifix, though she pretended to the world at large that she was one of our emancipated, free-thinking young women.' He lowered the cup into its saucer. 'Marie had innocence and charm. Love for

237

her had the same innocence, I suspect. She could make people love her very easily. Our hearts are perhaps too cold to understand that fully.' Then he wiped his mouth. His voice grew sterner. 'That much I learned from the crucifix itself. A poor wooden thing carved by a peasant, it had been made lovingly and devoutly. Only someone truly innocent of heart could treasure it for all its imperfections. The English policeman brought it to me. He wanted confirmation that it was her name carved on the back. I told him it was.'

'So where is it now?'

'He took it away with him.'

Their conversation passed on to other topics. They talked of their planned visit to the place with the unpronounceable name – Bournemouth, to be exact. They also remarked on the disappearance of the young Russian doctor.

'Here,' said Annenkov a little bellicosely, 'I entirely fail to understand you when you say you can't detect any ferocious, sickly arrogance in our new generation of nihilists. You seem inclined to endow them with a Plutarchian dignity. I simply can't see it!'

Turgenev laughed. What he enjoyed about his friend was the straightforwardness of his approach to life. Annenkov's standards were high and good and sober. Always so enthusiastic to taste novelty, he usually disliked its piquancy and hardly ever swallowed it whole.

'I have discovered one or two things about him,' said Turgenev. 'For instance, it is true he's been engaged in some original scientific research.'

'Then he is not a true Russian nihilist!'

'In which I believe you are entirely correct. He has made certain discoveries which impressed a local expert. He is reputed to have had a microscope and samples in bowls and correct documentation – in a word, a scientist. So you see,' and Turgenev extended his arms across the table in an expansive gesture suggesting magnanimity and approval, 'I believe he's started with the ABC of his subject. He's started from the beginning, whereas we've grandly and presumptuously assumed that our programme for primary education will receive the rapturous applause of the government and the people as soon as it's unveiled. I believe that what our people want is precisely his science. In a scientific age it is men like him who are needed, men who are full of strength and anger and honesty. We, you and I, are back numbers, you know.'

Annenkov frowned. 'Don't underrate yourself!' he declared. 'In a hundred years' time, who knows? Will they remember you or Chernyshevsky?'

But this question received no answer, for at that instant there was a tap on the door. It was Mrs Rees with a telegram. She apologised profusely in her high Welsh sing-song for what may have seemed a delay in delivering the orange envelope to their room. Turgenev tore it open.

SEREZ-VOUS ENCORE ANGLETERRE – VIENDRAI SAMEDI. SINE SENE VIENDRAI APES NEGONSTEEZ VUE. M.A.

'From Maria Alexandrovna at last!' shouted Turgenev. 'And in Chinese!' He handed the telegram to his friend. 'If you can decipher it . . .'

The SINE SENE VIENDRAI APES NEGON-STEEZ VUE proved to be beyond them. That afternoon they summoned to their aid the only supposed expert in the Russian colony (who at least knew something about early Christian art, if not about hieroglyphics), Alexis von Fricken, and after much further puzzling and debate they recognised that the

239

words should have read: SI NE SEREZ, VIENDRAI APRES – REPONDEZ MOI, or so Turgenev supposed in the letter he wrote to Maria Alexandrovna the next day before leaving for Bournemouth. The sad fact was, he admitted in the same letter, that her absence now remained beyond doubt. His holiday in Ventnor was, in any case, almost at an end.

It seemed to Guy that the time had finally come when they would be a family again. The twins, himself and his father, as one family, would no longer be dependent on the charity of Uncle Charles Augustus or the fond but sometimes irksome protection of Aunt Emily. His excitement at the thought of his father's arrival in Ventnor defied even the renewed rain and wind of the grey Sunday morning. It even survived the subdued, devotional atmosphere at the breakfast table. In the morning they all went to St Catherine's. Elizabeth was in the congregation, but not her father or Molly. She was accompanied by Susan Hodgson. Elizabeth's blue, clear-eyed look had a sharp and vulnerable brilliance against the white of her face. Exchanging a glance with her, Guy was suddenly overwhelmed by an uprush of such joy he wondered how he could ever have felt excitement at his father's arrival or pain and grief at the disappearance of his friend Zhenia. The sight of her reminded him of the exhilarant, buoyant happiness he had felt when he had kissed her. All he really wanted was to see her again and he assumed from the slight change in the light of her eyes as she returned his glance that she shared his feeling.

But he remained housebound meanwhile, on Aunt Emily's insistence. She did not intend to put herself to undue trouble on her brother's behalf and proposed to wait at Belinda House until word came from the

240

Esplanade Hotel. 'In such rainy weather,' she declared after returning from church, 'I can see no good purpose being served by waiting up in the High Street for the coach from Ryde.' When Guy offered to go himself, she reprimanded him for what she called 'a lapse in taste'. So he spent the early part of the afternoon staring out of the window at the grey sea and the rain-darkened sand and the occasional passer-by. Whenever his thoughts turned to the recent events and he remembered the water rising over him, he found it easy to think instead of Elizabeth and the softness of her warmth close to him. He knew it was an emotional betrayal of the friend who had saved him. Dressed in his smart new suit, delivered late last night, he found it much easier to anticipate the future than to contemplate the past.

By the time word came that Mr Seddenham had arrived, the rain had stopped. Aunt Emily, in her formal Sunday black, accompanied by Guy in his new suit and the twins in their best clothes, made a dignified little procession along the esplanade to the hotel. The rooms booked for the new arrival had been those previously occupied by Count Rostopchine. Aunt Emily had debated with herself in a fairly loud voice – and of course in Guy's hearing – whether or not her brother might have acquired a servant during his trip to Australia. That would have accounted for the rather grand way his telegram had demanded the booking of two rooms. They were none the wiser when they were shown up the stairs to the spacious room overlooking the sea where Rostopchine had received Rostovtzoff and Kruze, had refused Marie Valence's request for money and had done his best to humiliate Mr Ellis. The furnishings were exactly as they had been. As a matter of fact, the long thin curtains hanging in the balcony doorway fluttered in a sea breeze exactly as they had done two Monday mornings previously.

'Father! Father!' the twins cried with an exuberance which Guy found excessive and ran across the room into their father's outstretched arms. He was a tall man with a ginger beard, a round, firm-skinned face and light ginger-coloured eyes that twinkled behind the puckerings of smile lines at the corners of his eyes and the edges of his mouth. His hair was sandy and seemed to Guy sparser than he remembered it. He had a strong build, not exactly spare but not thick enough to make his waistcoat bulge, and his obviously new coat with velvet lapels hung upon his broad shoulders and frame with a look suggesting opulence and well-being. He swept both girls up in his arms and held them there shrieking and laughing with delight, giving each of them smacking kisses on their cheeks. When Aunt Emily intervened with 'Oh, Tom dear, you will get them so excited, they will be quite unmanageable!' he slowly lowered them to the floor and then stretched out both hands to his sister who, laughing with a smidgeon of embarrassment and pleasure, offered her cheeks to his kissing lips.

'Dearest Emily, you know how grateful I am to you. I have thanked God daily that I have been secure in my mind as to their welfare. In your keeping they have truly begun to bloom like the finest roses, haven't they? My dear, I am so thankful. . . .'

More kisses, a close embrace and even polite nose-blowing by Aunt Emily anointed the little ceremony of greeting and gratitude. The brother and sister drew apart and it was the turn of the father and son to greet each other. Guy had always assumed he would run directly to his father and they would clasp each other as they had usually done in the past. In the last year or so, of course, their embraces had been more manly, less effusive, even rather distant and respectful. But now Guy realised he was almost as tall as his father and when he looked him directly in the eye he noticed his father flinch very slightly in acknowledgement of their new equality and what seemed a new distance between them. At least that was the interpretation Guy put on the rapid fluttering of his father's eyelids and the faint stiffening in the line of his smiling mouth.

'Well, Guy, my boy, you've grown! I'm amazed!'

He took Guy firmly by the hand and shook it seriously, with a deliberate, slow movement, looking Guy a little unsurely in the eyes, and then they drew closer and embraced rather formally, in a way that showed how unfamiliar they were with each other. Guy noticed the strong masculine fragrance that came from his father's cheeks.

'We are glad to see you back, sir,' he said in a firm voice, though such firmness and formality, especially the 'sir', sounded too grandiose and Jane started giggling.

'I'm very glad to be back in England, my boy. Seeing all of you looking so well and cared for, I even wonder whether I shouldn't perhaps go away more often.' It was said in good humour, but its gruffness struck a wrong note. None of them wanted to talk about their father going away again. He hastened to allay the visibly startled reaction of the twins. 'Oh, my dears, I don't mean that at all! I'm planning to stay here a very long time, a very long time.' Even this did not sound as reassuring as it should and Edwina was prompted to ask:

'Aren't you going to stay in England always?'

Guy recognised that his father had misjudged the mood of the twins. They had grown used to understanding the faintest of slights from adults. They had

243

developed little antennae of discernment, as it were, with which they instantly detected the slightest quiverings of concealment or duplicity in an adult voice.

'I will most certainly not be leaving you again, my dears, whether or not I do stay in England,' he announced, bending down to the two upturned bright-eyed faces. 'We do not have to think of anything like that now, do we? I am here and you are here and we are a family again!'

'Yes, yes, that is most certainly so,' Aunt Emily agreed.

'And yet I cannot hide from you, all of you,' said their father, seeming to continue with what he had been saying almost without regard for his sister's agreement, 'that I do have some special, very special, news for you.'

Before he could tell them what the news was, the door opened and a young woman entered. She had a pink, healthy complexion and an outdoor freshness about her blue eyes and prettily curling fair hair. Her long blue dress caught up into fashionable scalloped folds at the front accentuated the line of her figure while also emphasising her youthfulness. To Guy she seemed no older than Marie Valence, although quite different in appearance. The young woman's boldness, the challenging way she entered the room, reminded him strongly of Marie and made him catch his breath for a moment.

'Ah, Mary, my dear!' exclaimed his father as she entered, clearly surprised and disconcerted by her sudden appearance. He immediately took her by the hand and led her towards the others. 'I thought it best you should all know at once you have a new mother. You will be surprised, of course, and it will take a little time for you to get used to the idea. But I would like you to meet her now. We were married in Australia shortly before leaving. I could not let you know sooner because there would have been no way and I thought it best that you should meet each other face to face as soon as we reached England. It will take a little time, of course, for you to . . .'

The young woman called Mary smiled broadly and, looking at each of them, but especially at the twins, said:

'Hello! I just had to come and see you all!'

She spoke her greeting in a ringing, vowel-rich, Australian accent. It was met by silence. Aunt Emily opened her mouth, closed it and leaned slowly forward in a respectful bow, but her silence clearly expressed disfavour and an accumulation of hurt dignity. The twins looked up at their painfully smiling father with strained faces. Mary's bright smile seemed to challenge them all to like her and its obviously warm, open invitation was hard to resist. Jane was the first to react. She slowly moved forward and held up her face to be kissed by their new mother. Then Edwina joined her. It was only Guy who found himself unable to respond in any way.

The idea that this stranger with her robust young womanhood and strong Australian accent should take the place of his mother so shocked Guy that he could no longer bear to look either at her or at his father. He turned and looked over his shoulder at the sea. A strong wind caused tufts of foam on the wave-crests and a flag on a pole just below the hotel balcony fluttered strongly and steadily as if on the prow of a ship. It was grey but rainless. Perhaps a dozen people, no more, could be seen walking on the foreshore. Guy stared hard at this external vista in an attempt to compose his feelings. He was disgusted at himself for being so rude and yet still more disgusted at his father for having apparently betrayed the sacred trust of their family unity.

'Guy,' he heard his father say, 'I'd like you to meet Mary.'

Guy held his head away, though he was not staring at the sea any longer but simply trying to fight down his emotions. It was Aunt Emily who spoke on his behalf. He heard her say severely:

'Guy was very fond of his mother, Tom dear, and I don't think you should expect him to make a quick adjustment. It is hard enough for me to know precisely how to take it.'

'Of course, of course, my dear,' came his father's worried voice. 'I realise it will take a little while . . .'

'It will most certainly take a little while,' said Aunt Emily.

But Guy forced himself to turn round and face Mary, his new mother. Her blue eyes were watching him carefully. When he looked into them, he saw in their smiling brightness not only her challenging youthfulness but also an amused womanly interest. This he acknowledged by smiling also, in shy unwillingness. Then he nodded curtly, stepped past her, walked to the door and turned the knob, just as Aunt Emily, raising a black-gloved hand, restrained her brother by saying: 'Let him go, Tom dear.'

Guy ran down the stairs. He could hardly restrain the upboiling rush of tears that gathered achingly in his throat and felt ready to spill out of his eyes. But at the foot of the stairs he almost ran into the hotel manager and the encounter was so ludicrous that he felt like laughing. He apologised and walked out on to the esplanade. The wind instantly blew his hair all over his face. It rushed through him, he felt, as if he had stopped existing. And emotionally he had become invisible, he thought, and it surprised him slightly that he could walk at all in such a dancing wind, with specks of dry sand beating against his cheeks.

A whiteness of far sunlit cloud gave the afternoon a momentary appearance of summeriness and clarity, but scudding smoky shreds of dark cloud from the west as quickly darkened the scene again. He faced into the wind and walked along the sand below the bathing machines the way he had walked on that early Sunday morning a week ago. He supposed it was Marie who called him. A voice was calling him, he was certain, but he knew it could not be real, and the difference between *that* Sunday and *this* Sunday was that then he was innocent and dreamy and now he knew so much and all of it seemed nightmarish. And the difference now was that the tide was rising. It was far up the shore and among the rocks where he'd found Marie's body the waves were bursting in tall, elaborate plumes of water.

Why hadn't his father done something to warn them? he asked himself. His father had most likely given long and careful thought to the problem and perhaps there had been no way of letting them know, but to have chosen someone with a name like Mary seemed to Guy unforgivable. He had supposed the name Marie would forever remain in the past, like his mother. Now the living and the dead would somehow be coming together and there would be no real separation. The idea was appalling. He tried to oust it from his thoughts. He could think only of the need to escape. What if he joined the navy like Miles? What if he decided to 'broaden his horizons' like Mr Prendergast? He knew the family fortunes had been restored and he would most likely be able to become a doctor if he chose. This thought naturally reminded him of Zhenia and he walked on steadily towards the rocks.

The conviction grew in him that his life would only be properly fulfilled and useful if he could always remember the Russian doctor's devotion to truth and the discovery of nature's secrets. Then he recalled the way in which his friend had talked about his nihilism as a denial of possession by name. He remembered his drunken shouts: 'We must simply *be – be* . . . be good, be helpful, be loving, but be nihilist, not possessing name, a naked person, simply working to find secrets . . .' and the shouts sounded in his ears as loudly as the violently detonating waves that sent up their shellbursts of water on the far side of the rocks. Now was the first time he understood their meaning.

They meant that each person had a personal task in life undertaken with love only for the task itself, not for self or for others. Love was a source of human weakness, so much romanticism – that had been his friend's message. But Guy had learned another message in the past week. He knew he would never understand his father's remarriage unless he understood that no one could live without love, just as he felt the love of his own mother clinging to him and recognised his love for Marie as a cross made upon his heart. The gulls' high-voiced shrieking just under the steep incline of the cliff came at that moment like a confirmation of his thoughts. In the same instant their shrieks seemed to contain his name shouted above the noise of the waves.

'Guy! Guy! Guy!'

He stared at the tall plumes of water. Was it Zhenia's voice? Could his friend have not disappeared after all? Had it all been malicious rumour? The waves beat strongly among the rocks. The green sea plunged over the shoulders of the lower, smoother rocks, mingling with the freshwater stream, and swept busily into inlets among the creviced slabs of the taller rocks. He turned and there behind him, almost in reach, stood Elizabeth, bare-headed, her beautiful hair streaming back from her intently smiling face, her eyes glistening. She said she had been calling his name. Her arms were stretched out to him. He offered her his own and suddenly she was in his embrace and they stood together rocked by the wind and covered by the fine spray of bursting waves.

Epilogue

Some days later Mr Ellis was taken by his half-sister to an outcrop of rocks. It was not far from Blackgang Chine, to the west of Ventnor, but isolated and known only to Molly Ford through her assiduous exploration of the coastline. If her hearing was defective, her eyesight was perfect. She pointed downwards and Mr Ellis slowly descended the steep sheeptrack of a path that led from the cliff-top to the rocky shore. By the time he was close enough, the sea grumbling and spitting among the boulders, he saw that the white shape was a corpse.

It was that of a naked man in his late twenties. The features had received serious injury from the effects of stormy seas and were barely recognisable. The limbs and general build were those of a man of considerable strength. Stopping on a rocky promontory, Mr Ellis signalled to his half-sister not to come closer and gazed down at the white limbs spread in an oddly relaxed posture. The whole body was turned a little away and the face, or what was left of it, was hidden by a web of long hair. The sea washed over the extreme pallor of the limbs, tingeing their whiteness with a faint green luminosity, yet hardly stirring them. In an uncanny way it suggested by its lapping motion the intake and expulsion of breath from the rigid, enmarbled torso. The constable's one thought turned on the strange word 'nihilist'. He thought of what he saw as the naked nihilist, seeming to be a creature of the sea that had emerged from unknown depths, from an incomprehensible past, and as naked as any other creature taken from the sea. The naked body struck him as possessing a graven, immobile beauty as of rock over which the sea had washed for centuries and had formed and moulded and brought to life in the whiteness of salt and had now deposited on this shore in acknowledgement of the true origin of humanity. If all life came originally from the sea, then the sight which greeted the constable's eyes seemed for a moment to suggest not death so much as a new vision of human perfectibility, the first, perhaps, of those who would become known as 'the new men'; though the constable himself had no inkling of this.

His deep fear of human remains when taken from the sea made him turn away suddenly, though just as strong an inducement was the curtain of rain already approaching from the west. As he scrambled back up the rocks it began to pour. There was another storm that night. No search was made after the storm had abated and the constable did not mention what he had seen to anyone. Nor did his half-sister. Within a short time he began to doubt whether he had seen anything of the kind. There was another consideration which reinforced his doubt. A Mr Holdsworth came from Torquay and at once took charge of all the doctor's instruments and specimens, claiming that he was the only person in the whole area who understood the doctor's contribution to science and that it had been the doctor' express wish, uttered in Mr Holdsworth's own presence, that all his work, and even his name, should be anonymous. And who was Mr Ellis to oppose such an authoritative wish when the doctor had scarcely spent three weeks in Ventnor, was known only to a few, had behaved so strangely and had seemed literally to dissolve into the sea before their very eyes? Could that faceless naked corpse really have been the doctor's?

251

Mr Ellis, like any normal human being, believed he could tell fact from fiction, but as he reflected on what he had seen he could not be sure. So he preferred not to raise objections.

In truth, of course, making all allowances for the vagaries of fiction, Bazarov did not die in Ventnor, he was 'born' there. He received life through the creative imagination of Ivan Turgenev who immortalised him as the hero of *Fathers and Children*. Turgenev spent three weeks in Ventnor in August 1860. While he was there he conceived his hero Bazarov and drew up a draft programme for primary education in Russia. Several other facts are to be gleaned from his reminiscences and letters, from memoirs and from other sources, including the *Ventnor Times* of August 1860. They have practically all been incorporated into this fiction. Marie Alexandrovna, for example, refers to M. A. Markovich (pseudonym Marko Vovchok) (1834–1907), a Ukrainian writer and translator; Rostovtzoff (the form of his name given in the *Ventnor Times*) refers to N. Ya. Rostovtsev (1831–97); Kruze refers to N. F. Kruze (1823–1901); all the other Russians mentioned as being in Ventnor have some basis in fact, except Count Rostopchine, his manservant Fedya and his mistress, Marie Valence. As for P. V. Annenkov (1813–87), Turgenev's close friend and trusted adviser, we would know much less about the Ventnor holiday without his admirable testimony.

For example, we would not know that, most likely on Monday 26 August, Turgenev and Annenkov left Ventnor to visit Alexander Herzen at his holiday home near Bournemouth. 'For a whole day,' Annenkov tells us, 'we wandered about on various roads and then came to a stop close to Southampton, found a public stage-coach and reached by nightfall the hill with the little house on top of it. The hill was close to the sea and bore the proud name of "Eagle's Nest". There was no eagle there, with the exception of the host whose jovial laughter greeted us at the door and accompanied us into the brightly lighted dining room where supper was already waiting. It would be hard to convey the amount of anecdote, jokes, comments and laughter expended during the meal.' And Alexander Herzen (1812–70), the jovial host who greeted them, mentioned in a letter of the following day that he was writing from the banks 'of *Bunmos* (as they pronounce it here) and, what is more, in the presence of a most frightful storm and Turgenev'. He had trouble with the pronunciation of the name Bournemouth just as everyone had trouble with the English summer weather.

A couple of days later Turgenev was back in Ventnor, partly to ensure that other members of the Russian colony had copied out the draft programme for distribution to leading figures in Russian society and partly to collect his belongings. On Sunday 2 September, six days after the Seddenhams, he left Ventnor for London and visited (so Herzen confided in a letter of 6 September) a lady described as 'Emilie Hermitage-blanc'. What odd sense of delicacy prompted Herzen to Frenchify the name? Perhaps Turgenev had spoken of his English acquaintances at Belinda House while he was visiting Herzen at his holiday home in Bournemouth, but the latter suspected some deeper or less respectable attachment than the innocent one which might have impelled Turgenev to visit the Lambeth house. He would have been greeted very warmly there, we may be sure. The twins would have come running along the dark hall as soon as his tall figure appeared in the doorway, and the mistress of the house would have come hurrying out of the morning room with a busy swish of skirts, and he would have bowed to her and kissed her hand. . . .

But to Aunt Emily's surprise and disappointment he

came in fact to see Guy. He insisted on speaking to him privately. Beyond admitting that they had talked about the Russian doctor and some of the things he had said, Guy was prepared to say very little about the visit. His reluctance was due to a sense that he had been responsible for the doctor's death.

And Guy Seddenham himself, what happened to him? After qualifying as a doctor, he married Elizabeth Fenton and they had six children. Most of his working life was spent in a country practice in Oxfordshire. Towards the end of his life he developed an interest in the paranormal, as an article in *The Lancet* of 14 June 1902 can testify. After his retirement, it occurred to him that he ought to repay a debt of conscience and he made enquiries in the Torquay area. James Holdsworth turned out to be still alive, though nearing seventy. From him he obtained the only remaining piece of evidence that his long-dead friend had ever existed. It was a leatherbound notebook. Closely-written Cyrillic script and some drawings, chiefly of the *peachia hastata*, made him fairly certain that it was Zhenia's but since there was no name on it he could not be sure. On the very day of his death he placed all the new-found remnants of his 1860 holiday, including the notebook, in an envelope marked 'Ventnor'.

His second son Charles kept the envelope, passing it on to his daughter Jane. When she emigrated to America in her forties she left it to her brother Thomas. He took the trouble to have the notebook looked at by someone who knew Russian. It was established what it was about and that it had a certain rarity and curiosity value. Perhaps that helped to preserve it.

In 1986 Thomas's grandson Donald, a student at the University of Durham, came across the envelope while clearing out a drawer of the desk his grandfather had bequeathed to him. The name 'Ventnor' on the envelope meant nothing to him. He was about to throw it away when something fell out. He picked it up and saw that it was a crucifix. Also in the envelope was a sheet of lined paper which had been carefully folded into an oblong shape. He unfolded it to discover a wafer-thin object, blackened and whiskery, which stuck to the paper and bore a faint resemblance to a dried plant. The name on the outside – THE ARROW MUZZLET – meant nothing to him. As for the notebook, he studied it carefully. In a part of the leather binding which seemed to have been neatly cut with a sharp blade he found another piece of paper, just as carefully folded. This had the name GUIDO printed on it in capital letters. He found that it was a kind of letter written in Russian in the same neat Cyrillic hand as the entries in the notebook. When translated, the letter read:

I am writing to you in my own language because it is easier. I want you to know that you are my only friend. I cannot return to my country and here I am a stranger among strangers. I had wanted to devote my life to a study of the natural sciences, but now I think that will not be possible. My eyesight is beginning to fail. That is why I asked you to look in the microscope. I want you to know this because sometimes it seems to me that Masha is happier than all of us and perhaps one day I too will be found like Masha in one of those deep pools. . . .

Remember me.

If this also meant nothing to Donald Seddenham, what did seem to have some meaning was the small wooden crucifix with the characteristic Orthodox slanted crosspiece. On the back of it two words were engraved. They were evidently a name. But whose name was it? Only Turgenev had understood, it seemed, and he had told Mr Ellis. As he had said, there were millions and millions of them in Russia with a name like that:

Марья Ивановна